the
Gravity
between
Us

the Gravity *between* Us

KRISTEN ZIMMER

bookouture

Published by Bookouture

An imprint of StoryFire Ltd.
23 Sussex Road, Ickenham, UB10 8PN
United Kingdom

www.bookouture.com

ISBN: 978-1-909490-13-0

To my mother,
For encouraging me to chase my dreams and believing
wholeheartedly that I could turn them into reality.
Thank you.

To Elizabeth,
My beacon of hope, my light in a dark world;
I love you.

To Oliver Rhodes, Jenny Hutton and Jena Roach,
You've all helped shape this story in such lovely ways.
I am so grateful to you for your dedication and guidance.

To Mark Falkin,
Thank you for finding this book the perfect home.

CHAPTER ONE

Payton

Kendall is sitting on my bed playing with my laptop. I'm hovering in front of my closet, looking for my favorite Montclair State University sweatshirt. "I hate your hair," I call to her over my shoulder. "Sorry, I couldn't keep that in any longer." I did notice right away that the reddish-purple tint of her new hair color made her blue eyes pop. Nonetheless, I don't like it. I mean, what natural blonde ever wants to go auburn? Women drop hundreds of dollars at hair salons trying to attain the golden perfection she was born with. It's ludicrous.

"It's for my next role." She laughs. "You could at least *pretend* to like it."

"No, I can't. And you shouldn't either. Lawrence made you do it. I know you didn't want to."

"Of course I didn't want to. You should have been there when he came to me with the idea. He was all like, 'You absolutely have to do this. Don't worry, it'll be great.' God, he sounded just like my mother. It took everything I had not to punch him in the throat."

I chuckle at that. There's a lot to be said about Kendall Betten-court. She's one of those people who were put on this earth so that the average human can give the word 'beauty' a definition. Between having the body of a Victoria's Secret model and a face that should be immortalized in a Da Vinci painting, she never stood a chance at living her life in the shadows. It didn't really come as much of a surprise that this girl—whose genetic makeup is, by no fault of her own, startlingly akin to that of a Greek goddess—would become one of Hollywood's most sought-after up-and-comers. But my fa-vorite thing about her is *not* her physical beauty or even the fact that she has genuine talent. It's that she doesn't take shit from anyone, including her legendary publicist, Lawrence Mackin.

"How did the *Today Show* go yesterday?" I wonder. "I didn't catch it."

"I didn't even want to do it. I honestly felt like saying, 'Well, Matt, I don't think anyone should bother wasting their money on *In Heaven's Arms*. It's a total gagfest.'" She sticks her finger in her mouth and makes this half-retching, half-gurgling sound. "'It's all Ghost Girl meets Living Boy. Ghost Girl falls in love with Living Boy, Ghost Girl tries to figure out how she can be with Living Boy without inhabiting a rotting corpse, which is sure to be a major turn-off to Living Boy. Blah Blah Blah.'"

I take a seat next to her on the bed. "Funny. If it's so horrible, what the hell possessed you to star in it?"

She shrugs. "I don't know. I guess I figured I couldn't sit around waiting for an awesome script to come my way. By the time someone writes a strong, intelligent, independent, twenty something female lead, I'd be too damn old to play her. Besides, everyone and their mother read the book it's based on. James thought it would really put me on the map. I know he's one of the best agents around, but I still can't believe he was right! It was such a piece of crap book, you can imagine how much shittier the movie adaptation is."

"So, we won't be going to see it tonight then?"

"Not unless you want me to upchuck violently in a public place. That would be a perfect headline for *The Inquirer*! 'Movie Star Visits Home Town, Vomits All Over Friends and Former Classmates.'"

I'm laughing so hard now, I'm afraid I might pee myself. *Oh man, I've missed her so much.* "We don't have to go to the movies, but we should do *something* fun. Otherwise, I'm just going to sit here obsessing over the sixty-four bars I have to write by Tuesday for my Piano Theory class."

"I don't care what we do. You know I'm leaving for a shoot next week. I have no idea when I'll be able to make it home again. The only reason I came home this weekend is because I was afraid I was forgetting what my *best friend* looks like."

I cannot argue that. The last time I saw her was around the Fourth of July. A few years ago it would have been unthinkable to go three months without seeing each other.

"Let's go to the Grind House," she says. "For some reason I've been craving their terrible coffee."

"Sure, as long as you make sure to put those hideous things on your face." I point to the metal-framed sunglasses sitting atop her head. "Otherwise, it'll be a mob scene. Everyone will be tripping all over themselves to meet you."

"Yeah right," she says. "Everyone around here knows me, Payton. It's not like I'm Angelina Jolie or someone cool like that." She throws me the keys to the sleek, silver Beamer she rented. "You're driving. I can't stand the potholes around here."

❋ ❋ ❋

The moment we walk into the coffee shop I become aware of just how off-putting small town New Jersey can be for a famous person, or an "almost famous person" as Kendall would say. People don't recognize her at first; she was still sporting her natural locks in *In Heaven's Arms,* as well as on her most recent press tour. She's still blonde on all the magazine covers. But it's easy to make out that the world around us is about to lose its collective mind. It starts with stares—everyone squinting hard in our direction. We're in line waiting to order by the time the real craziness kicks in. The atmosphere intensifies as the noise level recedes, until finally, the whole place goes dead silent. Then, with all the grace and subtlety of a falling H-bomb, the menacing buzz of whispering beings: "Is that Kendall Bettencourt?" "I think so. OMG!"

The barista knows exactly who Kendall is. He can hardly contain his drool as she begins her order. "Hi. Can I have a tall hazelnut latte, please?" She looks over her shoulder at me and raises her left eyebrow. I'm standing stiff and straight at my fully awkward height of 5'9," somewhat in awe of how she's managing to function normally in this preposterously abnormal situation. The attention that is on her right now is overwhelming. I mean, I get it. Her biggest movie ever just opened. She has more money than the Catholic Church, and she's gorgeous, but really? I want to scream at everyone within earshot, "I've been hypnotized by her much longer than you have! You all need to *get over it* already!"

It doesn't seem to faze her much, though. Maybe she's just gotten so used to being gawked at that she legitimately doesn't care.

She shoots me a grin. My rigid muscles instantly relax. "The usual for you, Pay?"

"Um, yeah."

"And a tall coffee, light and sweet," she continues to the barista. When she's finished, she turns back to me and whispers, "Ignore it. That's the approach I'm taking."

What a radical strategy! "Okay."

"Your coffee, darling," She hands me a piping hot cup and then takes off toward the large wall of windows. People continue to gape at her as she passes like she's a unicorn or some kind of exotic animal. She is stopped twice—first by two preteen girls who ask for her autograph, and again by a musclebound, gym-rat-looking guy who uses his iPhone to snap a few pictures of himself with his arm slung round her shoulders.

Once everyone gets over the titillation of her presence, we find a sunlight-drenched table in the corner where we can sit facing one another. She looks at me for what feels like forever before speaking. "I can't believe your hair got so long." She puts her cup down, reaches across to me, and winds a few brown strands between her fingers. "You should get bangs. Not those full in the front kind, but the asymmetrical side-cut kind. You'd look bangin'," she chortles. "Get it, banging?"

"You're such a dork," I say through my own giggle.

"You know, I meet new people every day, and they all have these great expectations of me." Her voice quickly goes from funny to serious. A hint of melancholy flashes in her eyes. "I'm supposed to be the cool new superstar, or the latest silver screen vixen. No one sees me as the dork who makes lame puns."

"But you *are* a dork who makes lame puns. You're just cooler and sexier than the rest of us. It's pretty awesome. You're like a chameleon."

"A chameleon?" She cocks her head. "Yeah, I like that. Thank you."

"Don't embrace it too much. You forget that chameleons are slimy reptiles."

"Wait a second. Did you just call me a slimy reptile? Nice, Payton. You're a master at backhanded compliments *and* completely ruining the moment."

I take a sip of my steaming coffee and examine her carefully. Her tone was both convincingly stern and mildly pained, but the look of anger on her face is so feigned that she isn't fooling anyone, certainly not me. "Yes, I'm particularly skilled at ruining moments. And *you* should consider taking acting lessons. Your 'rage face' is overly emotive."

"Shut up," she croaks. "Damn it. I can't pull anything over on you, can I?"

"Nope." I shake my head, reminding her that I know her all too well.

"While we're on the subject of ruined moments, I'd like to ruin your day by making you take me to the city."

"No! You know I hate Manhattan! It's loud and dirty and too big for its own good."

"Please? It's barely half an hour away, and I'll drive. I know how much you despise New York motorists."

I look at her skeptically. She reciprocates with a semi-adorable pout.

"I want to go to The Met. And afterward, I'll let you take me to lunch. I won't even try to pay."

"Wow!" I can feel myself smirking. "What a gift! Thank you so much."

"Whatever! You always complain that I never let you pay." She playfully slaps my arm. "Come on, look at my sad puppy face! You can't resist it! I am being *so* cute right now!"

"Okay, yes! We can go, as long as you stop with the face. I can't take it."

"Sweet!" She holds out her hand. "Car keys, please."

❊ ❊ ❊

The Met is much larger than I remember. It's teeming with tourists, which turns out to work in our favor. We walk the halls of the museum in silent anonymity, drifting through a sea of strangers. Not once does anyone stop to ask Kendall for a picture or autograph. I can tell she is relieved. Truthfully, I am too.

We reach the photography section and stop to sit on the floor. And that's when my senses are tossed into cataclysmic upheaval. Mounted on the wall in front of us is a print called "Lesbian Couple at the Monocle." Instantaneously, I'm anxious. It's like a sign from the universe telling me that I need to gather my guts, forget the past, and finally stop being afraid.

I've never said it out loud to anyone. I'm not sure I should start now. Will saying it give it some kind of molecular structure that permanently and visibly imprints itself on me? I doubt it. But saying it means that there is a very real chance I might lose friends and alienate people. Worst of all, I have no idea how Kendall is going to handle it. It's not exactly a topic we've discussed much or, like, at all. Will she still see me the same way she did this morning, last week, last year? At least if I tell her here, in public, she won't make a scene. She is notoriously too good an actor for that. Hell, that's what she gets paid to do.

I'm about to drop the bomb when Kendall's eyes wander up to the photo. "Lesbian Couple at The Monocle. What?" She stands up to get a closer look. "That's weird. I thought it was a picture of a man and a woman. Look at it." She bends down, offers her hand to help me to my feet. For an instant I think about refusing it for fear that my palms are sweaty. I decide I'm being ridiculous, but wipe my hands on my jeans just in case.

I clear my throat before speaking and immediately notice how annoyingly hollow and gruff that sounds. "I would think it was a man and a woman too, at first glance."

"It's interesting how old this picture is and how much society has changed since it was taken."

"What?" I'm so close to full-blown panic, I'm willing to bet it's written all over my face. "What do you mean?"

"Like, back in the day," she starts lightly. "I mean, she is clearly a woman," she points at the print, "but she is dressed like a man. I suppose there had to be that, I don't know that... dynamic back then. If it were a picture of two girls..." She's getting flustered, blushing a bit, but she presses on. "Okay, say it were a picture of me and you. That caption, 'Lesbian Couple at the Monocle,' would have sent people's heads spinning more than I'm sure it already did. Do you see what I'm saying? It's like there had to be one feminine woman and one more masculine woman for it to have been understood that they were a couple."

"Oh." I want to say 'what?' again, but know I shouldn't. "You're talking about stereotypes?"

"Yes! That's it! Like today, just because a woman has short hair or wears racer back tanks doesn't mean she's a lesbian."

"And on the flipside, just because a woman has long hair or wears skirts doesn't mean she's straight," I add.

"Right! Those notions don't apply to the world anymore is what I was trying to say."

"I get it. You can't go by what a person looks like."

"Exactly!"

Then it hits me. This is it. It's now or never, put up or shut up. I've gotta go for it. "So, if I were to tell you that I'm gay, it wouldn't be all that surprising—purely based on the fact that I have a feminine appearance."

"No, not based on your appearance. Based on the fact that I know you, maybe..."

I'm staring at her now. Blatantly staring. *Was that too indirect? Should I be more forward?*

"Wait," she says, her eyes narrowing in on me. "Are you trying to tell me that you..."

I motion *yes* with my head. "I'm gay, Kendall."

And then there is silence—a very deep, impenetrable stillness. I want to curl into the fetal position and die right here in the middle of this world class museum.

"Um, how about we do that lunch thing I'm letting you pay for? I need a beverage," She says finally.

It's not at all what I was expecting to hear. "Sure."

We walk down to the Rock 'n Roll Deli, neither of us uttering a word to the other. When we arrive, I order her favorite, tuna salad on a whole wheat wrap, and my tried-and-true staple, grilled cheese and tomato on rye, while she finds a booth in the back.

I haul ass over to her with our food atop a bright red, plastic tray. She snatches her wrap from the tray, but doesn't eat it right away. Instead, she is hell-bent on gawping at me for I don't know how long. I can't tell what she's thinking, but it's as if she is somewhere between eyeing up a piece of meat and staring down a rabid dog. "So, you're like, *gay* gay?" she asks after taking a few bites of her wrap.

"Uh," I pause to think over her question. "Is there some kind of *non-gay* gay?"

She laughs—the kind of good, hearty laugh that always gets me laughing, too. "What I mean is that you're gay, as in, exclusively. Not like bisexual?"

"Yes, exclusively. I'm an exclusive lesbian. Though, syntactically, that would indicate that I'm difficult to get into or something, like one of your hot LA nightclubs."

"It's impressive that you're able to maintain your hilariousness even when talking about serious, life-altering things."

"Well, it's not like some crazy Body Snatcher thing happened, but yeah, it is pretty life-altering."

"How long have you known?"

"For a long time, but I didn't start to think of it as a fact until I was sixteen."

At that, I see her expression change. She's offended, or hurt, or something. Maybe a little bit of both. "Seriously, Payton? You've known for 'a fact' for nearly *three years*, and you're only telling me now? Jesus, are you that scared of me?"

"No, not at all!" I shake my head fervently. Terrific, I have to tell her the story. *This is one memory I was hoping to never relive.* It might be old news, but it sucked enough to damage me irreparably. Every time I think about it, I start trembling like a dead leaf in the wind. "Do you remember Amanda Garrison? She was a year ahead of us in school."

"Amanda Garrison." She taps the table top as though trying to place a face to the name. "Yeah, I remember her. She was the captain of the soccer team the year before you were, right?"

"Right."

"Uh huh. What about her?"

Here we go. "I kind of had a thing with her. It wasn't, like, love at first sight or anything. I just knew that I liked her and that she liked me, too. We started talking a lot after practice, went out on a couple of dates. Eventually her parents found out about it; I'm still not sure how. They went through her text messages or something. Anyway, it doesn't matter. The point is, her mom totally flipped out. She dragged Amanda to my house and demanded to talk to my mom. Mom wasn't home—thank God—but when I told Mrs. Garrison that, she started screaming at me. She kept telling me that her daughter wasn't gay, and I had better stay away from her. She forbid Amanda from seeing me; she even went as far as making her quit the team. From that day on, Amanda wouldn't even look at me. It was so brutal.

After that, the thought of coming out to anyone was paralyzing. I pretty much dined on an unhealthy diet of self-loathing and terror. It took me a long time to get comfortable in my own skin—I'm still working on it. But at this point, I'm just too exhausted from keeping it a secret to even bother trying anymore."

Her revolted expression speaks volumes. It's enough for me to know what she's going to do next. She reaches across the booth and takes my hand in her own. "Wow, Payton. That's monumentally messed up. I'm sorry that happened to you. Some people are just so closed-minded."

"Some people are, and that's also part of the reason I've been hesitant to tell you. You're a celebrity now. Your face is already plastered all over the tabloids, and you're just doing normal teenage crap. What if it got out that some girl you're always flying cross-country to visit is a big old homo? I'm sure that would start some delightful rumors. Rumors create rifts between people. So you see, I wasn't scared of you. I was scared I might lose you."

"The tabloids are going to write what they're going to write regardless of what the truth is, Payton. I can't let it bother me. Plus, hello? I live in *Hollywood*. It would be insane to think that I don't have any gay friends! And lose me? That will never happen. I'm like a bad case of herpes—just 'cuz you can't see me doesn't mean I'm not there."

"Herpes! Eww," I roll my eyes. "That is a horrible analogy."

"Yeah, but it's kind of funny and also very true."

"So, we're okay then? We're cool?"

"Are we cool?" She drags out the "cool," leans back in her seat, and crosses her arms. "Yeah, dude, everything's cool. Everything's smooth." She's making fun of me, and I couldn't be happier about it.

"Sweet, *dude*. Finish your wrap."

She brings the last bite to her lips and abruptly stops. "Hold the phone. If you're into girls, what the hell was with you and Scott Strafford the end of junior year?"

"Let's chalk it up to a last ditch effort at heterosexuality."

She stuffs the bread into her mouth. "Yeah, you should've picked someone else. If I had to choose between that asshole and lesbianism, I'd go gay all the way. Seriously, I considered asking your mom to have you committed. Only a mental patient could've fallen for that jerk."

"I'm going to write *The Inquirer* and let them know that one of Hollywood's It Girls talks with her mouth full."

"See food." She sticks out her tuna-covered tongue. "It's all the rage."

"Charming," I lark. "No wonder all the guys find you irresistible."

"Harhar," she says and grabs the tray from the table. "Let's get out of here."

❊ ❊ ❊

Kendall picks me up at noon on Sunday. We have plans to play pool at the billiard hall, Eights, with our friends, Jared and Sarah, but elect to waste time driving around aimlessly for a while. It's nice to drive around in October; the trees are luscious shades of fiery orange and crimson. Kendall says she misses real foliage because practically all they have in LA are palm trees. I wouldn't know. I haven't had the time to visit her out there, which is funny when you think about how flexible my schedule is compared to hers. It's never a good time for me to visit her when she's in Los Angeles for any extended period. She is always in between projects when I'm swamped with papers or studying for a ton of exams. "You work too hard," she always says. I usually retort with witty comments about the pot calling the kettle black.

"Why do you stay at the Marriot every time you come home?" I ponder absentmindedly. "You could stay at your parents' place."

"I like having my own space." She crinkles her nose at the song on her iPod, Original Gabber's drum and bass tune "I Wanna Be (A Motherfucking Hustler)," and quickly skips to the next one. Her head begins to bob in time with the heavy beats and dissonant shrills cascading through the sound system. It's a diversion, a subtle indication that she is not interested in having this conversation. *Tough shit.*

"No, you like not having to see your mom."

"In case you haven't noticed, my mom has been kind of a nightmare since I fired her as my manager. I mean, it's been a year already. She is never going to let me live it down that I wasn't going to let her micro-manage my life and tell me what roles I was or was not allowed to accept."

"Kendall, did you ever stop to think that maybe it's hard for her? You've found so much success so quickly, and you sort of pushed her away to get it."

"I had to push her away to get where I am, Payton. She didn't want to let me grow up. If it were up to her, I'd still be on the goddamn Disney channel! That wasn't good enough for me. I wanted to be a serious actor."

"Put yourself in her shoes. Can you imagine your life being poked into by random people around town, nobody bothering to ask you how you're doing and going straight to, 'Oh my god, what is your insanely talented offspring up to now?' Would she even know the answer to that question?"

"No, she wouldn't. Truth be told, I can't even remember the last time I called her." She groans. "All right, I get it. I'm the worst daughter ever. Thanks for pointing that out."

I can see the guilt on her face. She knows it doesn't matter how many mansions or matching sets of red Mercedes she buys her parents. All the shiny toys in existence can't make up for neglect. "You're not the worst daughter ever, but when your friends run into your mom at Quick Check and she asks *us* how you're doing, I'd say it's time to pay your parents some attention."

She frowns. "You're right."

"Do they know you're here?"

"No."

"Why don't we stop by?"

She purses her lips together. "I can stand a short visit."

"Great. I haven't seen your dad in ages." Mr. Bettencourt is the coolest old guy ever. He used to play soccer at UNC and taught me how to slide tackle without getting field burn. I think it made him happy to teach me stuff like that. Like me, Kendall doesn't have any siblings. Unlike me, she was never very interested in sports. One time Mr. Bettencourt told me that I was the next best thing to having a son. It was sort of nice, seeing as he was the closest thing I'd ever had to a father—aside from my grandpa, of course.

"You see him more often than I do," she says in a begrudging tone that makes me want to remind her whose fault that actually is.

"True," I mumble.

We park in front of her parents' driveway, effectively blocking in both of their cars. I feel like we should've brought flowers, or wine, or something. My mom always says it's rude to show up at someone's doorstep empty-handed. Then again, Kendall bought them their doorstep, so that's got to be more than enough.

She rings the bell and steps to the side of the alcove, hiding herself from view.

"What are you doing?"

"Surprising them," she whispers. "Act natural, doofus."

"Okay," I reply literally two seconds before her mother's silhouette appears behind the frosted glass door.

"Hello, Payton! It's lovely to see you." Mrs. Bettencourt pulls me in for a hug.

I feel out of my depth, like, what the hell am I supposed to do now? "Hi, Mrs. B," I grin. "How are you?"

"I'm fine, thank you for asking. What brings you to our neck of the woods?" She's smiling at me, and I'm fairly certain this is the first time I've noticed how much Kendall resembles her mom. I can picture Kendall when she's fifty with slight, graceful creases around her mouth from years of good-natured laughter and inviting smiles.

"I brought you a present." I reach around the brick nook for Kendall's arm and tug her toward me.

"Hi, Mom," she says, rather unenthusiastically.

Mrs. Bettencourt seems about ready to burst into tears. She paws at Kendall, pulls her into a tight embrace. "Goodness, you're skin and bones!"

"I'm an actress, Mom," Kendall grumbles. "It's mandatory that I be skin and bones."

"Good thing you're here! You're right on time for dinner," Mrs. Bettencourt says, ignoring Kendall's smart retort. She pushes us through the threshold and hollers up the snaking staircase, "David, come downstairs! Our daughter is here!"

Half an hour or so into a rather silent meal time, Mr. Bettencourt decides it's time to make small-talk. "So, Pumpkin, you're filming in Louisiana next?" I notice that, unlike his daughter, he refrains from speaking until his mouth is free of food.

Kendall nods. "I'm leaving tomorrow, and I'll be there for a month. I had a substantial break between the press tour for *In Heaven's Arms* and this new movie though."

"Enough time to meet a nice young man?" Mrs. Bettencourt wonders.

"Wow, Mom," Kendall places her fork down on her dish and deadpans her mother. "That was artfully understated."

Mr. Bettencourt virtually gags on his salmon. He checks his watch and smiles at Kendall. "Well, at least you got nearly an hour into your visit before she started."

Mrs. Bettencourt turns to her husband. "Honestly, David! I'm just curious. She really ought to make time for a social life. If I were still in charge of her schedule, you'd better believe she'd have ample time for that. She's only nineteen, for goodness sake."

"Exactly, I'm nineteen!" Kendall growls. "I'm old enough to make my own decisions. I'm dedicating my effort to work, not 'meeting a nice young man.'" She sneers at me and says under her breath, "See, this is why I don't come home."

"Why can't you do both?" Mrs. Bettencourt gestures toward me. "I'm sure Payton has a boyfriend despite being busy at college."

Kendall lets out a single, reverberant chortle. "You don't even know what you're talking about! Payton is *gay*."

The instant the words fall from her lips, I am utterly mortified. Time seems to freeze and every sound around us is muted. My throat locks up so tight, I'm convinced I'll pass out. The horrified look on Kendall's face is so priceless that if I weren't so entirely embarrassed I'd burst into raucous laughter. This is the first time I have ever seen Kendall rendered speechless. Her mouth is slightly agape, her gaze clamped on me. I think she is almost as appalled as I am.

Mrs. Bettencourt's eyes scroll from Kendall, to me, and back. "Oh," she clears her esophagus with a cough. "Really, Kendall. I just want to make sure you're taking the time to enjoy your adolescence."

Kendall peels her gaze off of me and inhales deeply before acknowledging her mother. "I thought you'd be glad that I'm not a boy-crazy fifteen-year-old anymore."

"*I'm* glad," Mr. Bettencourt declares. "You had me worried there for a while, changing boyfriends more often than clothes."

"Yeah, well. There will be no more of that. I'm going to relax and revel in my freedom for a bit." She motions at her mother. "So give it a rest, Mom, all right? I have friends. I go to parties. I'm fine."

"You'd better be going to parties, young lady," Mr. Bettencourt says with a wink. "I'd expect nothing less from any child of mine."

❋ ❋ ❋

The resounding silence on the drive to Eights is as unbearable as it is persistent. Kendall doesn't even bother switching on her iPod. "I am so unbelievably sorry for outing you to my parents," she says after an eternity. "It was like word vomit or something. I didn't even comprehend what I was saying and then *bam*, the words are beating me over the head. Are you pissed at me? You should be pissed at me. *I'd* be pissed at me. I say the most retarded things sometimes!"

She's droning on like she usually does when she feels bad about something. I should stop her, but it's amusing and kind of cute when her feathers are ruffled. I let her continue for a few more seconds before cutting in. "Whoa. All right, chill out," I say, throwing my hands up dramatically. "I'm not pissed, okay?" I feel my face break into a giant grin against my will. "Better you blabbed about it to your family than mine. If it had been *my* mom sitting at the table with us, I would've gone straight into cardiac arrest."

"I know!" She sniggers. "I would've bitten my tongue off before I allowed that to happen, I swear." She takes her focus off the road, turns it on me. Suddenly it's a tangible thing, a lead bullet burying into my temple. I've never felt this uncomfortable around Kendall before, and I *do not* like it at all.

"What?" I'm not convinced I actually want to know what she's thinking, but I have to escape the lingering strangeness.

"Can I stay at your place tonight?"

The question throws me off completely. It's not the way we do things. She comes to visit, checks into the hotel, and then drives over to see me once she's settled.

"I thought maybe you could drop me off at Newark in the morning. Your classes don't start until the afternoon on Mondays, right?"

Blood rushes to my ears. I'm beginning to feel light-headed. I don't know why, but it's really distressing. "I thought you had to drop the BMW back at the airport rental place?"

"Nope. We can go get your car so you can follow me back to the hotel in this baby." She pats the leather steering wheel. "I'll leave the Beamer with the concierge, and he'll take care of it for me. We'll throw my luggage in your trunk and head to Eights from there."

I am absolutely positive logic is my enemy because it's completely evading me right now. "Sounds like a plan."

"Wicked." She presses play on her iPod sending Nero's "Me and You" blasting through the speakers.

❈ ❈ ❈

Eights is packed even though it's Sunday night. This is the place to be if you're not of legal drinking age. We're all sitting at a table, watching people shoot billiards. Kendall has her huge sunglasses on as a stab at flying under the radar. So far it's working, but it seems like her disguises are generally a crapshoot—sometimes they're successful, other times they're not.

"Hey Kendall, you have an extra pair of sunglasses I can borrow? It's so bright in here," Jared quips.

"So *very* bright," Sarah joins in.

"You two are hilarious." Kendall slips her glasses up into her hair and throws a crumpled napkin at Jared.

"Dude, I haven't gotten to bust you about your sorry disguises in months. I have a lot of catching up to do," he says.

It's like old times. Besides Kendall, my friends haven't changed much since we were younger. Jared still acts like a child despite having a "grown-up job" at the Department of Parks and Recreation. Sarah is still the only one of us who can calculate the tip correctly without assistance. I, on the other hand, am feeling strangely out of sorts for reasons entirely unknown to me. Maybe Kendall outing me to her family is a bigger deal than I thought it was? I don't know.

"Yo, Payton," Sarah calls. "Where are you?"

On the corner of Edgy and Cranky, that's where. Thanks for asking. "What?"

"You've been on another planet all night," Jared says.

Kendall doesn't say anything, but seems interested in whatever explanation I may give.

"No, I haven't."

"Yes, you have," Kendall agrees.

"Holy crap, I know what it is!" Sarah screeches. "You met a guy at school, didn't you? I bet he's a drummer!" To Kendall, she asks, "Is he a drummer?"

Kendall shakes her head and elbows me.

"Don't tell me he plays the violin," Jared says. "That would be too gay." Kendall's hand smacks him square in the chest. "Ouch. What the hell?" He rubs the spot where Kendall hit him.

I really do not want to have the epic "coming out" conversation for the second time in as many days. "Can we drop it, please?"

"Is it someone we know?" Jared persists. "And *is* he a violinist?" he asks Kendall.

"No, on all possible counts," Kendall says and signals at me. "Christ, enough with the twenty questions!"

"I haven't met anyone!" I burst out. "But if I had, the appropriate pronoun wouldn't be 'he.' It would be 'she.'"

"*She*," Jared repeats after a beat. "You mean to tell me I've got a hot famous friend *and* a hot lesbian friend, both of whom are sitting at the same table as me right now? Dude, I am *the man!*"

Everyone erupts into a cacophony of laughter. I'm chuckling so hard that my ribs ache.

"Wait. Quiet down, you guys," Jared says in a very serious tenor. "Payday, when's the last time you got laid?"

Kendall rolls her eyes at him. Sarah whacks his arm and says, "Don't be crude."

He scoffs. "Pardon me. When was the last time you had a sexual encounter with a lady-friend?"

Kendall balls her fist at him. "That wasn't any better."

"Never," I say, then instantly feel the heat of flush in my cheeks. *Did I really just admit to that?* "I've hooked up with a few girls, but never... to that extent."

"Never?" Everyone questions in unison, their voices steeped in amazement.

"How do you know you're gay if you've never had sex with a chick?" Jared asks.

Per usual, you can count on Jared to ask the asinine questions! "Have you ever had sex with a guy?"

"No," he says unaffectedly. I'm surprised there isn't a look of total repulsion on his face.

"Then, how do you know you're straight?"

He considers his answer much longer than he's considered *anything* else he's ever said. "I don't know, man. Girls are sexy as hell."

"So, breasts, thighs, butt, hips—girls just do it for you, right?"

"Yeah."

"It's the same for me. I'm just waiting to meet the right girl—someone I'm sure I'm comfortable with because I've had the chance to get to know her—rather than hop into bed with the first cute girl I meet."

"Word, I feel you. That's cool."

Sarah squints suspiciously at me. "Are you telling us you go to one of the biggest universities in the state and you haven't met a girl you're interested in?"

"Why is that so hard to believe? I've been flooded with work from the get-go. I barely have time to breathe much less date." It's not a lie, just the closest I can get to an explanation. I *am* usually trapped under a mountain of books and paperwork, but I have enough spare time to at least make an effort. So, why don't I?

"What would your ideal girl be like?" Kendall probes. "What's your type?"

Good question. I haven't given as much thought to it as I probably should have by this point in my life. "I don't think I have a 'type.'"

"*Everyone* has a type, Payton."

I allow myself to really speculate about it for the first time in a long while. My brain runs through a checklist of desirable character traits, mentally marking off the tiny boxes next to each. "She'd have to be smart, that's absolutely a requirement. Kind, but still a little feisty. Funny in the sense that she's okay with laughing at herself every once in a while. And she'd have to love music. Maybe not every bit as much as I do, but *a lot*."

"What about physically?" Kendall adds curiously. "Say you could pick your ideal woman out of a line-up of famous chicks. Who would you go for?"

The very first person who comes to mind is Kendall Betten-court. *What in the hell?* The thought torpedoes me into the most surreal panic. She is one of the most important people in my life, not some hotter-than-a-house-on-fire bombshell from a movie poster. I *know* her. She's a sweet, sassy, intelligent, beautiful-on-the-inside, *real* person. And… *Oh my god.* She is my type! She is the standard by which I assess every other woman on the planet. *Oh, this is so effin' bad. I need to get out of here. Bring the damn check, please!*

I'd pick you, Kendall. You are, in every possible sense of the word, the most breathtaking woman I have ever met. That would be the most truthful answer I could give, but I know when to keep the truth to my damn self. "You know that X-Men movie, the one where Xavier can still walk?"

Kendall furrows her eyebrows at me as if to say 'yeah, and?'

"The actress who played Mystique in that. Hello, blue body paint."

"Yes!" Jared shouts. "Nice, Payday. Fist pump!"

"Please," Sarah waves him off. "Refrain from fist pumping. That gives Jersey such a bad name."

"Whatever. You see more fists pumping in The Garden State than you do gardens," Jared says in defense.

"All right, all right," Kendall interjects. "It's time for this party to end. I've got an early start tomorrow."

❋ ❋ ❋

As we pull up to my house, I notice my mother's Honda is missing from its usual spot in the driveway. *She must be working an overnight shift again.* Head ER nurse is the crappiest job. Mom sleeps in the on-call room more often than in her own room. I don't normally mind, but tonight I'm dreading it. Suddenly, agreeing to let Kendall share my bed seems like the worst idea I've ever had. My stomach is doing backflips, and I'm sure I'm going to hurl. *This is going to be fun.*

Kendall drops her Gucci duffle on the floor and combs over the DVD tower in my room. "Oh, I *so* called it!" She slides *X-Men: First Class* out of its spot and dangles it in front of my face. "You are a loser. A LOSER!"

The fact that I own this dreadful movie makes my fabricated 'perfect woman' story slightly more believable, but it will never be true. Kendall remains in the forefront of my brain, all beautiful and perfect and real as ever.

Just sell it, you moron. "What," I say flatly. "Jennifer Whatshername has *impeccable* bone structure."

"Her bone structure," she scoffs. "Good thing *that's* what does it for you. She's gotten quite slim recently."

"Did *you* really mean to insinuate that someone is too thin? Yeah, skinny, you should talk." I want to squash the revelation that will surely doom our friendship. I need to act normal. With the intent of sending my stupid attraction to its grave, I press my fingers into her ribs and start tickling her. She squeals and squirms frantically while batting at my arms. I notice her sweater ride up her torso, but before I can pull my hands away I make contact with the soft, sun-kissed skin above her waist. That's around the time I realize how thoroughly screwed I am. I guess once you acknowledge the fact that you've got it bad for your best friend, there isn't a damn thing you can do to make it all okay again. *Dear God, if you're listening, please strike me down right this moment. It's easy to avoid awkwardness when you're in a coma or dead.*

I quickly stop touching her and snatch the DVD away from her. "This isn't even the crappiest movie in my extensive collection of crappy movies, okay? I own every film you've been in, to date."

She frowns. "Did you just call my movies bad?"

"Not *all* of your movies are bad. You have to admit that some of them are rather basic, though."

"Basic? That's Payton-speak for 'mind-numbing.'"

I draw in the deepest breath I've ever taken and try to keep my mouth from saying the most obviously obsessive fangirl things. "No, that's Payton-speak for 'the best friggin' thing ever.'"

"You're right, anyway. Thanks to my mom, most of the stuff I've done up to now *is* boring. But this new film I'm starting is surprisingly well written. Actually, it's kind of intense, totally the kind of film my mom would have absolutely insisted I have nothing to do with." She pauses sharply. "Did I tell you that my character is a drug-addicted bisexual rock star?"

This day keeps getting better and better! "No, you didn't tell me that. Do you get to kiss anyone interesting? That chick from those sparkly vampire movies, perhaps?"

"You know if I had been cast in that franchise, it wouldn't have sucked as miserably as it did."

"Not even you could have saved those movies."

"How jealous would you be if I said I got to kiss a certain someone with 'perfect bone structure'?"

I would be jealous that she *gets to kiss* you. Play it cool, I remind myself. "Do you, really?"

"No, just some fellow up-and-comer. I've never met your heart-throb, but if I ever do, I'll be sure to let her know how *sexy* you think she is when she's blue and covered in scales."

"Do that and I'll put a hit out on you, Dirty Jersey style."

She smirks at me and sits down on the bed. She's quiet for a while. It's unnerving. "A lot of people are saying that I'm going to be nominated for an Elite Award for *In Heaven's Arms*." She doesn't sound too thrilled at the idea.

"Isn't that a good thing?"

She shrugs. "It would change things for me."

"Yeah, from that day forward your name will forever be prefaced with 'Ellie Nominee.' That sounds nightmarish. It'll probably be carved on your tombstone, too! 'Here lies Ellie Nominated actress Kendall Bettencourt.' That's assuming you don't *win* the damn thing. That would be so much worse! 'Ellie Winner Kendall Bettencourt' has a hideous ring to it."

She reaches out for my arms and pulls me down next to her on the bed. I practically die at the sudden contact between us. "I'm serious. I don't have much privacy as it is now. I might as well keep my apartment door permanently propped open if I'm nominated."

"I'll make you a deal. If it happens, I'll move to LA to become your personal bodyguard."

"That's a good deal. I'll take it." She gestures for a handshake. Gingerly, I oblige her. Her hand is warm and smooth. I resist the urge to press my lips against it.

Damn it! These feelings for Kendall are fully freaking me out. They were never part of my consciousness before, but the more I think about it, the more I'm sure they have always existed—resting dormant just beneath the surface of perceptibility. Now that they've broken through whatever barrier kept them locked away, I've become so harshly aware of them that it's physically painful. It's like I'm treading on jagged glass, and I can't deal with it. All it takes is one minor slip up, one wrong footfall, and I'll be shredded into tiny pieces.

I'm quickly finding that I cannot wait for her to board that plane in the morning.

❄ ❄ ❄

Kendall yawns as the credits of *X-Men* scroll across the TV screen. She gets up to riffle through her bag in search of pajamas. Unfortunately for my sanity, her idea of comfortable sleepwear is a pink cami and a pair of black shorts designed to conceal the absolute minimum amount of butt-cheek allowed by law. *Please, not those. Don't you have track pants, or like, a snow suit in that bag?*

"Payton, your bed is beckoning to me, 'Kendall, fall into me. I'm so cozy!'" she says in squeaky, high-pitched voice.

It's eleven o'clock. I'm exhausted, but so terrified at the idea of sleeping next to her that I'm willing to battle the impulse to doze. Those damn shorts are not helping in the slightest. They have downright entranced me.

"Did you hear me?" Kendall snaps her fingers. "It's bedtime, unless you want us both to stumble around like zombies in the morning."

I snatch a pair of sweatpants from a pile of clothes in the corner then stop to look around. There are an endless number of textbooks and staff paper notebooks strewn haphazardly about the navy carpet. My closet looks like it threw up, and my wall-mounted rack of guitars is so dusty it could cause an asthma attack. I should have cleaned up before she got here. "I'm gonna change in the bathroom," I say as I scuttle toward the door.

She shoots me a sideways grin. "Giving me the boudoir are you? That's very sweet."

"You can thank me with a fruit basket," I call over my shoulder and bolt down the hall.

She is already huddled beneath the plush, green comforter by the time I've subdued my anxiety enough to reenter the room.

Her breathing is shallow and rhythmic, a sure sign that she's fallen asleep. I tiptoe over to the bed, gently lift the sheets and work my way into them. *Please don't wake up*, I think as I cocoon myself with a spare fleece blanket. If I'm swaddled tightly enough, there is no way I can accidentally make contact with her body while in the subconscious throes of slumber. I contemplate concocting some form of pillowy chastity fort to separate us even more, but that would be something I'd have to explain in the morning. I can feel my mind succumbing to fatigue, so I turn my back to her and allow myself to quietly nod off.

❅ ❅ ❅

Faint beams of early morning sunlight wake me. Reluctantly, I lift my head to read the bedside digital clock. It's 6:33. At some point in the night I managed to escape my blanket shackles. I'm lying on my back with my left arm propped under my pillow. Kendall's head is nuzzled into the spot where my shoulder and collarbone meet. Her arm is slung across my stomach—which, of course, is exposed because I don't own a single shirt long enough to resist creeping up my torso as I toss and turn in the night. It's a hairline past 6:30 in the morning, and I'm already freaking out. *That must be one for the record books.*

I draw in a series of quick, short breaths—preparing myself to move as lightly and slowly as possible. It's like that coyote ugly thing, except the girl I'm trying not to disturb is absurdly gorgeous, and we most definitely *did not* do anything sexual the night before. Or any night *ever*.

As I attempt to slide off the bed, Kendall slightly stirs, but does not wake. She makes a minor adjustment to the placement of her arm and instantly goes from lazily hugging my side to fully holding me. There *is* a difference between the two. It's a discreet longing—an added bit of effort—that turns a hug into a hold. I'm as sure as I've ever been of anything that I am being *held* right now. Without warning, I feel a hot, wet tear roll down my face. It splashes onto my t-shirt. I want this moment to last forever. I know it's the only one of its kind I'll ever have with Kendall.

I turn my head toward her and find myself unexpectedly peering into her snowy blue irises. She is very much awake, but has yet to move. "Good morning," she yawns.

"Hey."

She sits up, cracks her neck, and stretches. "I'm sorry. I slept, like, on top of you."

"It's okay, as long as you didn't drool." I pull at my shirt, pretending to check for any soaked-through spots. I know I won't find any save for the tiny tear mark at the collar.

"I do *not* drool," she says. "What time is it?"

I grab the clock off the nightstand and bring it close to her face. "This is a six," I point. "That's a three and that's an eight."

She rolls her eyes. "You're so cute when you're snarky."

"Get dressed." I slip off of the bed and pluck a pair of jeans from their spot on the desk chair. *I take it back, that whole 'I can't wait for her to leave' thing.* "You'll miss your flight if we don't get going."

❄ ❄ ❄

We pull up to the airport drop-off zone with barely enough time for Kendall to get through security and book it to her gate. If it weren't for me, she would've missed her flight for sure. It's always been this way. Kendall is fifteen minutes late; I'm fifteen minutes early. Together we cancel each other out and arrive everywhere right on time. She constantly says that without me around, she has no idea how she manages to be on time for anything. I joke that she doesn't manage it at all.

She hasn't even gotten out of the car yet, and I miss her already. "Text me when you land," I say as I pop the trunk so she can grab her luggage.

"Don't I always?"

Yes, you do. "Just a reminder."

She leans into me, gives me a peck on the cheek, and the tightest hug. "I'll see you soon. I promise."

I hate it when she makes promises she can't keep, but I know she'll try at least. "See you soon."

And then she's gone.

CHAPTER TWO

Kendall

I avoid travelling with an entourage whenever possible. Having that many people with you is a pitiful cry for attention, as far as I'm concerned. And it's not like the paparazzi need any help doing their job; if they want to track you down, they're like hellhounds on a mission. Besides, your entourage is only around to cater to your every whim and handle the transport of your luggage. I am perfectly capable of handling my own damn luggage trolley. It's so obnoxious when famous people allow others to do everything for them. I wouldn't be surprised if some of these A-Listers have their personal assistants wipe their asses for them, too.

Newark Liberty International Airport is a hot mess most of the time. I prefer JFK for business travel, but Newark is much easier to access from home. Today, however, security is running pretty smoothly. I'm through the checkpoint and headed to the gate fairly quickly. In the distance, I see a bunch of people seated in the lounge. They're presumably waiting for economy class to begin boarding. There *are* a few perks to my job—never again having to fly coach is one of them.

I throw my sunglasses on in hopes of dodging attention. It is *way* too early for me to be all smiley and receptive to any fans. Lawrence insists—like any good publicist would, I suppose— that there are two things every notable person should always have: A full face of makeup and a friendly disposition. Unfortunately, at 7:30 in the morning I generally have neither.

I'm recognized almost immediately by a group of guys in Louisiana State University attire. They make some noise and flock toward me. All of a sudden, there are pens, notebooks, and cameras being shoved in my face. *Really?* I plaster on the biggest smile I can muster as I pose for pictures and sign my name a few times. It's amusing how total strangers react when they meet somebody they consider a "celebrity." They always seem to go straight in for the hug, never mind the customary introductory handshake. I'm not sure how I feel about letting people I don't know get so close to me. I'm sort of OCD about being touched, though I don't usually have a say about it.

Once all the excitement of the spontaneous meet-and-greet dies down, I say goodbye to my new friends, gather my things, and hurry my way onto the plane. Sometimes I can't believe this is real life. I can't fathom how my presence is so astounding that people make a big deal out of getting my signature. Take flight attendants, for instance. Now, they are some awesome people. They normally couldn't give a damn about who the hell is on the plane as long as everyone sits down and shuts up. It's sort of weird that they always call me by name, though. "Can I get you something to drink, Ms. Bettencourt?" or "Enjoy your flight, Ms. Bettencourt."

One of the awesome attendant's voices booms over the loud speaker asking for all electronic devices to be switched off. I've got the drill down pat, so I don't wait for the announcement to finish. I pull my Blackberry from the pocket of my jeans, start for the off button and then pause. "Taking off now," I type to Payton. "Think I'll step up from texting to calling you when I land :)." I press send.

I still can't wrap my head around why it took her so long to tell me that she's gay. Yes, some people are assholes, but I'd like to think I'm not one of those people. How can you judge people based solely on their sexuality? That's only a small part of who they are! And it's not like they can change it, as though it were a bad dye-job or an unsightly outfit. I would never think any less of someone for being who they are. Doesn't Payton know me well enough to understand that? Of course she does... but I guess it doesn't matter how well you think you know someone, there's always a fear that they'll abandon you. After all, it's the people you care about the most who can cut you the deepest.

✼ ✼ ✼

The plane lands in New Orleans after three-and-a-half cramped hours, and I cannot wait to get my feet on terra firma. First class boasts extended leg room, but that is a crock of BS. I feel horrible for everyone on the flight who isn't in the "elite" seating.

I meet my driver at the baggage claim. He's holding a sign that says "Bettencourt," and I sprint toward him before anyone else can catch wind of it. He grabs my luggage from the conveyor belt despite my determination to do it myself and then checks his itinerary. "Ms. Bettencourt, looks like I'm taking you to the Windsor Resort first then to meet with Mr. Ryan at 3:30."

"Okay, firstly, the name is Kendall." I extend my hand to introduce myself properly.

He shakes my offered hand. "Ricky."

"Secondly," I flip through my organizer. *Of course, I can't find the damn schedule!* "Mr. Ryan? I don't know who that is."

"Oh," he looks at me, startled, and hands me the paper he was reading from. "Jonathan Ryan. He's a music teacher. You're supposed to meet him for a lesson."

A music lesson! I don't know why I feel blindsided; I signed on to play a rock star in this movie, after all. I knew I'd have to sing and mock-play guitar, which was almost reason enough for me to turn down the part, but now I actually have to pick up an instrument? I need to call Payton. She will be hysterical. I have *zero* musical talent.

"Okay, Ricky." I sigh. "Let's get this show on the road."

❈ ❈ ❈

The first thing I do when I get to my hotel room is call Payton in a tizzy.

"Land safely?" she answers.

"Yes, but I'm freaking out."

There's silence on the line for a moment. "You've been there for an hour. What could you possibly be freaking out about already?"

"Music lessons." I was right when I said she'd be hysterical. She's squawking like a murder of crows. "How is this funny, Payton?"

"The *one* thing you couldn't stick with, they're making you do."

"I couldn't stick with it because I knew I was crap."

"That isn't true, and you know it. I tried to teach you some piano, and you quit after, what, two lessons? You could have gotten it if you would've been patient."

"Patience is a virtue I've never had. You know that."

"That's because you're, like, instantly good at everything you do… and I bet you could've been good at the piano, too, if you would've stuck with it."

"The instructor's name is Jonathan Ryan. Payton, the guy has two first names! He's sure to be an ass."

"Um, Payton Taylor. Hello?"

"But…" I start in protest. She cuts me off.

"Kendall, I have to go to class. Here are your instructions, short and sweet: You're going to the lesson. You *will* pay attention, and you *will* put some effort into it. I'm sure they don't expect you to be an overnight virtuoso. They probably want you to get a handle on the logistics of it, is all."

"Fine!" I whine.

"Don't be petulant. You can do it. I know you can."

She has so much faith in me, and I have no idea why. I'm glad she does, though. Somebody has to. "I'll try." And I will try. For her.

"Good. Let me know how it goes... tomorrow, though. I've gotta read six chapters tonight for my History of German Douchebaggery class, *and* I have to start a paper for Modern Lit."

"History of German Douchebaggery," I say with a snort. "Okay. Kick ass on all that."

"Kick ass on your lesson," she replies then hangs up.

Once again, Payton has talked me off a ledge. I've lost count of how much I owe her.

❊ ❊ ❊

I meet Jonathan Ryan at a full-fledged recording studio. I'm talking wall-to-wall noise-cancelling glass complete with condenser microphones hanging from the ceiling. I only know what the hell a condenser microphone is because I dated a sound guy last summer.

I can tell this dude is a jerk from Jump Street. His hair is gelled into spikes, and he's wearing eyeliner. *Eyeliner, for god's sake!* I want to tell him that he looks like a poser, but that would only make this experience even less enjoyable.

"Hi. I'm Jon," he says in a thick southern twang and hustles me toward a black Baby Grand. Right away, I'm thinking of how easily Payton could rock out on that thing. Me? Not so much. "I know the character you're playing is a guitarist, and you're not expected to play," he continues, "but the director wanted you to 'experience the feel of the music at its roots,' whatever that means. I think the best way to go about this is with the piano."

Okay, I may have been wrong about this guy. There is a slight chance he won't be so bad. "So what do you want me to do?"

He pulls the bench away from the piano, sits down and motions for me to join him. "Let's find out what you know."

I look at him like he's dense. *What do I know? Something in the ballpark of nada.* I think back to all the times I'd sat with Payton at the piano in her living room. It was old and had belonged to her grandfather who'd played with the likes of John Coltrane and Miles Davis, she told me. She tried to teach me rudimentary things. Now, I wish I had paid closer attention.

I place my fingers on the keys and press down lightly on a few. One note in particular sounds familiar. Payton used to tap it over and over again. "Is that Middle C? I think that's what it's called, I don't know."

"That's right, it is Middle C. That's the beginning of the C Major scale. The scale, in whole notes, is CDEFGABC." He plays each white key as he names them.

Encouraged, I press the second white key next to Middle C, twice. "E, E," I say and continue. Before long I've played an entire series of notes, first with one hand, then with two. "That's Brain Stew by Green Day," I proclaim with pride.

"Is it?" He asks. "Who taught you that?"

"Payton," I say—just her name, as though everyone in the entire world knows exactly who I'm talking about and no further explanation is necessary. But then I remember that not everyone on the planet knows Payton. They know me, and I know her. "I'm sorry. A friend I grew up with taught me. Her name is Payton. She plays guitar and piano and everything else. She's completely into music. I think she's responsible for most of the artists I have on my iPod."

He nods. "Can you play anything else?"

I clear my throat. In my head, I'm hearing a song Payton and I used to play together. She taught me the simpler part, and she played the more complex notes. "Yeah, but I need some help with it." I press the keys slowly.

Jon knows the duet. He plays the part Payton usually does. I start humming along with the notes, then singing. We play the song through to the end.

"You have a nice voice," he says. "Right on key. That's the most difficult thing to teach, the concept of being on key. It's either something you have or you don't."

I shrug. "Thanks."

"It sounds like there isn't much more you need to know. You should thank your friend for giving you a solid introduction."

"I will."

He stands and steps away from the piano. "Well, it was nice to meet you. Good luck with the film." He extends his hand to me, and I shake it.

"It was nice to meet you, too. Thank you for your time."

"No problem," he says. "Take care."

I'm headed toward the door, about to reach for the handle, when Jon appears at my side. He pulls the door open, holds it steady.

"What is this, chivalry?" I laugh. "I thought that was dead."

He grins. "Not here in the South, it isn't."

"Thanks," I say and move to exit the room.

"Hang on. Since you're going to be in New Orleans for a while, I thought maybe I could take you out sometime—show you around the city and everything. I'm assuming that I wouldn't be stepping on your boyfriend's toes, of course."

I study him for a moment. He seems like a nice guy, and I'm impressed he had the balls to ask, as most guys would just stand there in a stupor, salivating all over themselves. But I really am dead set on taking a vacation from the dating scene to focus all my energy on becoming the best actress I can be; no boy who wears eyeliner is going to persuade me to do otherwise.

"Listen, Jon, I appreciate you asking, but my schedule is going to be packed while I'm here. I'll probably be so rundown that I doubt I'll be up for hanging out in whatever free time I may have."

"I understand." He seems disappointed, but cool. He hands me his business card. "In case you should find yourself in need of a tour guide, call me."

I take the card and put it in my pocket. "Okay. I'll do that," I say, but I already know I won't. The only thing I've gotten from meeting him is a bizarre urge to learn more piano.

Ricky is waiting for me by the car when I get outside. He opens the door to the back seat, and I climb in. According to the itinerary, I have the rest of the day to myself.

"Would you like to go back to the hotel, Ms. Bettencourt?"

"Kendall," I correct him. "Would you happen to know any-place I could pick up a keyboard or something?"

He laughs. "Kendall, you're in the Big Easy. We're knee-deep in music here. I can find you a wobble board if you'd like one."

I have no idea what a wobble board is, but it sounds like the coolest thing ever. "Excellent! Let's track one of those down, too."

❄ ❄ ❄

I text Payton when I get back to my room, "I bought a keyboard. It's a Yamaha PSR-E333. The guy at the store told me it's good for beginners. Think you can teach me?"

I receive a text back straightaway. "I'm guessing your lesson went well. I can try to show you some stuff over Skype, but you should hire a professional—someone to be there with you as you go along."

Nope. All the effort she put into trying to teach me, and I brushed it off. It feels wrong to let someone else pick up where she left off. "I remembered how to play 'Brain Stew' and 'Heart and Soul.' I remembered where Middle C was. If you could teach me that when I was so reluctant to learn, you're the only one who can teach me anything now," I send back.

"Okay," she replies. "Let me know when you're free, and we'll video chat."

Good. It'll be nice to see her face, anyway.

Her next text reads, "What's your call-time tomorrow?"

"I have to be in hair and makeup at 5:30."

"In the morning? Oh, how I envy you!"

I can practically see the sarcasm dripping from her words. "I know. I'm beat. Going to bed soon. I'll call you when I can."

"Sweet dreams!"

The first two weeks of shooting are horrendous. There isn't an unscheduled moment from dawn to dusk and to top it off, my co-star, Rebecca, is an amateur at best. Every scene we have together needs at least ten takes. She's sweet, has a ton of potential, and her amber eyes remind me of Payton's, but she clearly isn't ready for the big time yet. She keeps botching her lines—not because she doesn't know them, but because her confidence is lacking. I want her to succeed as much as I want this film to succeed, so I suggest we continue to workshop the script together. She shows up at my door after a long Friday on set with the most dejected expression on her face and a crinkled script in her hand.

"Nope! Nuh uh," I say. "I'm going to close this door. You're going to knock again, and when I open it I want to see some enthusiasm on your face, like this," I flash a huge grin. "Got it?"

She bares her teeth. "Is this good enough?"

"Perfect!" I invite her in and lead her over to the couch. "Want something to drink?"

"I'm okay, thanks."

"Sure." I click my tongue. "So, where do you want to start?"

She flips to scene thirty-two—a very angry build-up to a very hot love scene. "I think I'd like to run through this one. I've got the lines down, but I think we should work on the... I don't know."

"The chemistry," I agree.

"Yeah, the chemistry. I'm nervous about it. I've never shot a scene this *choreographed*. And it's my first on-screen love scene, so I want to get it right."

I know where she's coming from. Your first on-screen love scene is the most awkward thing in the entire world. It's supposed to look natural, but it's so ridiculously technical. If you don't handle it with care, it can easily turn into a total mess. I mean, you don't have anyone barking directions at you when you're getting it on in real life, do you?

"Okay. Let's go for it." I read the slug line aloud, "INT. KATIE'S HOTEL ROOM – AFTERNOON," and continue. Both of us need to be standing relatively close to a bed, according to the directions, so we stand. "You're wearing that?" I finger the collar of her shirt like it's the strings of a hoodie. "You could at least make an effort."

"We're going to an interview for a magazine, not the Grammys," she pushes my hand away. "What am I supposed to wear? Shredded jeans and a dog collar, like you?" She pauses. "Goddamn it, Katie! You used to be a musician. Now you're just some desperate rock star. Always gotta look the part. Always gotta be high on something."

That was good, very smooth. "Look the part?" I sniffle, per the directions. "I am the part! I've spent every waking hour trying to get exactly where I am right now! I crawled through the shit, played in every dive and gutter to get here. I worked my ass off. Now that I've made it, I'm enjoying it! What's the problem?"

"You think you were alone in those dives? Sam and Tracy and I were right there with you the whole time! The problem is you're the only one who's changed! I used to be so in love with your talent and with you. But you turned into a junky and before you know it, all you'll be is a has-been."

I'm supposed to push her onto the bed while kissing her passionately. But I can't. I'm frozen in place. Nothing like this has ever happened to me before. "I'm sorry," I stammer. I'm just me now; Katie has left the building. "That was great. I just like to save the actual physical part for when they call 'action.' It feels more genuine that way."

"Oh yeah, good thinking," she replies. "We're going to rock this scene."

"For sure," I concur. But I'm not so sure. There's an enormous lump in my throat that I can't seem to swallow.

"Hey, I'm starving," she takes the focus off the giant elephant in the room that apparently only I can see. "You want to head down to the bar across the street and try some of the black crawfish I've been hearing about?"

"Crawfish?" I am entirely grossed out at the idea of chomping on something that looks like a crossbreed between a scorpion and a lobster, but Rebecca seems fun and adventurous. I could use a bit of fun and adventure. "There isn't anything I'd like to try more!"

✳ ✳ ✳

It turns out Rebecca is exactly what I expected her to be. She's loud, rowdy, and quite a partier. I learn her entire life story while watching her inhale tequila shots. She's twenty-two, originally from Iowa, and has been living in Los Angeles for four years. She has a boyfriend named Tom, a dog named Chutney, and a father who never believed she'd amount to anything. I tell her that I'm single, that I don't have a dog, and that my mom is the epitome of a pushy "stage mom." Thanks to the Internet, she already knows all about where I'm from and how I got my start. It's strange to think that anyone who wants to can consult the web and magically know all about me.

It's after two in the morning when I decide I need to leave.

"I'm gon' stay n' make some new friends," she slurs. No one in the crowded bar is paying much attention to us, but I don't think I should leave a pretty, drunken girl by herself at a pub in the French Quarter. That screams disaster to me.

"Oh, no you don't." I slam some cash on the bar, stand up, and sling her arm around my shoulders. The second we try to leave, I see people pulling out their cell phones to capture us on video. *Wonderful. I'm underage, carrying an inebriated girl from a bar in the dead of night, and some crappy rag mag will have photo evidence of the whole event by the time the sun rises.* I'm tempted to deadpan a camera and say "Hi, Ma. Aren't you proud?" but that would almost certainly be the dumbest thing I could do in this situation. Lawrence is already going to shit a brick and beat me with it. I needn't say anything to fuel the fire.

By the time we stumble into Rebecca's room, I am thoroughly exhausted. She passes out almost as soon as her head hits the pillow. I roll my eyes and leave her to her own devices.

When I reach my room, I fall into bed without bothering to change into pajamas. I'm finding sleep elusive, though. The way the night ended is bugging me. I try to avoid nights like these. I kind of like my budding reputation as Hollywood's "good girl." I like to present myself as fun-loving, yet digni-fied. There are too many people in this business who strive to make themselves seem much "cooler" than anyone needs to be. Besides, if getting so sloshed that you need to be carried home is the public's idea of cool, I'd much rather be thought of as lame.

I click a text to Payton, although I know she won't be awake to answer it. "Sorry I haven't texted in a while. Things are insane here. Tonight was my first break from filming in forever, and my co-star got wasted. Pick up a gossip mag on Monday if you need a laugh. Have the day off tomorrow! Hope to talk to you. XOXO Kendall."

※ ※ ※

Saturday is the cast's first full day of rest since day one. I spend most of the day reading and lounging by the indoor pool with the rest of my cast mates. Lauren Atwell—the actress playing Tracy, the bassist—is beyond cool. I met her briefly once at a premier, but this is the first chance I've had to really get to know her. She's twenty. She likes to read and go to concerts. She's been acting since she was ten, though this is her first major studio production. I get her phone number so we can hang out back in LA. Spencer St. Germaine, our drummer, is the only one of us who can play his instrument for real. He's sweet, but spends most of his time on the phone with his girlfriend.

In time, Rebecca joins us. It becomes apparent to everybody that she is hung over when she keeps calling us by our characters' names.

"Someone had a rough night," Lauren says.

Spencer, finally detached from his cell, says, "Yeah, you look like you lost a match with an MMA fighter."

"I *feel* like I lost a match with an MMA fighter," Rebecca replies. "Thanks for getting me back to my room last night," she says to me.

"You're welcome," I reply while checking my phone for any texts I may have missed. It's late afternoon, and I still haven't heard anything from Payton. It's worrying. That's not at all like her. She usually gets back to me ASAP when she knows I have free time.

"Waiting for your boyfriend to call?" Spencer asks.

It's the most irritating thing that everyone assumes I have a boyfriend, like it's impossible for me to be happily unattached. "Why does everyone always ask me about the boyfriend I don't have?" My voice sounds much sharper than I intended it to. They all pick up on it.

"Sorry," Spencer nods. "It just seems like you're waiting for a call."

"Is that a sore subject, the boyfriend thing?" Lauren questions.

"I'm waiting for a friend to get in touch with me. I sent her a text last night, and I'd normally have heard back from her by now." I shrug. "And no, it's not a sore subject. I'm just not interested in a relationship right now."

Just then, my phone rings. It's Payton. I hop to my feet, distance myself slightly from everyone so that I can talk to her privately. "Hey. Did you get my text?" I wonder if maybe it got lost across the great, expansive airways of America.

"Yes, I did. Sorry. I had a study group this morning. I went for coffee with a girl from the group afterward."

"Oh." A spark of jealousy ignites inside me, though I'm not sure why. It's not like Payton would ever replace me. Would she? "You were on a date?" *That isn't any of your damn business. And shouldn't you be happy for her if it was a date?*

"Um, sure, if you consider a two-hour conversation about the Nazi occupation of Europe a date. That would be the worst date ever and likely put me off women altogether."

I laugh. "You're right, that would be the worst date ever."

We talk for over an hour and set up a video chat session for when I get back to LA. After she hangs up, I rejoin the pack by the pool. Rebecca and Spencer are horsing around in the water. Lauren is smirking at me. "Got that call you were waiting for?"

I plop into a lounge chair. "Yeah. My friend, Payton."

"That's good. I could tell you were worried."

"I haven't been able to talk to her much lately, since we've been so crazy busy with filming." I decide right then that I will never take another part in a film that's only in production for thirty-one days. It's too much, too quickly.

She furrows her brow. "Afraid she'll forget about you?"

"No." It's more me forgetting about her, though I know that could never, ever happen. "I just always think I'm missing out on things back home. Even in high school, when I was just doing TV shows and small films—I worked so hard, scooping up as many roles as I could get. People say high school is the greatest four years of their lives. When I actually managed to be there, it *was* great. Yet I know I missed some of the most important things. I wasn't there for prom. I wasn't there for graduation. I wasn't there for my best friend when she was dealing with what was, in all probability, the hardest thing she's ever had to deal with."

"Sounds like you didn't know what you were getting yourself into when you signed up for fame and fortune."

"I wanted to be an actress, strived to be a great one, but I was kind of ill-prepared to be *famous*. Like, there's this bizarre new thing that's been happening to me lately; I keep catching paparazzi hiding in the bushes in front of my apartment building!"

"Yikes." She laughs. "I haven't had to deal with that much absurdity yet."

"Want to trade lives with me?" I ask, only half-joking. "Mine's becoming kind of insane."

"No, thanks, I'm good with getting paid for being a tiny blip on the radar. If you think it's bad now, wait until award season comes around. *In Heaven's Arms* was incredible. If you don't get an Elite Awards nod, there isn't any hope for the rest of us."

"Oh god, that is the last thing I want. I'd be honored and flabbergasted to the point of muteness, but I don't want to deal with that kind of attention. It's gotten hard enough already to have anything that's *personal*."

She nods. "I guess that's how you know you've made it, when privacy becomes a mythical thing."

"I guess so. I suppose I'd better take a deep breath and hold on for dear life."

She laughs again. "Definitely."

❉ ❉ ❉

Finally, it's the last day on set. *Everyone* is beyond ready to wrap at this point. But today is the day I have been dreading—the filming of scene thirty-two. I've never enjoyed doing sex scenes, but this one is freaking me out much worse than any I've had to do before. It's a closed set, so only the most necessary cast and crew will be loitering around as it happens. Normally, that makes it easier for me, but this time, it isn't helping at all.

As my call-time approaches, I contemplate chugging some vodka or something to help loosen me up. I feel shoddy, like this is the ultimate assessment of my acting abilities and soon everyone will see what an unqualified fraud I am. I can fake playing a girl left dazed and lonely by her sudden shot to stardom because that isn't such a stretch from the person I really am. I can even fake playing the stupid guitar. But this love scene, the way it's written… it's too passionate, too real for me to counterfeit. I've never experienced anything like it in real life, so I've got very little to draw on. *I am going to bomb.*

We're standing around, waiting for the gaffers to adjust the lighting. I sneak off to the chair where I left my phone. I flip through the contacts and punch the key for "Payton" while wondering if she ever gets tired of talking me through my absurd crises.

"What's wrong, Kendall?" She questions as soon as she picks up. *She knows me so well, it's frightening.* Suddenly, a shroud of guilt takes hold of me. I start thinking about all the times she must have needed me to be a phone call away, and I wasn't.

"Nothing is wrong, per se. I just need a potent shot of reassurance. You were the first person who came to mind." *Nice going. Way to sound like a stage-five clinger.* "Remember when I told you I got to kiss that up-and-comer? We're shooting that scene in, like, five minutes, and the revised version involves much more than kissing."

"So, Kendall Bettencourt, the best actress in the business, is nervous. Is that what you're telling me?"

"I can't act. I can't do anything. Let's move on."

"Oh, please." She draws out the 'ease.' "Acting is like breathing for you, drama queen. Close your eyes and pretend you're in your own space, kissing someone you'd kiss if you weren't acting." She pauses. "Think of Jared."

"Jared?" I let out a boisterous cackle. The crew around me stops what they're doing to glower at me. Jared. Gross. That car crashed and burned when we were fifteen. Absolutely nothing was salvaged from the wreckage. "I would never kiss Jared again, even if he were the last living thing on earth. Seriously, I'd make out with a dead cactus first."

"Made you laugh, though," she says. "It can be anyone, anyone at all. Picture someone you're comfortable with. Hell, picture that dead cactus if it's easier than what you have to work with."

"Okay." The assistant director taps my shoulder. This is happening... like imminently. "Thanks, Payton. I've gotta go."

"Good luck."

Sure, I could picture someone I'm comfortable with. The problem is that the first person who pops into my head is the *last* person I should ever think about kissing.

Rebecca steps next to me looking über self-assured. "Are you ready to kill it?"

"Of course," I smile. *More like it's ready to kill me.*

Action is called. I steady myself before moving closer to her. "You're wearing that?" I tug at the strings of her sweatshirt, disgusted. "You could at least make an effort."

She slaps my hand away. "We're going to an interview for a magazine, not the Grammys. What am I supposed to wear? Shredded jeans and a dog collar, like you?" She pauses and so does my heart. "Goddamn it, Katie! You used to be a musician. Now you're just some desperate rock star. Always gotta look the part. Always gotta be high on something."

I wipe at my nose with my palm, sniffle. "Look the part? I am the part! I've spent every waking hour trying to get exactly where I am right now! I crawled through the shit, played in every dive and gutter to get here! I worked my ass off. Now that I've made it, I'm enjoying it! What's the problem?"

"You think you were alone in those dives? Sam and Tracy and I were right there with you the whole time! The problem is you're the only one who's changed! I used to be so in love with your talent and with you. But you turned into a junky... before you know it, all you'll be is a has-been."

She's right in my face, now. The heat between us is palpable. Suddenly, they're not Rebecca's eyes I'm looking into—they're Payton's. I gulp hard. What I'm feeling isn't comfort; it's something else entirely.

Do it! I close my eyes, reach behind her head, and grab her ponytail. The next thing I know, I'm voraciously shoving my lips against hers. She wraps her arms around me. Her hands settle on my back momentarily then abruptly move to the hem of my shirt. Her mouth breaks contact with mine for a split second as she pulls the shirt over my head, exposes my black lace bra to the camera. Then her lips smash into mine again. We move together in unison—still kissing—and fall back onto the bed. I'm on top. She's writhing against me from below. To everyone watching, I'm acting, but very much to my chagrin, I'm turned on *for real*. It's distracting in the worst possible way.

I force myself to concentrate on the script directions. I'm supposed to speedily unbutton her pants, but it feels totally wrong. *To hell with that.* Instead of pulling her jeans off in one quick motion, I slow it down. I slide the waistband down around her thighs, making a point to touch her skin in the process. I tug at the bottom cuff of each leg—first the right and then the left. I crumple the jeans into a ball and throw them to the floor. I slither up her body to look into her eyes once more. She bites her lip and curls her hand behind my neck. We meet half way and kiss again. She glides her tongue into my mouth, making this guttural moaning sound that reverberates deep in the hollows of my chest.

"Cut!" resounds from behind the camera. I have to force myself to stop. "That was perfect, ladies. It's a wrap, people!"

Everyone cheers except me and Rebecca. She grabs her pants from the floor. I pick up my shirt. We sit back down on the bed, avoiding each other's gaze as we dress.

She looks at me when we're both fully clothed. "That was…"

"Intense," we say in unison.

"I was thinking about Tom the whole time and getting thrown off. You know, due to the lack of stubble." She rubs her chin and giggles.

"Yeah, I bet." I don't want to tell her who I was thinking about. "So, wrap party?"

"Hell yes."

❄ ❄ ❄

I receive a wake-up call from the front desk at nine. Having left the post-wrap party a mere four hours earlier, nine in the morning seems like such an ungodly hour. I shouldn't have stayed out so late, and I *definitely* shouldn't have downed so much wine, but I really had to get out of my own obnoxious brain. Predictably, the brain I had to get out of so badly is currently paying me back by hammering incredibly hard against the sides of my skull.

Ricky arrives at 9:45 to drive me to the airport. I say hello to him and try to help him load my luggage into the car. He doesn't allow it. "Have yet to play this keyboard, huh?" He taps the large box as he places it in the trunk. I made a pact with myself that the first time I'd take the keyboard out of its packaging would be the start of my first official lesson with Payton. *Payton*. Her birthday is this Friday. I haven't been around to celebrate her birthday with her in years.

"I haven't had much time."

He opens the door. I scoot into the backseat.

"Are you ready to head on home?" he asks once he's in the driver's seat.

Home. Yes, I'm ready to go home. I grab my Blackberry from my handbag, scroll through the contacts, and press the call button.

"Wilhelm and Bettencourt Architectural," my father's secretary answers.

"Sandra? Hi, it's Kendall." Sandra is great. She's always so upbeat and makes a big deal when anyone calls the office, not just me. "Is my dad around?"

"Oh, hi honey! Glad to hear from you! Hold on a second. I'll patch you through to his office."

The line rings and rings and rings.

"Hey Pumpkin," my dad answers cheerfully. No matter how old I get or how long it's been since I've seen or talked to him,

I'll always be his Pumpkin. "You were all over *The Inquirer* a few weeks ago. Way to go." He laughs.

My dad. I miss him so much. And my *real* friends. And air that isn't so smoggy. And the view of New York City from across the Hudson. The list of things I miss goes on and on. "Yeah, I thought you'd be glad to see I was having ever so much fun on location."

"I was glad. Naturally, your mother was in shambles over it."

It's my turn to laugh before getting very quiet. "Daddy, I wanted to ask you something."

"Okay, shoot."

"I was wondering…" I feel peculiar, and it's completely unreasonable. This is the man I still call daddy, I'm talking to. "I was wondering if I could come stay with you and Mom for a while? Two weeks, tops. Maybe until a couple of days after Thanksgiving?" The only downside to this plan is that I'll have to spend more time with my mother than I'd like, but it'll be worth it if I get to hang out with my dad and my friends.

He's silent for a second. "Kendall, you don't ever have to ask to stay with us. It's your home, too. Is everything all right?"

I want to ramble off the list of things I miss, tell him that I feel unbelievably lonely even though the entirety of humankind seems to be fixated on me. "Everything's fine. I just need to get away for a while."

"I don't know why you'd want to get away to Clifton when you could go to Cancun, but we would love to have you with us for a while, especially for Thanksgiving."

"Awesome." I'm beyond thankful. "Okay, I'm headed to the airport now. I have to change my flight. I should be home later tonight."

"Okie doke. We'll see you when you get here." I can hear the smile in his voice and in my own as we say our goodbyes.

Once the call ends, I open the phone's picture folder and scroll through the photos: tons of me and the *Idol* cast clowning around, nearly as many of me and my Hollywood friends at parties and premiers, a few of me and my parents, a few of me, Jared, and Sarah, and one of Payton. *One.* She has always hated posing for pictures, but I managed to snap one when she wasn't paying attention at Sarah's Fourth of July barbeque last summer. She's sitting in a lawn chair with an acoustic guitar in her lap. She's facing the camera but looking at something out of frame. The sun is setting to the left of her, shining an ethereal glow across her face. *Beautiful.*

"Change of plans?" The sound of Ricky's voice startles me out of my thoughts.

"Yep," I nod. "I'm going home."

I catch him smiling in the rearview mirror.

CHAPTER THREE

Payton

I'm sitting at my usual spot in the student center café, reading through my World War II textbook and wondering why I have to bother taking all the standard academic courses. I wanted to go to Berklee to major in Film Scoring. I *should've* gone to Berklee, considering Montclair doesn't offer a single Film Scoring–concentrated class. In the end, it all came down to money. MSU offered me a much larger scholarship. And, I'll never admit to this if anyone were to ask, I was kind of scared at the prospect of being so far away from home. I wasn't ready for that back then. I'm not sure I'd be ready for it now, either.

I'm this close to finishing my last assigned chapter when a bothersome commotion erupts in the hallway, ripping my focus away from the page. I glance through the interior windows to see what the hell all the ruckus is about. There's a sizeable crowd gathered in front of the vending machines, but I can't catch a glimpse of what's got everyone so riled up. I slam my book closed, deciding to head to the practice rooms in the John J. building for some peace and quiet.

I'm about to pass the vending machines when I feel a hand grab my elbow and stop me dead in my tracks. "What the hell do you think you're–?" I start, ready to throw a fist. Before I can finish my sentence, I'm glowering into a pair of huge sunglasses.

My breath catches in my throat when I recognize who I'm staring at. "Kendall? Oh my god!" Instantly, I'm in her arms, hugging her tightly. I'm not even worried about whether or not touching her will make me feel all edgy inside. "What are you doing here?"

She smiles her glittering smile. "My mom gave me a ride, believe it or not."

"Cute, but you know what I mean. What are you doing *here*? I thought you were going home after you wrapped."

"I am home. LA is just where I hang my fabulous clothing on occasion. Besides, you've got a birthday coming up, duh." There are still a handful of people hanging around us, snapping pictures, and talking loudly amongst themselves. Kendall is observably annoyed by it. "Wanna get out of here?"

I want to, but really shouldn't. "I'd love to. I have class in an hour though."

"Skip it," she says lightly, like going to class has no bearing on my future whatsoever.

Damn it! She could ask me to jump into the flaming underbelly of hell, and I'd do it for her. "Let's go," I say. We loop arms and head for the parking garage.

The drive down to my house is too quiet for my liking. "So, I read in a magazine that you and Spencer Whatshisname were all over each other in New Orleans," I declare, forgetting that her confirmation would likely decimate me. *Bad choice for small talk, Payton.*

"That is such a lie! He's madly in love with the girl he's been with for years. Anyway, I was hardly anywhere but on set and in the hotel the whole time I was there. How could anyone claim to have seen us 'all over each other?'"

I smile. "Makes sense."

"What about you?" She picks at her cuticles. "Have you met anyone who hasn't bored you to death with conversations about the eastern front?"

Of course I haven't. I'm holding out hope for a girl who will never, ever have a romantic feeling for me as long as she lives. It's foolish, really, that I'm prepared to die alone when I know for a fact there's a sea of lesbians somewhere I could be swimming in. "I haven't put too much energy into meeting Ms. Right or Ms. Right For the Moment either. I've been concentrating on school and writing music."

"Oh, that's good," she says like she's surprised or relieved or something. I can't really tell. "Being career-minded is a big hit with the ladies, once you're ready to find one for yourself."

I don't want to say anything I shouldn't say, but I'm ready to lament about how I already found someone amazing.

"Hey, so what's the plan for Friday night? Will there be a slew of awesome birthday festivities?"

"The plan? Outside of spending the day acclimating myself to a 'nine' in front of the 'teen,' there is no plan. My mom has to work. Sarah has to work. And I really do not want to spend the night talking about random girls' racks with Jared."

"Okay, no. That will not do at all." She scoops up my hand from the gear shift. I quiver and hope she doesn't notice. "You leave it to Kendall. She will make sure you have the best birthday ever."

I smile. I haven't spent my birthday with Kendall since I turned sixteen. "I'm sure it will be the best birthday ever, provided Kendall doesn't refer to herself in the third person all night."

She drops my hand, pretending my words have offended her. "Kendall cannot guarantee such things."

"Okay, miss 'I'm so awesome I call myself by name,' what do you have in mind?"

The mischievous look in her eyes sends my ability to reason packing. "That is classified information Kendall is not at liberty to disclose. Be ready to go by nine."

"Can you at least give me a hint on what to wear? I don't want to be under or overdressed."

"Wear something in between."

She clearly isn't going to give anything away, and I am not about to push the issue. "Okay. I will be ready to go by nine on Friday."

"Good. I promise you won't be disappointed. I have something…" Her phone rings, interrupting her train of thought. She checks the caller ID and looks back at me as though she's thinking about ignoring the call. "Damn. It's James. I'm sorry, I have to take this."

"Hello," she answers and sticks her tongue out at me. "I'm home. No, home, as in New Jersey. What the hell am I doing here? I'm visiting. No, I have no intention of being back in LA by Friday. There's no reason for me to be in LA right now. It's called *downtime*. Gee, I'm sorry. I didn't know I had to clear every decision I make with you or Lawrence. Dude, you should be very careful about what tone you take with me. I fired my own mother for less."

I don't know what he says to her, but her attitude changes in a heartbeat.

"James, please. All I'm asking for is two weeks. I really need a break," she pleads. "The day after Thanksgiving? All right, I can do that. Schedule the meeting. Yes, I swear, I will be on the Red Eye. Great, thank you. Bye."

By the time she ends the call, she is completely deflated. "I'm sorry. He's got his boxers in a bunch over some part I've been offered."

"Does it at least sound interesting?"

"Who knows? It's based on some Tolkien-esque young adult novel. I might do it simply because I'll get to play with swords," she grins.

"Sounds cool, but I'm glad you decided not to rush back."

"And cancel your birthday plans? Over my rotting carcass!"

I quickly turn to look out my side window so she won't notice the stupid grin taking hostage of my face.

✳ ✳ ✳

We stroll into the kitchen later than I had planned, but my mom is so excited to see Kendall that she doesn't complain about us being late. She actually skips over me and goes straight to hugging Kendall, cooing the whole time about how the California sun agrees with her.

Kendall spent so much time at my house while we were growing up that my mom practically adopted her. "My other daughter," Mom called her. I'm glad she doesn't call Kendall that anymore; being attracted to her would be way more psychologically scarring for me than it already is.

"Sorry to break up the happy reunion," I say, pushing my way through them to the fridge. "What's for dinner?"

"*So* rude," Kendall scowls at my mom.

Mom snickers. "Manners, Payton."

I place three cans of soda on the kitchen table. "Man, two minutes in the same room with each other and they're already ganging up on me," I say to no one in particular.

"Psssh," Kendall says, "you know your mom and I don't even have to be in the same room to gang up on you."

Mom nods, slipping her way over to the stove. "This is true."

"Here." I pull some plates from the cabinet and hand them to Kendall. "Make yourself useful."

"Sure, put me to work. I'm supposed to be on *vacation*," she mopes as she sets three places at the table.

"This is nothing. After dinner, we begin your ear training."

"That's nice, Kendall," Mom chimes in. "I never knew you were interested in learning music."

"Until recently, the idea sort of horrified me."

"And what changed your mind?" I ask.

"I thought it would be good for my career if I was an artistic triple threat. You know… acting, piano, some third thing I have yet to figure out."

"I could show you how to take someone's pulse," Mom jests.

"She said *artistic* triple threat, Mom."

"If she hums while taking someone's pulse does that count?" Mom asks over her shoulder while stirring a huge pot of spaghetti sauce.

"It's not nice to tease your mother," Kendall says. "Anyway, not *everyone* can be a musical savant like you." She makes a face and jabs at my stomach with her pointer finger. I grab her hand and lace my fingers between hers, trying to get her to stop poking me. Our hands remain clasped together longer than they need to be, but she keeps a firm grasp. She glimpses down at our entwined digits then back up at me. She's peering deep into my eyes, deep into *me*, and the room is spinning.

The thought distresses me so much that I drop her hand straightaway. She pretends not to have noticed how swiftly I pulled away. There's this emotion on her face I can't quite place—not exactly freaked out, but nowhere near calm, either.

"Okay, girls." Mom's voice puts an end to the moment. "Dinner is served."

❋ ❋ ❋

Kendall presses the C4 key on the piano. "Middle C."

"Good. What comes after that?"

Her finger lingers over the next white key. "D," she says and presses it. "EFGABC," she plays the remainder of the C Major scale and exhales.

"Nice."

"Will you play something for me?"

"No. This is your lesson, not mine."

"I know, but I'd like to hear something other than random notes and unfortunately, that's the best I can do at the moment."

"Fine," I sneer. "What do you want me to play?"

She flips through one of my staff notebooks, stops on a half-finished composition temporarily titled "This Might Not Suck." "This one," she points. "It looks like it sounds very angry with all those notes and slashes everywhere."

"It's not finished yet, though."

She tilts her head, like 'yeah, so?'

"Okay. Put it there." I gesture to the music shelf on the top of the piano. She places the book down, already open to the page she wants me to play. I begin slowly.

She's wrong about it sounding angry. It sounds incredibly sad. It's in B-flat minor, like a modernized Adagio for Strings only nowhere near as remarkable. When it ends, I catch her staring at me. "Yes?" I question.

"Holy wow."

"Shut up." I knock my shoulder into hers.

"You have to finish it. Promise me." She touches my forearm. "I want that in one of my movies someday."

"Get out of here."

"I'm not kidding, Payton," she says, poker-faced. "It's beautiful and I want it finished, so please finish it."

"Yes, ma'am," I answer sarcastically. Her expression doesn't change. "You're serious, aren't you?"

"Do you think I'd joke about having your music in one of my movies? I could make it happen, you know. With the right scene, there isn't a music supervisor in the industry who wouldn't love to use that piece."

Okay. All I've ever wanted to do with my life is make music for films, but the notion that it could ever actually happen is overwhelming. "I will finish it."

She smiles. "Excellent! Well, now, I feel utterly impotent. I think that's the end of the lesson for tonight." She stands up and heads for the front door.

"Same time tomorrow?" I'm not about to let her quit on me again.

"I can't tomorrow," she says disappointedly. "James is going to e-mail me that screenplay in the morning. I have to read it and give him my decision and any script notes by tomorrow night."

"Friday?"

"Absolutely not! We will not be doing any work at all on your birthday, comprende?"

"Got it. Want a ride home?"

She shakes her head. "It's a nice night. I feel like walking."

I look at her skeptically. "Would you like me to walk you home?"

"I'd like you to keep your butt on that bench until you're done writing the rest of that song," she answers as she reaches for the doorknob. "See you Friday."

❉ ❉ ❉

I wake up Friday morning to my mom sitting on my bed. She's holding a chocolate cupcake with a lit candle stuck in the middle. The cupcake thing has been a birthday tradition since I was a little girl. Every year, Mom rouses me from peaceful slumber at 7:12 to commemorate the exact moment of my entrance into the world after forty hours of hard labor on her part.

"Happy birthday," she says and kisses my forehead. "My baby is all grown up."

"Thanks, Mom." I blow out the candle. "I'm really not that grown up though."

"You're not married with children yet, but nineteen is pretty much an adult."

Maybe it's because my brain is only half-awake that I am unable to stop myself from completely ruining my whole day, but the second I process the phrase "married with children," verbal diarrhea begins. "Mom, you know I'm gay, right?" *Holy flaming crapballs! Did I really say that out loud?* Oh my god, I want to hurl myself off the closest, tallest building and fall to my doom. *What a tactless imbecile!*

She laughs. She just flat out laughs. I am categorically dismayed, and she is laughing! *What the hell is so funny?* "Oh, honey,

I know." She pats my head. "But, thanks for telling me. It certainly took you long enough."

I'm baffled. "Are you *kidding* me? You've known all this time?"

"You're my kid. I pay attention," she replies baldy, like it's the most obvious thing to ever happen in the history of the universe. "I've watched you beat yourself up about it for years. I was waiting for the day you'd finally realize that there's nothing to beat yourself up about."

"Mom," I say, suddenly petrified. I can feel tears forming in the corners of my eyes. "I think I'm gonna end up alone." If I keep going the way I'm going, I'm definitely gonna end up alone.

"Oh, Kiddo. Just hang in there. Someday you will meet somebody who is as crazy about you as you are about her. It'll happen when you least expect it, trust me."

"I don't care about someday. *Someday* doesn't exist to me. All I've got is right now, and right now, I'm…" Do I tell her about my feelings for Kendall? No, not "feelings." Anything that hurts this much can't be generalized in the classification of "feelings." Being in this much agony can only mean one very specific thing. I'm flat out in love with her. "Right now, I'm so screwed up."

"All right, that's a bit vague. You know what I think you should do? I think you should try expanding your social circle. It's great that you're still friends with the same kids you grew up with, but there's a whole wide world of people out there you haven't met yet. You have to be open to meeting those people, exploring what they have to offer."

So that's the solution? Go into the world, meet new people, and everything will be roses and sunshine? That's helpful. "Sure. I'll work on that. Thanks."

She smiles and thumps my leg with her knee. "Good. Start right now. Get out of bed and go do something fun with your day."

Right, do something fun.

I forego my mother's suggestion and instead hole up in my room, strumming my guitar with the amp turned up as loud as it can go. I pause now and then to scribble down chords that strike me as sounding anywhere close to good.

❊ ❊ ❊

Kendall shows up at my door twenty minutes before nine. I nearly pass out—not because she looks incredibly sexy in her silver off-the-shoulder top, skin-tight black mini skirt, and knee-high leather boots, though that's as good a reason as any—but because this is the first time in her whole life she has ever been early for anything. "Sorry I'm early. I wanted to make sure you were dressed appropriately."

I check my reflection in the hallway mirror. I'm wearing light jeans that hug me firmly at the hips but fan out into bells at the bottom, a fitted baby blue polo that clings to my curves in all the right places and shows the perfect amount of skin at my midriff, and a crisp, new pair of white Pumas. I've even taken the time to straighten my hair and put on some eyeliner. This is about as dressed up as I get, with the exception of weddings and funerals. I think I look all right.

Kendall examines me for a moment then takes my hand. "Twirl," she says. I fire a questioning look at her. "No interrogation. Do as I say."

I spin around slowly. "Do I meet with your approval?"

"Yes." She reaches for my hair and rolls a few ends around her index finger. I tremble. "You should wear your hair down more often."

"Maybe I'll start to." *If you keep playing with it like that, I will gladly give up my signature ponytail for the remainder of my life.*

"Good. You've passed inspection. We can move on. Are you ready?"

As long as you're standing next to me, I'm ready for almost anything. "I think so."

"Marvelous." She ushers me out the door.

I expect to see a rented BMW or her dad's Mercedes parked in the driveway, per usual. But she's leading me toward a long, glossy stretch limo, complete with blacked-out rear windows and a suited-up driver ready to open the door for us. I'm at a loss.

"Your chariot awaits," she turns to me.

"Are you *sure* I'm dressed okay?"

She chortles. "I'm positive. I wanted you to have the star treatment tonight, that's all."

Seriously? I am excruciatingly aware that she doesn't feel the same way about me as I do about her, but sometimes the incredible things she does for me make me wonder what she would do for someone she's actually in love with.

"I don't deserve…" I try to get a full sentence out, but she covers my mouth with her hand.

"Do *not* say that to me." She drops her hand to her side. "You're the best friend I could ever have. You deserve more than I can give you."

Oh, man. I am going to cry. There is no escaping it.

"No!" She points at me. "No crying on your birthday. Not even happy tears."

I wipe at my eyes and nod. "Fine, then no more sappy stuff."

"Okay," she agrees. "Get in."

We get into the limo. Kendall pulls out a thin, dark cloth and folds it long ways. She holds it taught and reaches for my head. I freeze upon recognizing it. *It's a blindfold.* I grab her wrist. "That is *so* not gonna happen."

"Yes it is," she counters. "It's part of the plan. You can't see where we're going. The mystery is half the fun!"

I shake my head, more than reluctant to oblige. "No."

"Come on. Don't you trust me?"

Of course I trust you. With my life, I trust you. "All right, damn it," I relent.

She wraps the cloth around my head and ties it just so. "Can you see anything?"

I shake my head back and forth, up and down. "Not a thing."

"Perfect," she says and pushes me back against the seat. I can feel the warmth of her palms on my shoulders through the sleeves of my shirt, the heat of her breath against my face as she leans over me. Her long, soft locks brush against my cheek, and I can feel myself blush. I'm aware of every movement she makes and of the airy, fresh scent of her perfume. It's like I'm in sensory overload, compensating for my lack of sight. Even though I can't see her, I can still tell she is unambiguously spellbinding.

We drive for a while. My anxiety grows with every passing moment. *I've got to do something to take the edge off.* "Sarah called me earlier," I blurt out. "She said something cryptic about missing me, and told me to tell you that you don't play fair."

She snickers. "Playing fair is overrated. Feel free to tell her that is my official response. I'll have a press release drawn up for you."

"If you'd take this blindfold off, I could text her."

"Nice try." She knocks her knee into mine. "Relax. We're almost there."

"Where's 'there'?"

"Payton! Stop trying to get it out of me! Would it kill you to let yourself be surprised, for once?"

Surprised for once? I've been plenty surprised as of late. In fact, I think I've had enough surprises to forever satisfy any sense of adventure I may have had.

The car comes to a staggering halt. The hinges squeak as the door opens. Kendall takes my hand, guiding me from the car. "Watch your head," she gently palms the top of my skull to ensure that I don't bang it against the doorframe. I hear her heels click-clacking against asphalt. "I told you we'd be here soon."

"Cool." I try to swallow my discomfort. "So why do I still have this thing on my face?"

"Have you always complained this much?"

"I don't know. I've never been blindfolded before."

She slips her arm around my waist. "A few more steps." We walk a bit more, and then she stops me. "Okay," she says and undoes the blindfold.

We're standing in a dark room. All I can see is Kendall, eyes wide and glued on me.

"Now!" She yells out enthusiastically. And I'm blinded by bright fluorescent lights. It takes my pupils a minute to adjust and focus on my surroundings. We're standing alone in a music store I've always wanted to go to but could never afford, surrounded by instruments and electronics that are beyond my wildest imagination. In the center of the store is a recording studio display filled with microphones, monitors, computers, sound boards and various instruments. In the middle of the studio setup, there's a small table with two place settings, a silver serving platter and a bottle of champagne. I must be deeply asleep, because this is the sweetest dream I've ever had. I can feel Kendall's gaze all over me, which is the only reason I know this is real.

I walk across the room to the table. She follows.

"We're having dinner in Ralph's Music City? How the hell did you swing this?"

She grins. "I'm amazing, didn't you know?"

Yes, I have always known that. Everyone who knows Kendall Bettencourt knows that. "Seriously, though, how did you pull this off?"

"I made a few calls, asked if I could set up a quiet meal for two after they'd closed for the night. I had to swear on my unborn children that we wouldn't spill anything, so let's try to keep it tame." She smirks. "Are you happy?"

"If I hadn't got chastised for crying earlier, I'd be a sniveling heap right about now."

"Happy tears though, right?"

"Absolutely." Then I'm hugging her so tightly that I can feel her heart thrashing against her ribcage. She's holding me again, the way she did that night when she shared my bed—only this time, both of us are completely awake.

She lifts her chin from my shoulder and looks at me in a way I've never seen her look at me before. "Happy birthday."

It's a test of my strength not to kiss her. And I mean it is taking every last bit of willpower I have. "Thank you," I reply in a near whisper, then force myself from her arms and pull a chair out from the table. "Sit," I motion to her.

✳ ✳ ✳

Dinner is delectable. Kendall had the meal prepared by some highbrow French chef. The result is the best macaroni and cheese I have ever tasted. "I didn't know there was more than one way to make mac 'n cheese," I say between bites.

"Michele bakes the noodles and then browns the top with bread crumbs. Plus, there's a secret ingredient." She wiggles her eyebrows like she's all *in the know.*

"Is there?"

"Uh huh," she beams. "You'll never guess it."

"Oh, yeah? You forget that you are speaking with a culinary connoisseur."

She crumbles into laughter. "Sure, I am! You just said you didn't know there was more than one way to make mac 'n cheese. I bet you can't guess."

"Is that a challenge?"

She nods, her mouth stretching into a sly smile.

It's true I don't know the first thing about cooking, personally, but she must have forgotten about all those tasty dishes my mother made us when we were younger. Those meals earned my mom the nickname The Spice Queen. "What's the wager?"

"Hmm." She taps the tabletop. "If you're correct, you get to accompany me to the greatest awards show on earth."

She could ask me to accompany her to friggin' Siberia, and I'd be ecstatic about it. "And if I'm wrong?"

"If you're wrong I'm not going at all, even if I'm nominated."

"So, you're planning to be absent when they announce your victory? I don't think so. I'm eagerly anticipating being thanked in your acceptance speech. I'll take that bet."

"Go for it." She puts her fork down and folds her arms stubbornly. "I'm gonna enjoy watching the show from my big, comfy couch."

I take a sip of champagne to clear my palate, and then take another bite of the cheesy noodles—this time allowing myself to savor the various flavors. Straightaway, I pick up a very warm, pungent taste that definitely has a kind of sugariness to it. "Mmm," I say, taking a page from the *Kendall Bettencourt Handbook for Eating In Public* and talking with my mouth full. "I know what it is."

"Liar." She chuckles. "Come on, let's have it, then! What is it?"

"It's a mix of brown sugar," I pause, bring a forkful to my nose for dramatic effect before continuing, "And cayenne pepper."

There's a semblance of astonishment on her face, somewhat like the pout a child has when they realize they've lost their favorite teddy bear. "I *cannot* believe it."

"I nailed it right? Guess I'll have to take a few days off of school to fly out to LA in March."

"Um, about that. I think–"

"Oh no," I cut her off. "A bet is a bet, and I won fair and square. You are going."

"Whoa there," she says. "Yes, I am going." She reaches under the table, pulls out two pieces of paper—one white and one yellow. She places the yellow paper in front of me. I pick it up and read it. On the top, it says "Ralph's Music City." Below that is a list of SKU numbers, item descriptions, like CAD Black Pearl mic pack, Pro Tools 11, Dual Sound monitors, and MK2 pad controller, and the words "gift receipt" in big, bold letters.

"Kendall!" I squeal once the amazement dissipates. "You bought me a recording studio!"

"Not an actual building, but all the equipment, yeah." She gestures like a game show host to the display around us.

"Are you out of your mind? I can't accept all this. It's amazing, and I love it! But it's too much. Where the hell would I put all of this stuff, anyway? You've seen the closet I call a bedroom."

"Good thing my penthouse is so spacious," she replies matter-of-factly. She hands me the white paper—an application to the Music Academy of Los Angeles. "It's a formality. You have to fill out the paperwork and have your academic records sent to them, but I spoke with the Dean of Students a few days ago after I e-mailed her a video of your MSU audition. She told me you need to send your application to the Immediate Decision Department, and they will notify you of your acceptance into their Film Scoring program the same day they receive your application. They'll figure out how your credits transfer when you make your class schedule for the spring."

I am so thoroughly overwhelmed. My mind is finding it impossible to comprehend what she's saying. "What are you talking about?"

"I'm hiring you to be my full-time music instructor. That means you'll have to move to Los Angeles with me and attend MALA."

Move to Los Angeles with her. Go to MALA. Sounds simple enough. There is only one problem: with my stupid heart aching for her, and my retarded hormones raging all over the damn place, there is no way I could survive being that close to her all the time. It would be sheer torture. I'd be perpetually living on the precipice. The smallest incentive could push me from normal human being to bat-shit-crazy psychopath. I can't tell her that though. *So tell her something else, moron.* "Kendall, the tuition for MALA is outrageous! They only give partial scholarships and even with that I could never afford it."

"I will handle the monetary details of your education."

"No. I can't let you do that. We're talking, like, thirty grand a year for the next three years."

"Shhh," she says quietly. "Since you'll technically be my employee, consider it payment for services to be rendered. It's a business transaction."

She is unbelievable. My teeth clench instinctively. "Why do you have to be so damn smart? You always have a solution to my every moral dilemma."

"There is no moral dilemma here. You've invested so much time and energy in me over the years, specifically when I felt like I was losing faith in myself. I am paying you back the only way I know how."

I don't think she really understands what she is asking me. I'm not sure I really understand either. "To clarify, you want me to leave my school, my friends, and my mom to move 3,000 miles away and be your live-in music teacher. Do you know what kind of commitment that is?"

"You're making it sound like I asked you to marry me," she says nonchalantly. Her face then pales ghostly white. She snatches her champagne flute from the table and takes the longest gulp. "Look," she begins slowly. "You happen to be the most talented musician I know. You want to get into the film industry, and I think MALA will help you do that. Plus, I'm tired of missing you. I feel weird when you're not around for these long stretches of time. I thought we should try a different approach."

Okay, Payton. You already know the cons, now weigh the pros against them. 1) You totally understand where she's coming from when she says she's tired of missing you. Despite the idiocy of letting yourself fall for her, she's still your best friend. 2) MALA is an extraordinary school. 3) The weather in SoCal is supposedly beautiful year round. 4) A change of scenery might do you good. Crap! Logic sure as hell picked a great time to return to me. Where the hell was it a month ago when I really needed it to talk myself out of falling for Kendall? "I can't do it until the end of December. I have to finish the semester and spend Christmas with my mom, or she will murder me."

"Is that a yes?"

"I guess it is, yeah."

She throws her hands in the air triumphantly. "Woo! We are going to take Hollywood by storm, you know that?"

"I do now," I reply and raise my champagne glass in a toast. "Here's to us taking Hollywood by storm."

"Cheers to that." She clinks her glass against mine. "Oh, I almost forgot!" She snaps her fingers. From behind a curtain, a man in a chef's uniform wheels out a cake in the shape of a guitar. 'Happy Nineteenth Payton' is scrawled across it in icing, and two sparkling candles are on top.

"Kendall," I start. *It's all too much.*

"Shut up and make a wish."

I'm pretty sure the cosmos doesn't grant wishes where matters of the heart are concerned, but I blow out the candles and silently wish to become numb to all emotion. Something tells me I've got a better shot at getting a pony. "There."

"Good job." She hands me the cake slicer. "Milk chocolate fudge, your fave."

"I don't think I can fit one more bite of anything into my stomach. Besides, you've provided more than enough sweetness for the evening."

"There's no such thing as enough sweetness." She skims some icing off the cake with her finger and offers it to me.

I shake my head. *No. I will not have any part of your body anywhere near my mouth. Ever. That would end very badly. Or very pleasantly, if I think about it…*

"Fine." She rubs the icing on my nose and giggles. "Use it as a facial."

"I can already feel the exfoliation."

She pulls a napkin from the table and passes it to me. "Clean yourself up so we can get out of here."

CHAPTER FOUR

Kendall

The full weight of the evening crashes into me as we're leaving the music shop. This is happening. Payton is coming to live with me. She's right that it's a commitment; our lives will basically become intimately intertwined. No matter where I go or how long I have to be away, I will ultimately come home to the place where she is—the space that we share. It's nice, the prospect of having my best friend right there with me in the thick of it, keeping me rational when I come close to losing it.

"Hey," she says, grabbing my attention once we've reentered the limo. "Do you think you can be with me when I tell my mom? I'm sure the news that I'm moving across the country will come as a much bigger bombshell to her than my homosexuality."

"You told your mom?"

She nods. "This morning. It came out of nowhere. She woke me up to wish me a happy birthday and all of a sudden I'm like, 'Gee, Mom, thanks for the cupcake. By the way, I'm a raging lesbian.'"

"Wow, that's not awkward or anything. What did she say?"

"Um…" She pauses and chews her bottom lip. "She said she already knew."

Really? I never would have known if she hadn't told me. I'd be forever waiting for the invitation to her wedding to Prince Charming that would never come. "How did she know?"

"She said something about 'paying attention.' I don't know."

Paying attention? Is that it? I thought I was paying attention to you, but apparently not close enough. "I suppose congratulations are in order, aren't they? I'm proud of you." I move to put my arm around her shoulder, but settle for patting her on the back. "Of course I will be there with you when you tell your mom you're moving. Can we do it Sunday? I've been roped into a father-daughter day tomorrow."

"Sure, Sunday works for me," she agrees. "Oh, did you decide whether or not you're going to take the role in that action movie?"

"Yes, I'm going to do it." I jumped at the chance, if I'm honest. There's no sex in it at all, just lots of blood and violence. Is it bad that I'd rather stab people to death and blow stuff up than have to kiss anyone, like, ever again?

The limo pulls up to Payton's house shortly after midnight. Our driver opens the door for us, and we hop out.

"Thank you for tonight. For everything," she says once we've reached her porch. She has this look on her face that speaks much more than gratitude. It makes me want to wrap my arms around her and hold her until the sun comes up. The thought makes my stomach flutter. It's the most jarring, inexplicable thing. *Okay, seriously? What the hell is that about?*

"It was my pleasure." I want to hug her. I *should* hug her. But for some reason, I can't. I'm just standing here, feet shuffling like they've got a mind to run far and fast. The funny thing is, I *know* she feels it, too. She wants to hug me, but something won't let her. *Do it, Kendall! She isn't some random stranger who recognized you on the street. This is Payton.* I don't move. It's like there's an invisible wall between us, and it isn't going to come down any time soon, even though I long to chip away the bricks and mortar. "All right. Well, good night," I say finally. I try not to roll my eyes at how completely witless I sound.

"Good night, Kendall."

I'm about to walk away when she seizes me by the wrist. Her hand moves up my arm to my shoulder and settles delicately on the crook of my neck. She takes a step closer to me. Oh my god, is she going to kiss me? *Yes, she is!* But she doesn't. She hugs me—quickly and lightly—before disappearing into the house.

I admit to myself that I'm creeped out only after I'm through my own front door. I'm creeped out not because I thought she was going to kiss me, but because she didn't and I wanted her to. I *really* wanted her to. Where is this coming from? I'm not gay! I'm merely curious about Payton—about how the whole lesbian thing works. Until recently, I thought I knew everything there was to know about her. Finding out I was wrong has thrown me for a loop. Or maybe it's because I am so paralyzingly afraid of losing her. I know someday she'll fall in love, and I'll lose her. She'll meet a girl who will give her everything that I can't. *That isn't any excuse!* It isn't fair of me to try to make her see me in a way that she doesn't. And it definitely isn't cool that I'm trying to talk myself into being something I'm not, right?

"Have a nice night, Pumpkin?"

"Jesus, Dad!" I nearly jump out of my skin. "You scared me." *It was a nice night. Until, it kind of wasn't.* "Yes, I had a nice night."

"Sorry, I didn't mean to sneak up on you." He smiles. "Are you okay? You look like you were deep in thought."

"I was deep in thought."

"Want to talk about it?"

Do I? With my dad? Hell no, I don't. At least not right now. "Not tonight. I'm exhausted."

"Okay. Are we still on for tomorrow?" He makes a putting motion with his invisible club. "Mini golf!"

"You bet." I kiss his cheek, then bolt up the steps to my room.

"Good night," he calls after me.

※ ※ ※

Saturday morning I wake up from a restless sleep in a cold sweat to disheveled sheets. I had this crazy nightmare where I was being chased by zombies down the highway. I was on foot, trying to zigzag my way through heaps of wrecked cars and piles of lifeless bodies. It's the kind of dream I used to have when I was a kid and had watched a scary movie right before going to bed.

I don't feel well. I'm worn out, and the last thing I want to do is play stupid miniature golf with my father. But I made him a promise, so I force myself to get up and grab some clothes from my dresser.

I catch a glimpse of myself in the floor-length mirror on the way out of my room. I look perfectly revolting in my old, threadbare track pants and an MSU hoodie I stole from Payton last summer. If Lawrence knew I was considering going out in public like this, he'd have my hide for sure. *Screw it. If anybody truly cares enough to examine what I wear while I'm on vacation, they can all have a good time and go to hell while doing it.*

I hobble down the stairs to the kitchen where I find my dad sitting on a stool at the chic, slate coffee bar. He's fully engrossed by his newspaper. "I made coffee," he motions toward the countertop without looking up at me. I pour myself a cup before taking a seat beside him.

"You're my savior," I say after taking a sip.

"Of course I am." He grins. "You look awful."

That's my dad! Always straightforward. "Then I look exactly how I feel."

"Would you like to skip father-daughter day?"

I shake my head. "Not on your life. A date with Dad is one of the best dates a girl could go on."

"Should I assume that you've had your fair share of bad dates recently?"

"You've been spending too much time with mom!" I wag my finger at him. "You've picked up her tendency to get on my nerves."

He raises his hands as though he's been caught in the middle of a bank robbery. "I'm just being a dad."

"Sure, sure," I say. "Can we go play golf now?"

❄ ❄ ❄

I'm mobbed at Mini Golf Palace the second we walk through the entrance. My dad is so alarmed by it. This is the first time he's been out with me since the hype around *In Heaven's Arms* began. Prior to that, I had to deal with the occasional fan, and I was happy to do so. I guess when you star in a multi-million-dollar movie that starts its PR *months* before its release—and that has been deemed "the must-see movie of the year" by nearly every film critic in existence—you should learn to anticipate an insane reaction from people when they recognize you. It would have been nice if someone warned me this would happen *before* I took the role.

I sign some autographs and pose for pictures. Once I get all the obligatory celebrity BS out of the way, we pick out our clubs and mosey over to the course.

"Does that always happen when you leave the house?" Dad questions as he putts and sinks the ball into the first hole.

"Sometimes it's worse than others."

"It must be hard, not being able to do much of anything without being noticed."

"I'm getting used to it." I putt and miss the hole completely.

"So," he says with a long pause. I always fear that pause. It usually means he is either gearing up for a big speech or a series of nosy questions. "Do you want to talk about what was on your mind when you came home last night?" he asks as I am smack in the middle of a putt. I miss the hole again.

I need to talk to somebody about the million things going on inside my head or I'll go nutterbutters. Since Payton is *unquestionably* out, that really only leaves my dad. "I don't know where to begin."

He places a reassuring hand on my shoulder. "Whatever it is, Pumpkin, you can tell me. You know that."

I take a quick glance around to make sure there is no one in hearing range. The last thing I need is some crazed attention whore relaying a private conversation between my father and me to the media. "I've been thinking a lot about Payton recently."

"All right."

"I mean, I've been thinking, like, a lot of *weird* things about her." *Please comprehend what I'm getting at so I don't actually have to say the words.*

"Explain 'weird things,' please."

Damn it. There is no way to handle this discretely, is there? "It started when I was on set in New Orleans. I had this racy scene that I was enormously freaked out about so I called Payton to calm me down like I always do. She gave me great advice—picture that I'm being intimate with someone I'm comfortable with. And the person I pictured was her. Ever since then, I've been on edge around her. I can't stop thinking about her in *that* way."

He shifts his weight from foot to foot, clearly uneasy. "So, you're saying the weird things you've been thinking about Payton are sexual things?"

This is too weird. Talking to my father about anything even remotely resembling sex has always been out of the realm of reality for me. But sex is kind of what my whole malfunction is about, isn't it? "Yes. Physical things, I guess."

"And you've never had these kinds of thoughts about her before?"

"No!" I blurt out. "I keep telling myself that it's because I'm scared of losing her. You know, because someday she'll find a girlfriend and leave me behind. But the more I think about it, the less I'm sure that that's actually what's going on. I'm so friggin' confused, even more so after last night when I thought she was going to kiss me and…"

There's a flash of concern in his eyes. "She tried to kiss you?"

"Dad, are you listening to me? She didn't *try* to kiss me. I thought she may have wanted to."

He scratches his chin. "Perhaps you should be having this conversation with your mother?"

"That's never going to happen! I need someone to listen to me, not freak out about how I'm making poor decisions, sending the wrong signals, or whatever stupid thing I know she'd say."

"Sweetie, what you're talking about now is kind of a big deal. I think she's better suited to–"

"You're out of your mind if you think mom is the right person to go to when something is 'kind of a big deal.' She has a meltdown if I wear a dress with a low neckline. How do you think she'd react if I so much as hint that I have feelings for a *girl*?"

"You're right." He hesitates to say it, but I'm glad he does. It means he finally gets that his wife is ill equipped to deal with anything she doesn't like. "When you told me the other day about your big plan to have Payton move out to LA with you, I thought it was a great idea… But now I'm not so sure. Living with her might just serve to confuse you even more."

"It might, I don't know. What I *do* know above all else is that Payton is the only person who manages to make me feel like I'm not an alien from planet Glamouria. She doesn't treat me any differently now that I have fame and money."

"Well, if she makes you feel normal and grounded, I'd say stick with the plan."

"Right." I should let this heart-to-heart die right here, but I need to know that no matter what happens my daddy will have my back. He's the only parent I have that I can really count on. "If I came home six months from now and said, 'Dad, I'm gay. I'm never going to be with another guy again,' promise you wouldn't hate me?"

If I were to stroll up to him and coolly smack him in the face with my golf club, I don't think he'd be any more surprised than he is at this very moment. "Kendall, you're my daughter. I could never hate you. I will always love you and be proud of you. Unless you were to become a career criminal, then I probably wouldn't be so proud."

I laugh. "Don't worry. I'm not into crime."

"Good! Are you feeling better now?"

Astonishingly, yes. I give him a quick nod. "Thanks, Dad."

"You're welcome," he says as I swing through the sixth hole and again fail to sink the ball. "Let's forget about golfing and go to lunch."

"Yeah," I agree. "I like that idea a lot."

❊ ❊ ❊

Payton calls me early Sunday morning. I don't pick up. Avoidance! It's yet another first in our friendship. This whole thing is seriously messing me up. It's too complicated. I never should've come home in the first place. If I would've gone back to LA after wrapping like I'd originally planned, none of this would be happening. *And you've reached a new low by lying to yourself!* I could be in LA, New Jersey, or on the freaking *moon* and it wouldn't make one iota of difference. I'd be dealing with this regardless of my location. This is a life thing.

My phone buzzes again. *Payton.* I take a deep breath before answering. "Hey."

"Hey. My mom is home, finally. Are you coming over?"

I sigh inwardly. "I'll be there in twenty minutes."

"Are you okay? You don't sound right."

Are we so close that we're psychically connected or something? I hope not, or keeping things to myself is going to end up taking a huge chunk outta my ass. "I'm okay, a little tired." *And a smidge homosexual, apparently.* Wait, what? For crying out loud, Kendall, stop obsessing over it!

"Okay," she says. "See you in a while."

"Bye." I disconnect and scramble to get dressed.

I never used to care about looking awful around Payton. She's seen me with a stomach virus. She's seen me without any makeup, wearing sweatpants. She's a *girl*. Now I'm dressing up to the nines with the specific intent of getting some kind of reaction from her? If she doesn't think I look smoking in this get up, she won't ever have a single carnal thought about me. I'm wearing a short, backless drape dress, white knee-high buckle boots, and a full face of makeup. Basically, I look like I'm headed to a photo session for the cover of some fancy magazine instead of across town to have a serious sit-down conversation with my best friend and her mother. I've come to the conclusion that if I *were* into girls, it wouldn't be any easier than being straight. I'd still have that 'dress to impress' nonsense embedded in my brain.

A few minutes later, I knock on Payton's door. She opens it, eyes wide and wary. *Good*. I'd like her to be as uncomfortable around me as I've been around her lately, which is about the meanest thing I've ever wished on anyone.

"You look nice," she says casually.

Nice? I was aiming for hot to the extent of blood boiling. "Thanks," I reply, feeling somewhere between oddly disappointed and sort of relieved.

"Mom's in the kitchen. I told her we needed to talk, so she's pretty much bracing herself for nuclear fallout."

"She should take the news of you moving out fairly well then."

"Somehow I doubt that."

We walk into the kitchen. Mrs. Taylor is at the table, looking precisely as Payton described. "Hello, Kendall."

Payton pulls out a chair for me.

"Hello," I return.

"Okay, Mom," Payton begins as she sits down. "Let's skip the pleasantries and get right down to the issue at hand." She sounds like she's in a business meeting. It's strange hearing that tone from her.

Mrs. Taylor searches my face for some kind of hint as to what may be coming. I make sure to divulge nothing through my expression. "Okay, Payton," she says. "What is the issue at hand?"

"After the semester is over, I'm moving to California with Kendall. Before you get upset, let me just say that I'm not quitting school. I'm transferring to the Music Academy of Los Angeles."

Mrs. Taylor is staring at me like she's thinking about ripping my throat out for taking her baby girl away from her, which, I suppose I am. She gestures to Payton. "This isn't exactly what I meant when I said you should expand your social circle."

"Mom, I really want this. Do you have any idea how many MALA alumni have gone on to make music for movies and TV? This could be my shot at turning my dreams—which I always felt were kind of unattainable—into reality. Grandpa would support me if he were here. I think he'd be proud of me for following in his footsteps and for being so completely dedicated to music. He's the one who had me banging away at the piano by the age of three in the first place."

Oh, she's playing the 'ridiculously talented grandpa' card. That's smart. Mrs. Taylor can't possibly argue that. And she doesn't. She huffs, defeated. "Kendall," she says pointedly, "you take good care of my kid, you got it?"

Like there's a chance I wouldn't? I smile. "I got it."

"And Payton, you're going to call me at least once a week, right?"

Payton nods. "I will, I promise."

"I guess there isn't anything left to say." Mrs. Taylor pushes away from the table and moves toward Payton. She pulls her into her arms and holds her close. "My baby really is all grown up."

"It was bound to happen sooner or later," Payton says.

"I was hoping for later." Mrs. Taylor releases Payton from her grasp. She moves to exit the kitchen, but stops as she's about to pass me and pulls me into a hug. "Be careful with her," she murmurs into my ear.

I want to ask her what she means by that. What, is Payton breakable? But I let the inkling pass. "I will."

She lets me go and leaves the room.

"That went over much more smoothly than I thought it was going to," Payton mumbles.

"I have no idea why you were expecting anything less." I nudge her. "Your mom has a long history of being rational."

"True. Thanks for being here."

"You're welcome," I say as she leads me from the kitchen, through the living room, and right to the front door. "Are you kicking me out?"

Her face contorts into a startled expression. "What? No. I assumed you had somewhere to be." She shrugs. "You're all gussied up. I thought maybe you had something to do in the city today, important people to meet with or whatever."

"I just met with them."

"Then I guess you've got the rest of the day free." She laughs a sweet, throaty laugh, and my heartstrings come undone. I realize at that moment how completely helpless I am against her. She's like a cyclone, this fascinating yet deadly force of nature that carves a path straight through my defenses no matter how hard I try to fortify them. So, why do I bother trying at all? I'm not sure if I'm ready to be swept away. I'm not ready to leave the sorry, little shelter I've built myself. Once I step into the storm, everything changes.

"Actually, I have to help my mom with something. I'm sorry, I just remembered. "

"It's cool." She says it as if she means it, but her eyes say otherwise.

"I'll call you tomorrow," I say, though I already know I won't.

"Sounds good."

I don't hug her goodbye. I simply get into my father's car and drive.

❇ ❇ ❇

Looking at myself in the rearview mirror, all I can think of is how downright ridiculous this whole situation has become. It isn't just about Payton anymore, is it? Beyond her, it's about an absolute reclassification of my sexuality. And I am *not* gay. I'm just... not. How can I be? I've dated more guys than I can count on two hands and ten toes. Lesbians don't date men, and I do. End of story. So what if the physical attraction I've felt for the dudes I've dated thus far has been lackluster, lukewarm at best? Maybe they've all been too pretty to incite any kind of serious desire in me. Maybe I need a cowboy—some ruggedly handsome, Stetson-wearing, scruffy-faced macho man. *Or maybe you've only dated pretty boys with soft, feminine features because you're genuinely attracted to um,* females. No! No, goddamn it, I am not! Shut up, brain, or I'll lobotomize you!

I fiddle with my hair, watching my reflection and forcing myself to not think about this anymore.

CHAPTER FIVE

Payton

Kendall doesn't call me for three days. It's Thursday afternoon, Thanksgiving, and she's hopping on a Red Eye back to LA before the sun is up tomorrow. I guess it's good that I've been busy helping my mom prepare dinner all day. I'd probably be going out of my mind if I had a tick of idle time.

Mom's got this idea in her head that she has to teach me absolutely every last recipe she's ever made before I move out, or else I'll starve to death in LA. At the moment, I'm not sure I'm moving out there at all.

"Mom, this stuff is gross." My hands are covered in turkey filling. The wet, sticky consistency is making me cringe. "I'm not gonna go hungry because I don't know how to stuff poultry."

She looks at me as though my words have wounded her. "You let your grandfather teach you everything he knew about music, but you can't let me do the same with food?"

"I love music. And I'm good at it. I've never been any good at cooking. That's why I've always left the mastery of meal-making up to you."

"It's a useful thing to know. Wouldn't you like to impress a future girlfriend with your culinary skills?"

"Why would I want to do that if I could just serenade her? She'd be putty in my hands!" I fake a maniacally sinister laugh.

"You are so cocky sometimes," she says with a smirk. "So much like Grandpa."

"That's a good thing, isn't it?"

"Of course it is. If anyone stood a chance of making it in music, it was him. You've got his tenacity."

I smile at that. Being compared to my grandfather is probably the biggest compliment I could ever be paid. I'm about to launch into a big speech about his awesomeness and how much I miss him when the doorbell rings. My aunt, uncle, and cousins are joining us for dinner. "I'll get it," I say and clean the bready goo off of my hands with a dish towel.

I'm taken aback the second I open the door. Kendall is leaning against the railing. She's in a pair of yoga pants and one of my cozy oversized hoodies looking like she hasn't slept a wink in days. It's such a stark contrast from the last time she was here that I'm immediately worried about her health.

"Hey," she says, her voice hushed.

"Hi." I don't know what to say to her. I'm slightly angry that she's been blowing me off. Never mind not calling me for days, she hasn't even bothered responding to my texts. Here I am, planning the single most significant move of my life, and we're totally incommunicado? Wasn't this her brilliant idea in the first place? "Are you sick?"

"No." She kicks off the railing and steps closer to me.

"Are you sure? Even movie stars are allowed to have colds once in a while."

"I know. I don't have a cold."

I cross my arms. "Then where the hell have you been?" *Gross! What are you, her mom?* What the hell right do I have to be mad at her? She's a busy person. She has a life that's so much bigger than mine, so much bigger than *me*. It would be stupid to think otherwise.

"I'm sorry," she says delicately. "I've had a lot on my mind lately."

And she hasn't said a thing about it until now? I don't like being left in the dark. *Payton, you should talk. You haven't exactly been an open book lately.* "Anything I can do to help?"

"Not really. It's stuff I need to figure out for myself. I just wanted to let you know that I'm sorry I haven't been able to involve you in any of it. It's been hard for me, feeling like I couldn't pick up the phone and discuss everything with you."

"Why couldn't you?"

She sucks her bottom lip between her teeth and bites down. "Some problems can't be solved by talking about them."

"You're not pregnant, are you?" I ask jokingly.

She chuckles. "God, no! There's zero possibility of that."

"Phew." I wipe my hand across my forehead in mock relief. "Glad to hear that."

She smiles. "I've got to get home. The 'rents are hosting their illustrious Turkey Day Banquet, and they invited every person they've ever met. It's going to be huge this year, first holiday I've actually managed to make it home for in a while."

"Yeah, my family is coming over soon, too."

"Do you think you can get away later? I'd like to hang out for a while before I have to head to the airport."

Yes, I can get away. If I have to crawl out my bedroom window and climb down the garden trellis, I will get away. "Sure. I'll swing by around eight?"

"Perfect. You'll be saving me from the part of the evening where my mother hassles us into a circle and forces us all to share one thing we're thankful for."

"Wicked."

Without reluctance, she hugs me. The anxiety I've been feeling due to our unusual lack of communication is calmed for a moment. All too quickly, she releases me. "Later," she calls from the sidewalk.

"Later." I watch her speed down the road in her dad's bright red convertible.

❊ ❊ ❊

Luckily, I don't have to sneak out of the house via my bedroom window. I'm pretty sure I would've fallen to my death, or at the very least broken every vertebrae in my spinal column. Mom lets me leave after dinner without much of a fuss. It's surprising. She is usually adamant that I subject myself to the full extent of family time on holidays. She says I'm allowed a brief respite because "I was so lively and interactive during dinner." In actuality, I know it's because she doesn't want me sitting around the house sulking while my aunt is over. I say goodbye to everyone and quickly book it out the door before Mom has enough time to change her mind.

I'm running late. It's twenty after eight when I ring Kendall's doorbell. Her mom answers with a contented smile.

"Hi, Mrs. B! Happy Thanksgiving," I say while peering over her shoulder into the living room. *Okay, wow. Kendall wasn't joking about the whole sharing circle thing.* There must be about twenty people seated around facing each other. Kendall spots me through the archway. Her eyes launch daggers at me as if to say "The *one* time you're late, and it had to be tonight!"

"Happy Thanksgiving," Mrs. Bettencourt replies. I know before she says another word that she's going to invite me inside. "Kendall is in the family room. Go on in."

Oh, damn it! I so do not *feel like sharing right now.* "Thank you." I skulk by her.

Kendall meets me at the archway and whispers, "Really?"

"I know. I'm sorry."

"Have a seat, ladies," Mrs. Bettencourt directs as she reenters the room.

Kendall seizes my elbow and yanks me toward the loveseat. "We're not getting out of this unscathed. Keep a straight face and say *anything* when the time comes."

"Okay." It's kind of funny that she's acting like this is some kind of live-or-die situation. How hard is it to talk about something you're glad to have or have done? It's not like she has stage fright or anything.

Mr. Bettencourt starts off the circle by talking about how he's thankful for his wonderful family. Then it's Kendall's cousins, aunts, and uncles. Before long, it's Kendall's turn. She must have been spacing out or something while everyone else was speaking; her mother calls her name twice before she responds.

Kendall looks like she's thinking hard about what she's going to say, as though the fate of world peace depends on her words. "I'm thankful for love," she mutters, looking square at me. "I'm thankful for all the people in this room who love me and whom I love more than anything."

My mouth suddenly goes drier than the Mojave during a drought. Out of the blue, I feel as if I've been gnawing on a mixture of sandpaper and kitty litter for at least a good year. And then I'm coughing an incessant, obtrusive cough. It sounds more like choking than coughing, really.

Mr. Bettencourt rushes across the room with a glass of water in his hand and thrusts it toward me. "Here, drink this."

I take the offered glass, put it to my lips, and sip it deeply. After a few swallows, the hacking stops. I take a long breath. "Thank you," I say to him, then clear my throat. "In case anyone was wondering, I'm thankful for water."

A chorus of delighted laughter rings throughout the room. I've never been happier to have excellent comedic timing. If anyone were to ask, there would be no feasible way I could explain what just happened. Anyway, was Kendall even talking about me? Am I included in that small collection of people she loves more than anything? Sure, I am. She loves me like a friend, or worse, like a sister.

Kendall places her hand on my back and rubs gently. "Better?"

"Yeah, I'm fine."

"Good." She hops off the sofa and takes my hand. "Let's go upstairs. It's too loud down here."

Just shut up and go. "Yes," I say as I get up to follow her.

The first thing I notice when we enter her room is the colossal stack of packed bags at the foot of her bed. I know she was away on a shoot for a month, but really? I don't remember her having her entire freaking wardrobe with her when I dropped her off at the airport the last time. "Is it me, or have you acquired a whole lot of new baggage to bring back to Cali with you?"

She falls onto the mattress, giggling like mad. I wonder if she's having some sort of mental breakdown, because nothing about my question could've possibly caused that kind hysteria. "You have no idea how much baggage I've picked up since I've been home," she complains.

I don't know. From the looks of it, I'd say I have a pretty fair idea. "Is your dad driving you to the airport? There is no way he can fit all this stuff into that tiny hot wheels thing you bought him."

"Hell no," she shakes her head. "I called a car service."

"You probably should've called U-Haul."

She harrumphs as she sits upright and pats the mattress twice. I seat myself beside her. "Speaking of U-Haul…" she says as she stretches to the foot of the bed to riffle through a duffle on the top of her luggage pile. I seize the opportunity to admire her perfect posterior, which is accentuated by the stretchy material of her yoga pants. She pops back up and almost catches me ogling her. I was never before aware of the danger of near-misses. I'll be more careful to avoid them in future. "This is for you." She hands me a blue box about the size of a deck of cards. A thin, red ribbon is tied around it.

Another present? Damn it, I don't want your presents! I want your presence. Don't you get that? I flash a contemptuous look at the box and slide it back toward her. "Whatever that is, take it back. I appreciate the thought, but I'm not going to accept one more gift from you."

"It's not a gift. It's a necessity."

"A necessity? I wasn't aware oxygen could be boxed."

"Believe me, it's something you'll need and use often. Open it."

I'm skeptical, but she's managed to peak my curiosity. I undo the ribbon and flip the lid off. Inside, there is a lone key attached to a metal 'P' keychain.

"It's for my—for *our* apartment. I was going to wait until I picked you up from LAX, but I was way too excited about it."

I don't know what to say. After that vanishing act she pulled, I was beginning to think she was having second thoughts about the whole thing. "So, you still want this to happen then?" I'm not prepared for her to answer my question with a no, but it's a major thing, and I need to know one way or the other.

She palms her knees and remains noiseless for a few moments. "I can't apologize enough for disappearing on you," she murmurs. "Yes, I still want this to happen."

I'm relieved even though I know it's going to be difficult at first, living with her while endlessly battling this menacing ache I have to touch her. *That's the last straw! I am going to get over these feelings for her if it takes blunt force trauma!* Getting over her—it's the only solution to an impossible problem, a fantastical love that won't ever be reciprocated. I need to bury my grief before my grief buries me. But there is something else I have to get out of the way first. "I finished that song like you asked. Where is your keyboard?" I need to play it for her. It was written about her all along, right from the opening measure.

"Over there," she points toward her closet.

I stumble over, retrieve the keyboard from its box and carry it back to the bed. I plug it into the wall then settle myself down in front of it. I don't have the sheet music with me, but it isn't necessary. I know every note and rest by heart.

The keys are plastic. The feel of them beneath my fingers is different from the ivory keys of my grandfather's piano. It doesn't matter, though. The song sounds every bit as forlorn and haunting as I intended. Each bar I play is like another excruciating stab to the chest. Music. This is how I bleed.

"I renamed it," I utter once I've played the last note. "It's called 'Melody for the Dying.'" I look up from the keyboard to see her wiping tears from her cheeks. *Now you know what it's like. That was the sound of love, unrequited.*

"That was incredible," she whispers. "I could actually *feel* the sorrow."

"Thank you." But now it's time to put the pain away, stuff it into a folder marked "forget," and tuck it into the obscurest recesses of my mind.

"Hollywood is going to fawn over you someday. Seriously, you are the next Danny Elfman."

"I want to be the next Hans Zimmer. Maybe with some of The Chemical Brothers mixed in."

"Then that's who you'll be." She smiles and throws her arms around my neck. I collapse sideways into her. I'm practically lying in her lap, and she's nearly cuddling me. I should move and break the contact. Instead, I turn over slightly until I'm fully on my back. My head is resting on her stomach. Her legs are folded beneath my shoulders. This is no way to begin the "getting over her" process, but god, does it feel fantastic.

She's playing with my hair again—lightly brushing her fingers through it. For the first time in the longest while, I'm actually relaxed around her. I close my eyes and listen to her breathe. In and out. In and out. The sound is soothing like whitecaps crashing against the shore.

"Kendall," I say, disturbing the serenity of the moment. "I'm gonna fall asleep if you keep doing that."

"So, fall asleep."

I check my watch. It's almost ten. "Don't you have to leave soon?"

She leans over me and peeps at my watch. "Not until one."

"You want me to waste the last few hours I have with you napping?"

She yawns. "It's not a waste if we're both napping."

I sit up to study her. She seems like she could definitely use some shut-eye. If I was able to last an entire night sleeping next to her, what damage could a few hours do? "Lie down." I nod and set the alarm on my watch for half past midnight.

She turns off the bedside lamp, finds a cozy position, and fluffs a pillow behind her head. I stretch out beside her. She inches closer and rests her temple against my shoulder. I'm resolved not to let my angst return and screw everything up, so I shut my eyes and enjoy the warmth of her skin against mine.

CHAPTER SIX

Kendall

According to the clock on my bedroom wall, it's 12:20. I've been awake for close to fifteen minutes, but I haven't moved except to breathe. It's worse than the last time I woke up next to Payton. At that point, I hadn't quite figured out what I was feeling. But now I am hyper aware of it. I squandered hours and hours trying to put a name to it. When I finally got a firm grasp on what to *call* the thing I was feeling, I wasted even more time trying to make it go away. I say I wasted time because it was the most futile attempt I ever made at anything. Watching her now—lying here so peacefully, looking as beautiful on the outside as she is on the inside—it should not have come as a surprise that my feelings for her are anything but platonic.

I'm not talking about the physical aspect at all. Yes, she has the same biological makeup as I do, and I'm still struggling to get beyond that, but I honestly think that anatomy has fundamentally *nothing* to do with love. That isn't to say she's *not* attractive. I mean, duh! Look at her. The girl has amazing cheekbones, sumptuous lips, radiant olive skin, and abs toned to perfection. I don't care if you're gay or straight, male or female; you would literally have to be blind not to find her attractive. I don't know if physical chemistry would be an issue for me, but right now I'm not concerned with that. It isn't as simple as a fascination of the flesh. It's everything about her that I love: her intelligence, her ambition, her talent, her sense of humor, her dependability, her kindness.

The *real* problem is that she's my best friend. We have an undeniable connection that's more intense than 10,000 Kelvin heat, more dynamic than seismic activity. It's like there's gravity between us—she's the *only* thing anchoring me to the world, keeping me from floating off into the upper stratosphere and getting lost in space. I can't risk losing her. I would be an empty shell of a person if she weren't in my life.

Payton's wristwatch alarm sounds off at 12:30. She slowly begins to stir. I shut my eyes in a hurry. She can't catch me watching her sleep. That is *way* too creepy, and not to mention, obvious.

The mattress beneath her contracts as she pushes herself up on her elbows. She's looking at me. I've still got my eyes closed, but I can feel her gaze like it's a corporeal thing. "Kendall," she whispers, lightly pushing my messy bangs behind my left ear. *Do that again. Touch me anywhere.* "Kendall," she repeats, "it's time to wake up."

I open my eyes to find her leaning over me. She's bathed in the dim, far-away glow of street lights. The greenish-white sheen illuminates her enough that I can just make out the curvature of her lips. She's smiling. *God, Payton! Why do you have to be so dazzling, even in the dark?*

"Hey there, Sleeping Beauty," she says.

"Hey, yourself," I whisper. My brain is screaming, "Kiss her, kiss her, kiss her!" But there's a knock on my bedroom door.

Without waiting for a response, my dad walks in and flips on the light. I am flush on my back and Payton is still slightly leant over me. The shock on my dad's face is precious. I know what he thinks he walked in on. I want to say "Nice going, Dad. We could've been butt-naked, screwing like jackrabbits, and you would've ruined the whole thing!" But I don't want him to have a stroke or anything, so I keep quiet.

He coughs. "Sorry, I didn't mean to interrupt."

"Um, no, you didn't interrupt anything," Payton stumbles over her words. "We were just waking up."

"I see," he replies. "Kendall, I wanted to see if you needed any help bringing your things downstairs. Your car will be here soon."

Both Payton and I sit up. We dangle our legs over the side of the bed and kick our calves against it the way little children do. "Sounds good, Dad. Thanks."

My dad grabs two suitcases. Payton shuffles over to the pile and grabs two more.

"Everywhere I go, there's room service," I joke.

"No there isn't." Payton hands me a duffle. "Here you go."

"So surly." I chortle, pick up my keyboard, and follow her out of the room.

I'm pleasantly surprised the three of us manage to get all my crap down to the foyer in a single trip. "Thanks for the help," I say to both my dad and Payton once I've reached the bottom of the stairwell.

"You're welcome," they reply in tune.

Outside, a car door slams. I hustle to the front door and peer through the windows to find what I feared: my ride to the airport, the first step back to La La Land. Hollywood—the home of big dreams and big names. I'm very quickly figuring out that it's only a fantasy coated in glitz and glamour. Out there it's constant commotion, endless parties, and red carpet events. It's hardly ever quiet, almost never calm. It's all about style and money and being seen. No one cares about you unless your face is on billboards or your name is on VIP lists. *I kind of don't want to go back.*

"Mom's asleep," Dad says. "Do you want me to wake her so you can say goodbye?"

"A world of no." *I don't even like her when she's fully awake, let alone when she's crabby from being woken up.* He flashes a little grin then heaves a few bags out to the car. Payton follows his lead.

Dad takes the keyboard from me and places it in the trunk. He turns to me and pats my head. "Okay, Pumpkin, you're all set."

I hug him and kiss his cheek. "Thanks for everything, Daddy."

He nods. "Call your mother in the morning. She always worries when you travel." He turns toward Payton. "And you! Don't be a stranger. Come visit us before your big move."

"Yes, sir," she salutes him and smiles. We watch him as he retreats into the house.

And then there were two.

Payton is quiet and much too far away from me. I want her
right here—in my face and in my arms. Leaving her has always
been the hardest part for me, long before I became aware of exactly how much she means to me. There's sadness in her eyes
whenever I have to go, like she's convinced it's the last time she'll
ever see me. This time around, the sadness is killing me.

I reach for her. "Come here." She steps to me and wraps her
arms around my waist. I cling to her shoulders, resting my head
against her chest. I listen to the steady pitter-patter of her heart
and think about how glad I am for the extra four inches she has
on me. "I'll miss you most of all, Scarecrow." I take a small step
backward so that I can look into her eyes.

She brushes her hand against my cheek. "It's okay. I'll see you
again in thirty-two days."

"Thirty-two days," I repeat. Somehow, countdowns make everything better.

"Right."

"Okay." I slowly pull myself away. If I don't leave now, I'm
afraid I never will.

"Bye."

I slip into the back seat, and the car starts down the road. I
watch her through the rear window, shrinking as the distance
between us grows.

❋ ❋ ❋

I wake up startled to find myself in my own bed. I've forgotten
where I am and how I got here. The first reminder I have that I'm

back in LA is the panoramic view from my bedroom windows—palm trees as far as the eye can see. It's early morning, yet I can already tell it's going to be a warm, sunny day. It's a shame the weather in LA is rarely anything but beautiful. I love fall on the East Coast—the sharp chill in the air and Payton offering me her sweatshirts to keep me warm. *Payton. Thirty-one days.*

I recognize that I'm caught in a daydream and reprimand myself. I need to get my ass in gear if I hope to avoid running late. I hurriedly get dressed and am in my car in record time. I'm on my way to meet with James and the executives of this phenomenally big-budgeted action movie, *The Relishing*, when I figure I'd better stop at a bookstore and pick up a copy of the novel it's based on. I haven't read it yet, but apparently it has a massive cult following. If I don't portray this character correctly, I risk being hated by millions of zealous teenagers. I don't need that kind of stress on top of everything else that's been driving me insane lately.

Speaking of nuts, I was crazy to think I'd be able to casually stroll into a bookstore in Culver City and pick up a best seller without drawing any interest. Every last soul in the store is in an uproar once they see I've grabbed this book. Apparently, everyone is already aware that it's being made into a film. I am surrounded by people asking questions about it.

"Is the script true to the story?" a young girl asks.

"Are you playing Ciara or Emily?" another one chimes in.

"Who's been cast as the Mongrel King?" a bookstore employee questions.

I have no answers for anyone, so I smile politely, pay for the damn book, and push my way back to the car.

As I drive away, I seriously begin to wonder what the hell I've gotten myself in to. I thought the attention I've been receiving because of my last film was bad, but clearly, that was just the beginning. I feel like I'm biding my time, waiting for the other shoe to drop. I expect my star to extinguish at any moment, but it keeps getting brighter and brighter. Sometimes I wish I were still Kendall Bettencourt, the ordinary girl next door, instead of Kendall Bettencourt, the Hollywood darling. Then I could wear what I want and date who I want, and no one would care in the slightest.

All this thinking causes me to nearly speed clear past the studio. I manage to pull into the parking lot right at the last minute. I hand my keys to the valet and head inside.

James greets me in the hallway outside our designated meeting room. He insists on briefing me on the situation. "Okay, we're meeting with the producers and the director."

"Yeah, so?" I know the routine. I've gone through the motions more times than I can count. All I have to do is amp up my charm as high as it can go, lay the ass-kissing on real thick, and then let James handle the negotiations. When I'm satisfied with the terms, I sign on the dotted line. It's simple: James presents me as the hottest commodity on the market, and informs them that I can be bought if the price is right. Integrity is little more than an afterthought.

"Don't curse, and we'll be fine."

Seriously, that's what he's worried about? Occasionally, these Hollywood people bring out the ill-mannered troll in me, but that doesn't mean I am *always* an ungracious wretch. "I know how to conduct myself during business meetings, you jackass."

"Wonderful," he sneers and guides me into the room.

The meeting goes smoothly. After a spate of reluctance on my part, and the producer's ardent reassurance that I can be both a serious actress and an action star, I sign the contract. Landon Stone, the director, gushes over me the entire time. He calls me "the ultimate driving force behind the next sensational teen franchise." He goes on to say that my face is going to be everywhere—on posters, button pins, and t-shirts. There will be an action figure *and* a life-sized cardboard cut-out in my likeness, as well.

James is thrilled. I am scared to death. I don't *care* how astoundingly large my paycheck will be, I'm more concerned with my face being plastered all over the place. I'm going to be so sick of seeing myself on magazine covers, I doubt I'll ever want to look in a mirror again.

"Why don't you seem happy?" James disrupts my fit of angst as we're heading for the parking lot.

"I *am* happy."

"You should be elated. You've landed your most coveted female lead, to date. Forget about everything you've done in the past, this is going to make you *huge*."

I groan. "I thought I was already huge."

"You are, but you've reached the very top tier, now. It doesn't get any bigger than a Stone-directed adaptation of one of the best-selling books of all time."

Excellent! I'll never have a moment of peace again.

"Kendall!" I hear my name called from somewhere close behind me. I stop to say goodbye to James, then turn around, hoping that I won't find a fan looking for an autograph. Happily, the voice belongs to Lauren Atwell. She saunters toward me, a brisk pace to her step.

"Lauren! Hi!" I throw my arms around her neck. "How've you been since we wrapped?"

"Great! How are you? What are you doing here?"

"I'm pretty good. I just signed on to play Ciara in *The Relishing*. What are you doing here?"

"That's so cool! I just read for Emily!"

"Nice! I hope you get it. We would make the coolest, most ass-kicking movie ever!"

"We would," she agrees. "What are you up to now? You want to get a drink or something?"

I nod. "Love to." I planned to call her soon, anyway.

The valet pulls our cars around. I hop into mine and follow her off the lot.

❃ ❃ ❃

We end up at a tiny Irish pub called the Cloverleaf Tavern. It's in a quiet part of West Hollywood, and it's remarkably dead for a Friday.

"This place is cute," I say as we seat ourselves at the bar. "How'd you find it?"

She orders us both a cocktail. I'm impressed that we aren't asked for IDs, since everyone who knows us also knows that we're not quite old enough to legally drink alcohol. "My ex lives around the corner," she answers.

I laugh. "I guess you're not worried about running into him?"

"Her," she says. "And no, I'm not. We're cool. Anyway, this isn't her scene."

I regard her carefully, as though she might be able to sense whatever gayness I've got lurking inside me if I get too close. Isn't there a word for being able to sniff out homosexuality like a trained police dog? *Why the hell are all the cool girls lesbians, anyway?* "I wouldn't have guessed you were gay," I blurt out before recognizing how unbelievably asinine that sounds. *Brilliant.* I may as well have said "Gee, you sure are purdy for a lesbo," while clacking my ill-fitting dentures together and relentlessly drooling on myself.

She shakes her head. "I'm not gay. I just like who I like."

Wow. That's so bohemian! She can just jump from one orientation to the next without concern? I didn't even know people like that existed, that bisexuality is an actual thing… I always thought you had to check one box—gay or straight. "That's cool."

"Does it bother you?"

"What, that you're bisexual?" Does it seem like I'm bothered? I hope not. We're in West Hollywood! If anyone thought I was a homophobe, I'd be bashed and rightfully so. Besides, that would make me an utter cretin, wouldn't it?

She nods.

"No, it doesn't bother me at all. My best friend from back home is a lesbian. I was just curious about how you deal with the media. I mean, are you open about it?"

She nods. "I've always been open about it. I figure in our line of work, it's better to be straightforward about who you are and what you want. If you try to keep it a secret, it becomes a weapon. You know better than anyone how brutal the press can be."

That makes so much sense. But it takes a much braver person than me to be *that* honest with the entire world. "I prefer to keep my business to myself. I don't think my dirty laundry is all that interesting to begin with, so I don't know why anyone else would want to get a whiff of it."

She takes a sip of her drink. "You're beautiful, talented, and wealthy. I think people like to know that you're less than perfect so they can feel better about themselves."

I snigger. "Less than perfect? I am *so* far from perfect. I'm a neurotic mess most of the time." *And I have skeletons in my closet like everybody else does.*

"The average person doesn't see any of that. When they look at people like you and me, they only see what we have, not who we are."

I nudge her with my elbow. "You're a bit of a philosopher, aren't you?"

"That's nothing but a big Greek word for someone who thinks too much."

"Hey, that makes me a philosopher, too!" I laugh. "You're right, though. People don't get to see who we are. Maybe I should make a documentary about how boring I am when I'm not on screen."

"You totally should! Video yourself hanging out at home in your underwear," she says. "Interview your family and friends about what you do in your spare time. I'll sign on for that project! I'll tell everyone how dull you are and that you read an entire trilogy of books and talked on your phone the whole time we were in New Orleans."

"Nice! But don't you think that would be too much of a stab to the heart of the American dream to find out that famous people aren't much cooler than everyone else?"

"Probably, but you can throw in some kind of speech about how if you can make it in America, anybody can. I think that's the truth, anyway."

I come to the decision right then that I really like her. I wouldn't be at all surprised if we were to become very good friends.

CHAPTER SEVEN

Payton

The list of things I need to do before I move grows longer and longer in spite of my best attempts to check stuff off of it.

I got the whole MALA ordeal out of the way three weeks ago, submitted my application and transcripts. I received a call a few days later from the Dean of Students, saying how talented she thought I was and that I'd make a great fit for the school. She offered me a place in the advanced freshman Film Scoring program. My GPA is high enough that I was also offered the maximum scholarship the school awards. Of course, I accepted right away. I'm scheduled to meet with an academic advisor in early January so I can pick my classes according to the sight reading assessment I was asked to complete. My score was "roughly a prima vista"— able to play any piece of music nearly perfectly at first glance. Nearly perfect. In my vocabulary, that just means I have *a lot* of work to do. I'm most nervous about Performance 200: Composing for Orchestra. I've never written a piece for an entire orchestra before, but I guess I'll have to deal with it when the time comes.

With classes at MSU finally finished, I'm trying to concentrate my energy on packing up my room. It's proving to be quite a daunting task. Why is it that you never realize how much crap you have until you attempt to stuff it all into cardboard boxes? The mountains of clothes I own are not included in the aforementioned crap! My bookshelves are crammed with paperbacks and DVDS. I'm not sure where I had the room to fit all the CDs I've thrown out since the invention of the iPod. Most of my trinkets and knickknacks are going to have to stay here. I don't see the point in taking any of the soccer trophies or medals from various music competitions I've won. All those things are mementos from the past, and I want this move to be a new beginning for me—a renaissance of sorts. I'm hoping that once I've had the chance to marinate in West Coast sunshine, I'll be miraculously transformed into a new and improved edition of myself. Payton 2.0 will be confident, alluring even. She's going to take her mother's advice and meet new people and impress the hell out of them.

I didn't initially intend for my relocation to be any kind of major catharsis, or the catalyst that pushed me from one state of mind to another, but it makes sense that it would be. No one in LA knows me. I'll have the opportunity to be *anyone* I want to be. I'll start out as the mysterious girl who is always being photographed alongside Kendall Bettencourt, but I could act like I'm some kind of rock star and probably become one if I wanted. The issue is, I really don't. I want to be me, only happier. So, that's what I'll aim for—happiness. It's an achievable goal, right?

"Hey, Kiddo." My mom sticks her head through the door, interrupting the packing process. "I don't think your room has *ever* been this clean."

I look around in astonishment. I've managed to fit nearly everything I'm taking with me into two large boxes. My acoustic and electric guitars are nestled safely in their travel cases. Most of my clothes are already in suitcases. I've opted to leave the bulk of my winter clothes here, since I likely won't need them in sunny southern California. Snow boots and heavy sweaters probably won't be very useful out there, but every last one of my hoodies is coming with me. I don't care if it never drops below 80 degrees; I love hoodies too much to give them up.

"Packing is a glorified game of Tetris."

She nods. "We both know how good you are at Tetris." The expression on her face clues me in to the fact that she didn't wander upstairs merely to check on my progress or talk about Tetris.

"What's up?"

"I want to make sure that you're doing this for the right reasons. You're chasing your dream career, not your dream girl, correct? I doubt you need to move clear across the country to find her."

"Yes, Mom. I need to steer my life in the right direction, and MALA is *for sure* the right direction."

"That's good. Dedicate yourself to what truly matters, and you can achieve anything."

"Thanks."

She wanders over to me and envelopes me in a hug. "I sure am going to miss you. It's going to be so quiet without you around making a ruckus."

"Call me whenever it gets too quiet. I'll put you on speaker and play some power chords for you."

"Let's not get ahead of ourselves." She laughs and lets me go. "I'm off to work. Glad we had this talk."

"Me too. See you later."

By the end of the day, my room is transformed into an almost barren wasteland. Little remains of the clutter I used to live in. I've left enough clothing in my closet to get me through the next few days.

I'm tired and sweaty and about to collapse on my bed when the doorbell rings. I hobble down the stairs, open the door to find a man in blue coveralls standing on my porch. "Hello. I'm looking for a Ms. Payton Taylor. Is she at home?"

"I'm Payton. Can I help you?"

"I'm going to need to see your auto insurance card to confirm the VIN on your car. I also need the keys so I can pull it onto the rig."

"Excuse me?"

He consults a sheet of paper on his aluminum clipboard. "It says here that I'm supposed to pick up a white Volkswagen GTI coupe for delivery to an address on Hamilton Drive in Beverley Hills, California."

I look beyond him to the street. There's a massive black truck with the words "Express Transport Depot" scrawled across its side. It seems legit, but this guy must be a loon if he thinks I'm going to hand my car keys over to some dude I've never seen before. "Um, can you hold on a second?"

"All right," he huffs.

I grab my cell and dial.

"I guess the shipping company showed up on time," Kendall answers.

"What's going on?"

"You're flying to LA, not driving."

"Right, so what's up with this?"

"You need a car in LA. The public transportation here sucks more than the traffic."

I groan into the receiver. *I wish you'd stop buying me things.* "Do I even want to know how much this is costing you?"

"It's your Christmas present." Her voice has a twinge of impatience to it. "Sorry it's early. I wanted you to be able to get around without depending on a bus schedule."

"I would have gotten around to having my car sent out eventually." *After finding a minimum wage job and saving up for three months.*

"Hush up and give your keys to the nice man, Payton."

I dig my keys from my pocket and hold them out to the delivery guy. "The insurance card is in the glove box."

"Thanks," he says and heads toward the driveway.

"You didn't have to do this."

"No, I didn't, but you'll be glad I did. Trust me."

"Okay. Thank you."

"You're welcome. I'm getting really excited!"

"I know. I'm excited, too." I am, but I'm also sort of scared. I've always played it safe. So many things have changed for me recently that I'm finding it difficult to cope. That's the trouble with life. It's merely a series of moments, each one completely different from the last. I can't stop any of it from happening. "Listen, I'm really tired. Cleaning and packing totally kicked my ass. I need a nap."

She giggles. "Yeah, I bet. I've got a bunch of charity stuff to do this week, so if I don't talk to you, have a Merry Christmas. Wish your mom one for me, too."

"Okay, I will. Merry Christmas!"

❄ ❄ ❄

Christmas Day is ridiculous. Mom spends the whole day hugging me at random points and going on about "the very real intricacies" of empty nest syndrome. Her present to me is the title to my car, which she paid off six months early. She reminds me at least ten times that I need to insure it before I drive on the streets of Los Angeles. God forbid I get into an accident. I give her a gift set of her favorite perfume, which, of course, seems like the most pathetic thing ever. I promise her my presents to her will be much cooler someday, when I can afford it. That sets her off on a tangent about how she doesn't care about what I buy her, as long as I make it home every Christmas from next year until the end of time. We wrap up the holiday in our usual manner: snuggling on the couch, fireplace ablaze, watching *It's a Wonderful Life* on cable. As usual, she cries her eyes out. Seriously, if an angel got its wings every time my mother cried over this movie, heaven would be teeming with cherubs.

The next day, I head over to the Bettencourt's to wish them a belated happy holiday and to say my goodbyes. I told Mr. Bettencourt I'd stop by before my move, and Kendall warned me that I'd better follow through. This is the first time I've had to walk across town since I got my license. I already miss driving, so it's probably for the best that I won't have to go without a car in LA.

I catch Mr. Bettencourt wheeling garbage bins out for tomorrow morning. I dash down the driveway to help him. "Hi, Mr. B. Let me give you a hand." I move to grab the handle of one of the bins and find myself absentmindedly wondering whether or not Kendall takes out her own garbage. She probably has a boatload of eager ~~man-servants~~ neighbors willing to do it for her.

He smiles up at me and relinquishes his grip on one container. "Hi, Payton. Thank you."

Once we place the trash on the curb, he shakes my hand. It's weird. I've known him practically my whole life, yet I can't recall ever shaking his hand. "Come inside," he says. "Have a glass of wine with me."

"Wine," I repeat, startled.

He chuckles. "Don't worry. Grace isn't home, and I certainly won't tell your mother."

I give in and follow him into the house.

"Red, white or blush?" He asks, standing in front of the open wine chiller.

I wouldn't know, truthfully. I've hardly ingested enough wine in my lifetime to have a preference. The high school parties I used to attend rarely provided anything more sophisticated than half-flat beer from a keg. "Um, blush?"

"Good choice." He nods toward the dining room table. I sit. "I'm glad you're moving in with Kendall. I worry about her out there by herself."

I take a sip of my Zinfandel. "You shouldn't worry about her. She's got it all figured out."

"She has *some* things figured out. But she's still young, and she's still my daughter."

"My mom says the same thing about me."

"You'll understand when you're a parent. No matter how old your children get, you worry about them—the decisions they make, the possibility that someday they'll get their heart broken."

I'd never break her heart, not that I'd ever be given that opportunity. Anyway, I really don't want him to know that I have more than amicable feelings for Kendall. I know I love her for all the right reasons, but it would be a lie to say that I'm not interested in her in other ways. I'm pretty sure Mr. Bettencourt would slaughter me with an axe if he ever found out about the lust I harbor for his daughter. "Kendall is smart. She's got a big heart, but she's also a great judge of character. I don't think she'd surround herself with the kind of people who would hurt her."

"You're right. She has a good head on her shoulders." He eyes me carefully and sips his wine. I'm uncomfortable under his gaze, like he's judging my character. I'm curious what his verdict would be.

I had intended to stay longer, but I suddenly feel like I've over-stayed my welcome. "Thank you for the wine, but I should get going. I have a lot of stuff to do before I leave in the morning."

"It was a pleasure." He stands to walk me out.

I hug him instinctively once we've reached the door. "Please tell Mrs. B I said goodbye."

He nods. "You take care of yourself and Kendall, all right?"

"I will."

Take care of Kendall. The instruction embeds itself in my brain like it's a mission I've chosen to accept. Failure is not an option. If I can only learn how to take care of myself first, everything will be fine.

❄ ❄ ❄

Moving day has arrived. I'm awake long before my alarm goes off. It's quarter to seven, but my mind is racing much too quickly for me to go back to sleep. My flight takes off at 11:45. I've got a whole lot of time to kill before then, so I head down to the kitchen.

I pop some waffles in the toaster and brew a pot of coffee, then slip quietly to the front door to retrieve the morning paper. As I'm making my way back to the kitchen, I stop to look around the living room. A sensation of sadness takes hold of me. This is the last time I'll get the paper off the porch, or stand right here in this spot, or make breakfast in this kitchen. I'll never be able to say that I'm doing all these things in *my* house again. I know it will always be my home, the place where I grew up and made a lifetime of remarkable memories, but from now on, when I'm here, I'll merely be visiting. It's completely odd to know that I won't be living here anymore. *I hope Mom will be okay without me.*

"Good morning."

I turn around, notice my mother watching me from the landing of the staircase. The sight of her in her fluffy pink bathrobe makes me smile. "Good morning. Sorry, I didn't mean to wake you up."

"You didn't. I could smell the coffee in my sleep. I thought I was dreaming." She waddles into the kitchen, and I trail her through the door. "Would you like some real breakfast instead of those tasteless frozen things?"

Oh man, would I ever. "You don't have to cook for me, Ma."

She opens the refrigerator, pulls out a gallon of milk, a package of bacon, and a carton of eggs and sets them on the table. "Don't be silly. I won't get to make you breakfast for a while, so I'll make a big one for you today. Pancakes, eggs, and bacon sound good?"

"Yes. That sounds amazing."

She grins. "Set two places."

I do as I'm told, then pour two cups of coffee—mine with milk and two sugars, hers black. She has already fired up the stove-top when I hand her a mug. She takes a swill and sighs. "You make the best coffee."

"That's what you'll miss the most," I joke.

"No, Kiddo." She ruffles my hair like she used to when I was little. "I'm going to miss everything."

Yeah. I'm going to miss everything, too.

❄ ❄ ❄

We arrive at the passenger drop-off. Mom puts the car in park, and I hop out to find a luggage caddie. We take turns placing my stuff on the cart—she grabs a box, I grab a bag—working in tandem as a team like we always have. Five minutes later, I'm ready to go. Physically, at least. Emotionally, I'm not so sure.

I fall into her arms like the frightened child that I am, clinging to her for dear life. She squeezes me snugly. I tear up. She doesn't. My mom: The paragon of sturdiness when it counts the most. "You'd better get a move on, Kiddo."

"I'll call you later," I say before making my way into the terminal.

"I love you!" She hollers after me. "You're gonna be fine!"

I turn around just in time to watch her image melt away behind the sliding Plexiglas doors. *I hope she's right.*

CHAPTER EIGHT

Kendall

Apparently, a storm over Chicago forced Payton's flight behind schedule. I've been waiting in the airport lounge for nearly two hours. I sit patiently, trying to pay full attention to my book, but the anticipation of Payton's arrival is making me antsy. Lately, I've been inundated with press events and compulsory appearances at insignificant award shows, but I've still had more than enough time on my hands to miss her terribly.

At this point, missing her has become so overpowering that it's starting to get in the way of my obligations. The other day I had an interview for a syndicated morning show, and I could not for the life of me concentrate on the questions the interviewer was asking me. Fortunately, Lawrence was on the sound stage with the camera crew. He kept snapping and motioning with his pointer and middle fingers, reminding me to maintain eye contact with the host. Somehow, I managed to regain my bearings and make it through the interview. Afterward, Lawrence congratulated me on coming across as slightly brain damaged rather than completely brain-dead. If he hadn't been there, I would have been so consumed by my thoughts that I surely would have come across as having the IQ of a comatose goldfish. But Lawrence can't be around every moment of every day. Sooner or later, I'll be caught completely off guard, say something perfectly idiotic, and screw myself for sure.

"Excuse me. Come here often?"

I'd know that sensual, lightly graveled voice anywhere. *Payton.* I look up from my page, and she's towering over me. I spring to my feet and embrace her eagerly. "Funny you should ask that. Yes, it seems like I'm here all the time."

I take a step back and study her for a while. I am altogether captivated. It feels as though I'm staring into the eyes of some kind of apparition. But she's real. And she's here. And she's unequivocally gorgeous. She's wearing a body-hugging black hoodie and paint-splattered jeans with holes in the knees. Her hair is down. I get the familiar urge to play with it but don't allow myself to reach out.

She, however, goes straight for my freshly trimmed, side-swept bangs. Gently, she pushes them out of my face. "I see you're back to blonde. Very nice. You look like you again."

"Thanks. I couldn't deal with it anymore. Red fades too fast. It takes way too much effort to upkeep."

"You know what's really too much effort? Flying. That was the longest six hours *ever*. I have no idea how you spend half your life on airplanes."

I chuckle. "The day isn't anywhere near done yet. We have to round up all your stuff, get to the apartment, and unpack everything."

"I'm exhausted just *thinking* about it," she pouts.

"Come on. Let's get a jump on it." I take hold of her hand and lead her toward the baggage claim. She weaves her long, thin fingers into the spaces between mine. Our hands fit perfectly together, like they were created to complement each other. I don't ever want to let go.

✻ ✻ ✻

She told me she was packing light, but she has *a lot* less stuff than I was expecting. Her two military-style duffle bags and two guitars fit easily into the trunk of my car. We toss the pair of cardboard boxes into the back seat.

"How far is the drive?"

"That depends. About twenty minutes, but with traffic it could take much longer."

She fans herself with her hand and checks the in-dash temperature display. "Seventy-five degrees! It was only forty when I got on the plane at Newark."

"Seventy-five is unusual for LA in December. Normally, it tops out at around sixty-six."

"Ugh," she says and unbuckles her seat belt. She leans forward and pulls her heavy sweatshirt up and over her head, revealing a clingy white tank top. The cotton shirt is so thin, I can see straight through it to the lace bra she's got on beneath it. She's sweating a little, but in that extraordinarily sexy way girls do when they're dancing in a crowded club. I remind myself to keep my eyes on the road. If I gawk at her like I want to, we'll probably die in a fiery car wreck right here on the 405. The thought is horrifying—not the crashing part, the thinking she's incredibly sexy part. I could've gone my entire life without ever thinking that about Payton and been just peachy with it.

"You look hot." The phrase slips out before I have a chance to think about how wrong it sounds. "Uncomfortable, that is. We could stop somewhere to pick up some spring water if you want."

She gestures *no* with a headshake. "It's okay. I feel better now. I just want to get home."

Home. My home, her home, our home. Amazing. "The freeway is looking kind of packed. Getting home might take a while."

She switches on my iPod. "No worries. We've got good tunes."

❄ ❄ ❄

I watch Payton's reaction as we're pulling on to Hamilton. Her body language is plain adorable, kind of like a puppy's. Her window is down, and she's resting her chin on the doorframe. I can tell she is scrutinizing every little detail of the block from the huge houses and luxurious condos to the lofty palm trees lining both sides of the street.

"Well?"

She peels her eyes away from the outside world and glues them on me. "Well, what?"

"What do you think of the neighborhood?"

She groans. "I think I'm too poor to live here."

I feel a laugh brewing in my chest, but suppress it. "Oh, stop it."

"I'm serious. One look at me, and you can tell I'm way out of my league."

"What? Like you're going to be walking down the street one day and someone will call the cops on you 'cause they've confused you for a hobo?"

"Yeah, something like that," she says.

"Please. You think everyone is all haute couture all the time? Famous people like jeans and Converse as much as anyone else."

"In that case, I should fit right in," she says as we approach the underground garage of our apartment complex.

I press the switch on the remote and pull the car into the space marked "PH1." Payton's GTI is parked in the spot next to mine. "Here." I pop the glove box, hand her the keys to her car, and a remote to the garage door. She removes the apartment key from her pocket and fiddles with it until it's securely fastened to her car keys.

"Thanks." She gets out, unlocks the passenger side door of the VeeDub, and clips the remote onto the fold-down sun visor. Then she turns back and starts unloading her boxes from my back seat. "Can you open the trunk for me, please?"

"Let me call the concierge first. He'll send down a cart." I grab my Blackberry from my purse.

She flashes a sour expression at me. "We have a concierge?"

Was she expecting otherwise? This is Beverly Hills! I nod. "On weekdays we've got Rob, weeknights it's Jason, and on the weekends it's either Mike or Brandon. You should see what some of the people in this building make those guys do. I saw Brandon walking somebody's dog once!"

She arches her left eyebrow conspicuously. "And what do *you* ask them to do?"

"Hardly anything." I shrug. "They'll usually grab my bags for me without my asking them to."

She folds her arms and considers it for a minute. "Okay, make the call."

I dial. Rob agrees to have a luggage trolley sent down for us.

Payton surveys me as we're waiting. "You take your own garbage out, right?"

"What?" I ask with a snigger. *Where did that bit of randomness come from?* "We have a trash chute. But yes, I take my own garbage to it." I'm about to mutter something about curiosity killing the cat when the elevator opens behind us. Rob emerges, cart in tow.

"Here you are, Ms. Bettencourt."

"Thanks, Rob. This is my roommate, Payton Taylor."

"Hello. Nice to meet you." I can see that he's eyeballing her furiously. I want to say, "Yeah, she's scorching, but it's impolite to stare." Instead, I simply chuckle.

"Nice to meet you, too," Payton responds politely despite the fact that it seems that she's noticed him ogling her. "Um, I'm sorry, Rob. Can you put the brakes on this thing while I load it up?"

He steps on the foot brake. "Please, let me get that for you." He diligently begins shifting her stuff from the trunk to the caddie. When he's done, he closes the trunk and escorts us to the elevator. He rides with us to the first floor lounge and turns to us before stepping off. "Ms. Taylor, please call down to the front desk should you need anything."

"I will, thank you."

"Have a nice day, ladies."

As soon as the door is closed behind him, we're both in stitches. "I think you've got a fan," I sputter.

"Right, he's a fan of my C-cups like every other guy."

"Pssh, you're a beautiful girl." *Go on, Stupid! Say something else that'll give you away! Tell her that* you're *a fan of her C-cups, too, why don't you?* With breakneck speed I add, "In this town that will get you anything you want."

"I'd rather get what I want by working for it," she scoffs.

The elevator dings and the "PH" light illuminates. "Here we go." I take the handle of the cart—mostly so I can show her that pretty girls aren't afraid to do actual work—and push it down the hall. She follows close behind.

"There aren't any other apartments on this floor?"

"It's a penthouse thing," I say, then slide the key into the lock.

The second she steps foot through the door, her eyes go wider than an anime character's. She spins in a slow circle and looks up the winding glass staircase leading to the study. She marvels first at the high, glass ceiling then shifts her attention to the first floor.

Admittedly, the apartment is a bit excessive. It's 5,500-square-feet and kind of resembles something you'd see on an episode of MTV Cribs. When I bought the place, it had a skate ramp smack in the middle of it! I had that removed and replaced it with a sensible billiards table and lounge area. Now, the first floor is wide open; its flow is extraordinary. The exterior walls aren't really walls, but huge windows, and there is no division between the kitchen to the left and living room to the right. The bedrooms are separated from the kitchen and living room by a glass partition. Both the master and guest bedrooms are accessible through sliding doors in the sheet glass and are separated from each other by a wall made entirely of black bamboo. Each bedroom is equipped with floor-length privacy curtains, which can be pulled across the panoramic windows and the glass partition.

I wheel the cart through the living room to her bedroom. "You've got your own bathroom," I call out to her. When I reenter the living room, I catch her gliding her hand across the arm of one of the white leather couches.

"Where's the pool?" she asks, a hint of sarcasm to the question.

"Through the ranch sliders right there," I point to the doors opposite the wall-mounted flat screen TV.

"I was joking."

"I wasn't," I reply and motion with my finger for her to follow me up to the study.

She stops dead at the top of the steps and gasps. "Holy fuck!"

A roaring cackle escapes my lips. In all the years I've known her, I don't think I've ever heard her drop an F-bomb. For some reason, it's the funniest thing she's ever said. "I didn't know anything about how to set up a studio," I say once I've recovered from my laughter. "I asked Mark Carter to come in and put it all together. He tried out all the equipment, made sure it all works properly."

"Mark Carter, as in, the producer?" Her voice is so low, it's like she's merely mouthing words.

Could you be any cuter? "That would be him, yeah."

"You're saying one of the world's most badass electronica musicians put this whole thing together, and also actually *used* all this stuff?"

"Yep, that's what I'm saying."

Tears well up in her eyes. I can't quite describe the way she's looking at me, but if she doesn't kiss me *right now,* she won't ever kiss me. *Please! Please, do it! I swear on all that is good and holy, I will kiss you back.*

"Wait here." She takes off down the stairs.

Okay, that is so not the reaction I was hoping for.

A few minutes later, she reappears. In her hands, she holds a present wrapped in shiny green paper. "It isn't much, but Merry belated Christmas."

I slip the foil off. The box reads "Lenox." Inside the box is a framed 8x10 photo of Payton, Sarah, and Jared in front of the tree at Rockefeller Center. They are all smiling. *She is smiling.*

"I thought you could stash it away in your room or something."

"Nope! No way. This is going right on the mantel over the fireplace in the living room where every last person who enters this house can see it."

"Oh, great," she smirks.

"Seriously, it's awesome. Thank you."

"You're welcome. Thank *you* for all of this." She sweeps a gaze around the room.

I stare at my feet. I can't look at her, or everything I've got bottled up inside me will come spilling out in waves. "We should probably get you unpacked."

"Good idea. I'm gonna throw on a pair of shorts first, though."

"Cool," I say, though it's really not. My head is still reeling from the sweatshirt thing earlier. *Lord, help me.*

❋ ❋ ❋

We've been unpacking her stuff for a good hour. Every time she moves or bends over to pick something up, the goddamn shorts ride up and expose more of her impeccable thighs. Obviously, there is some kind of nascent physical lure going on here, and I doubt it's a passing inkling because I seriously feel the need to find out who designed those shorts so I can write them a long, heartfelt letter of gratitude.

"Houston to Kendall. Come in, Kendall."

"Huh?"

"I asked if it would be cool for me to mount a guitar rack on a wall upstairs."

"Yeah, duh, it's cool. It's your place now, too. Go crazy."

"Cool," she says and then leans over to grab a pair of shoes from her suitcase.

I clear my throat and remind myself not to stare. *Kendall, if you need to remind yourself of that, there's a good chance you may be royally screwed.* "So I was thinking we could take a drive downtown tomorrow. I want to show you where MALA is and all the cool stuff there is to do around there."

"You don't have to work?"

"I'm taping an interview with MusicTube at ten, but I'm free after that."

"Okay, that sounds awesome."

"Great. It's a date!"

"Hold on," she lifts an empty duffle up to me. "I think we're finished!"

I exhale a sigh of relief. "Thank god for that. I'm crazy thirsty. You want some water?"

"Definitely."

I snap my fingers and head into the kitchen. She tails me out to the living room then curls up in a ball on the couch. I'm filling a pitcher of water at the sink, about to hobble over to join her, when my Blackberry buzzes. I check the caller ID. It's Lauren. I contemplate sending her to voicemail, but decide that would be kind of rude. "Hey, hun," I answer.

"Hey. Guess what?" Her voice is cheery. I'm intrigued.

"What?"

"My agent called. It seems you and I will be working together again."

"You got the part? That's awesome! Congratulations!" Working with her will make this project infinitely more fun. "Are you excited?"

"Hell yeah, I'm excited! I was thinking I could celebrate with my co-star over dinner. Are you busy tomorrow night?"

Tomorrow night? I should probably check with Payton before making any plans. I can't go out and leave her home when she's only been here for one day. And anyway, I would love to celebrate her arrival by taking her out for a night on the town. It's probably a good idea to introduce her to new people, help her make friends. "That sounds great, but my roommate just flew in from Jersey. Would it be cool if she came out with us?"

"Absolutely. I'll make a reservation for three at Diamante's at eight?"

"Diamante's at eight? That's the hottest place on Santa Monica right now. You can get us a rez on such short notice?" I feel like that's a stupid question. If I called there tomorrow at seven for a reservation at eight, they'd go all Rain Man on me. "Ms. Bettencourt, we can definitely, *definitely* do that." It's yet another perk of the job. Shallow, I know, but convenient.

"Remember the ex I told you about?" Lauren questions. "She's the Sous Chef there. She owes me one."

Awesome. Friends in high places are so much more convenient than fame. "Hang on a sec," I say, then cover the mouthpiece and peer out into the living room. "Payton, think you'll be up for a night out tomorrow?"

She shrugs, "Yeah, sure."

I smile and bring the phone back to my ear, "Lauren, you're on."

"Cool. I'll see you girls then. Ta-ta," she replies and hangs up.

I grab two glasses with one hand and the pitcher in the other, totter out to the living room, and collapse onto the couch. Payton relieves me of my full hands and fills the glasses.

"My friend Lauren found out she got the second lead in *The Relishing*. We're all going out for a celebratory dinner."

She smiles apprehensively. "That's cool."

I pat her thigh without thinking about the tremors I will inevitably experience at the contact. "What's with the sheepish grin?"

"Well, my first full day in town is going to end at a Hollywood hotspot with two movie stars. That's sort of daunting."

"Ridiculous. Lauren is totally down to earth. You'll like her, I promise."

She huffs. "Okay. We'll find out."

"Yeah, we will. Now, what do you say about a quiet night with Chinese food and *Alice in Wonderland*?"

She smiles. "I say let's do it."

❊ ❊ ❊

Lawrence meets me at MusicTube Studios. He surprises me with coffee while I'm in hair and makeup. I'm not sure why he's here, let alone why he's bringing me coffee. In the very early days of his employment as my publicist, he bombarded me with instructions at every press event, but for the last little while he's pretty much trusted me to do and say all the right things without having to babysit me. Over the last few weeks, he's been attached to my hip. "What did I do wrong now?"

He examines my reflection in the mirror. I guess he's pleased with what he sees, because he straight up lies to me. "You haven't done anything wrong."

Yeah, like I buy that. "Then why are you here?"

"Moral support."

"I'm calling you out on your bullshit. You're here to make sure I don't blank out again, aren't you? Look, Lawrence. I've already got a father, okay? I don't need *another* one."

"Sweetheart, I don't know what's going on with you lately," he says, his voice clearly annoyed. "But you've been about as responsive to these interviewers as a fresh corpse. Your mind is elsewhere when it needs to be in the moment."

He can be a real ass sometimes, but even then, he's usually right. "I know. I'm sorry. I'll try harder to focus."

"Kendall, if there's something you need to talk about…"

"There isn't," I say sharply.

"Are you sure? I could call your mother if you'd rather talk—"

"No!" *Hell* no. I'd rather stick a fork in my eye than talk to my mother about pretty much *anything* other than the weather. "I'm dealing with it, okay? But thanks for your concern."

"Hey, that's my job."

An assistant enters the dressing room to give me a five-minute warning. I walk toward the sound stage. *Here we go. Don't mess it up.*

"Remember to smile," Lawrence says, sending me on my way with a pat on the back.

The host asks me routine questions about *Idol*: Can I describe my character, did I have fun on set, how did I feel about having to sing in a film, did I need any special music training? But then he gets down to the good stuff: How was it filming the girl-on-girl sex scene?

My instinct is to be honest, tell him it was the scariest experience of my life—that it was the moment I realized I might have been wasting my time kissing boys when maybe I've always wanted to be kissing girls—but my jaw clenches up faster than a bear trap can snap shut. I glance over the host's shoulder and see Lawrence backstage. "Be vague," he mimes.

"You know, all sex scenes are technical. It's pretty much up to the director to tell you where to touch your scene partner and how to kiss them. Basically, sex scenes are the total opposite of sexy."

I look over to Lawrence again. He gives me two thumbs up. The host laughs and finishes up the interview by thanking me for being on his show. I thank him for inviting me. End Scene.

"Great job," Lawrence says when I meet him backstage.

Really? It felt like a total bomb to me. "I'm going home."

He nods. "Good idea. Get some beauty rest."

❋ ❋ ❋

By the time I get back to the house, Payton is ready to go exploring. I insist that she drive downtown. She protests. I tell her that it's the same as driving in New York City, but that makes her more hesitant. After a good twenty minutes of arguing about it, I convince her that she needs to get used to LA roads if she's going to live here.

Finding a parking space in Bunker Hill is usually nothing short of a miracle, but Payton manages to do it, nearly cutting off another car in the process. I tease her about being a "goddamn Jersey motorist." She retorts with a sassy, "you know it, baby."

We find MALA and explore the campus for a while. She seems happy with its size and location and impressed by the number of students we spot carrying instruments of all shapes and sizes. There's an excited light in her eyes. *God, I love that light.* "It's like you belong here already."

She nods. "Yeah, but now we need to get out of here. I'm *starving*."

I agree wholeheartedly. "There's an awesome Peruvian restaurant around the corner. I guarantee they've got the best flan you've ever tasted."

She smiles at me. I liquefy like ice cream in the hot summer sun.

"Okay, but you gotta take those ridiculous glasses off your face while we're eating."

I accept the condition.

We walk down the street side by side. I'm so tempted to grab her hand, but I know I couldn't justify it. I keep hoping for the bulls of Pamplona to come rampaging down the sidewalk so I'd have a reason to lace my fingers with hers. Seeing as we're in LA, I know that isn't going to happen. *I should take her to Pamplona for the San Fermin festival. I think we'd both get a kick out of watching the sad attempts of silly people at dodging the deadly horns of one-ton monsters.* "Do you want to go to Spain with me next summer? I say next summer because I know I'll be filming *The Relishing* this summer, which is a bummer because I'd much rather be on vacation."

"Spain?" she questions as we arrive at the restaurant. She holds the door open for me, I note.

I slip my sunglasses off and dangle them from the collar of my t-shirt. "Yes, next July. I'd like to see the running of the bulls."

She chuckles as we are being seated. "Sure. I've always wanted to watch a bunch of idiots get trampled to death."

"It sounds cool as hell, doesn't it?"

She snatches the menu from the table and scans it over quickly. Her features contort with confusion. "I can't read any of this," she sighs. "I should've taken Spanish in high school."

"It's cool." I reach across the table and rub the soft skin on the back of her hand. "Leave it to me."

Our waitress comes over. I say, "Me gustaría que el pollo saltado, y mi amiga tendrá el pollo de gallina. Y dos refrescos de dieta, por favor."

Payton's jaw drops so low it nearly hits the table. "How did you do that? You didn't take Spanish in high school, either."

"I've picked it up here and there."

"Uh huh." She folds her arms. "So, what did you order for me?"

"Pollo de Gallina, chicken cooked with eggs, peanuts, milk, and cheese. And a diet soda."

"I'm impressed. Nice job."

"I need to practice for our trip to Pamplona."

She grins. "You should teach me."

"Okay. That's a fair trade for piano lessons."

❄ ❄ ❄

We get back to the apartment around six, leaving us just enough time to get ready for our night out with Lauren. I take a shower, blow dry my hair, and slip on a black, one-shouldered cocktail dress. It's designed in such a way that it looks like I'm wrapped in a body cast made entirely of lace. I'm checking myself out in the mirror when Payton knocks on my door. I don't spot it at first, but on second glance I see she's in a towel. Her hair is damp and draped over her shoulders. *This is not good.*

She's staring at me with such intensity that, for just a second, I wonder if maybe we're both thinking the exact same thing. I want to say "Let's do this and get it over with already," but she speaks first.

"I, um, I don't know what to wear."

Anything! Please, put something *on. I don't care what.* "You've got those black dress pants," I suggest. "With a white button down and the little vest that has the buckle in the back. That will be perfect."

"Right. Thanks," she says and heads for the door.

I think the moment has passed, but then she stops and turns back to me. "You look beautiful by the way."

I swallow hard. "Thank you." *Now please leave. This is too bizarre.*

She nods and walks away. I narrowly escape with my sanity intact.

❄ ❄ ❄

We arrive at Diamante's fifteen minutes after eight. Payton's fretting about showing up late, and I tell her to relax. In LA, being late is fashionable. The host recognizes me right away and leads us over to the table where Lauren is.

"Hi!" Lauren stands and faux kisses both of my cheeks. It's the most cliché Hollywood greeting, but I return the gesture anyhow.

"Lauren Atwell, this is Payton Taylor," I motion between them. "Payton, Lauren."

Lauren examines her meticulously. The look on her face! It's like she's a starved wolf about to pounce on wounded prey. She beams warmly and extends her hand. "Hello, Payton. It's a pleasure to meet you."

Payton flashes her most charming smile. "Congratulations on getting the part," she says as she shakes Lauren's offered hand. The very instant their palms meet, the air around us thickens. The sparks between them are practically visible from space. *Typical!*

"Ladies, I've gone ahead and ordered us a bottle of Château," Lauren sits and signals for our waiter to pour the wine.

"Lovely," I mumble as I take a seat. I realize very quickly that I need to keep my tone in check; it has a serious bite to it, totally capable of doing irreparable damage. I grab my glass of wine, nearly down it entirely in one gulp, and motion for the waiter to refill my glass.

"Thank you," Payton says to both Lauren and our waiter.

"So, Payton," Lauren starts, "you're a model?"

Payton's face reddens. She giggles nervously. "No. I'm a college student."

"You *should* be a model."

As soon as she says it, I get a hankering to lunge across the table and choke the ever-loving shit out of her. It's startling. I am *not* a violent person, and she hasn't even done anything wrong. *Yes, she has! She dropped a line on my girl!* Not *my* girl, just… oh, fuck me sideways! Of all the stupid things I have done in my life, introducing Payton to a tall, blonde, *sometimes* lesbian with high cheek bones might be the dumbest.

"She's starting classes at the Music Academy of Los Angeles soon," I butt in, trying to lighten my own mood while simultaneously informing Lauren that Payton has much more going for her than a spectacular physique.

The look of surprise on Lauren's face irritates me to no end. Was she expecting Payton to be another brainless, pretty girl who came to LA in hopes of being discovered? "MALA. That is very impressive. I hear they only cater to prodigies," she says.

Payton grins. "I wouldn't classify myself as a prodigy."

"I *would*," I interject. Payton glares at me. "What? You're amazing. You have to hear the music she writes. It's superb, extremely moving."

Lauren nods. "And what are you majoring in? Classical? Contemporary?"

"Film scoring, actually," Payton replies before taking a sip of her wine.

"You definitely chose the right school for that."

Throughout the entire meal, the two of them go on and on while I silently observe. I am little more than a fly on the wall, a stalking shadow. They are hitting it off famously, and I'm fading into the background. What's worse than Lauren's flirtation is that Payton is playing off of it—she is flirting *back*. I want to tell her not to fall for it, the smooth-talking starlet bit. But there's a real chance they might honestly *like* each other. If that's the case, I have no right to stand in the way. I've laid no claim to Payton; she can't be stolen from me if she was never mine to begin with. *Oh, look, there's more wine!*

"Oh, Kendall," Lauren says, "are you going to the Time Zone Ball?"

"Are you kidding? My publicist requires it. He went as far as to mandate that I accompany Gunner Roderick."

Lauren chortles. "Kendall Bettencourt and Gunner Roderick, now *there's* a match made in gene pool heaven."

I nod. "Oh, yeah, we'd procreate and pop out beautiful blonde-haired, blue-eyed heirs to the Tinsel Town throne if Lawrence had his way. Seriously, he's shipping us so hard. Gunner will probably get stuck escorting me around for a while."

Payton furrows her brow. "What is the Time Zone Ball?"

"It's the annual New Year's Eve party at the Beverly Regency Hotel," Lauren replies.

"Basically, it's an excuse for celebrities to dress in couture, get completely hosed, and make out en masse," I add.

Payton rolls her eyes. "That sounds like a *blast*."

"It's not so bad," Lauren says, "except that I'm going solo."

I already know where she's headed with this—someplace that is sure to infuriate me. I contemplate excusing myself to the ladies' room so that I can throw a fit out of public view, but I stay seated, exposing myself to the fullest extent of punishment.

"Payton, would you like to be my date?" Lauren asks slickly.

Payton is entirely flummoxed, like she's the ugly duckling who just realized she's a swan. "You want *me* to be your date?"

Lauren titters, amused. "Yes, I want *you* to be my date. Why do you sound so surprised?"

"Because… I'm nobody."

Lauren reaches across the table, takes Payton's hand and says, "Everyone is somebody. And you happen to be somebody that I'd like to get to know."

Jesus Christ, I'm going to pass out! I am seriously going to have a nervous breakdown right here in the middle of the restaurant. More fodder for the tabloids. *Just say no, Payton, like you would to crack cocaine!*

"I'd be honored, but I don't have anything high-fashion enough to wear to that kind of thing."

She didn't. I can feel my blood pressure skyrocketing.

"Minor detail," Lauren says, shirking off Payton's fret. "Who is your favorite designer? We can have them dress you."

Payton looks at me, and I shrug. *I am so not down to help you throw yourself at anyone.* "I don't really have a favorite," she says.

"I think you'd look amazing in Vincenzo Montebello," Lauren remarks. "What do you think, Kendall?"

I think you should drop it before I sink my claws into your pretty little neck and rip your tongue out through the gashes. Say what now? No! *Kendall, for real, what the hell is wrong with you?* I lean back in my chair, fold my arms, and fake the most undaunted expression that my facial muscles can form. "I think she'd look amazing in anything to be honest."

Payton blushes again. "I do like Victoria Westfeld."

"She is *very* punk-rock sexy," Lauren replies. I can tell by her tone that she approves. "All right, so if I can get you in a Westfeld, you'll be my date?"

"Sure," Payton smirks as if she doubts that it could happen. I know what she's thinking. New Year's is three days away. It's such short notice. She has no idea how things work in this town, but boy, is she about to find out. When Hollywood comes knocking, designers haul ass.

Lauren grins. "Great. I'll pick you up tomorrow, and we can go down to Rodeo to get you fitted. How does one o'clock work for you?"

Payton coughs on a mouthful of wine. "Are you serious?"

Lauren nods. "I'm as serious as a heart attack."

Okay, enough! I gesture to the waiter for the check. He slips a leather bill presenter on the table. I quickly place my Amex Black inside. I know it's showy to the point of tasteless to toss in Lauren's face the fact that I command bigger paychecks than she does, but it's the last thing I've got in my favor. Not that Payton cares at all about money. When it comes down to it, Lauren is more charismatic and daring than I am. That's what counts the most.

I fake a smile. "She'll be ready to go by one if I personally have to drag her out of bed."

"Cool. Can I get your number?"

"Yes," Payton nods. They exchange phone numbers.

"Great. I will see you tomorrow."

We say our goodbyes and bolt out of there with a quickness. The valet pulls my car around, opens the door for me and then for Payton. I gun the engine and blast the car onto the road faster than I should. When I look over at Payton, I see she has a firm hold on the "oh shit" bar on the passenger-side door.

I say through clenched teeth, "Stupid Bentley. Sorry, sometimes I forget how much power it has."

"It's okay. Just please don't kill us."

"I'll try not to, but I make no promises." I sigh. "So, you and Lauren seemed to hit it off well."

She shrugs. "I guess."

"You guess? She asked you to the Time Zone Ball. She's taking you for a Westfeld fitting. She obviously liked you enough for you to do more than *guess*."

"Okay, so she likes me."

"What about you? Do you like her?" I ask like I have a right to know. She's got this dreamy, far-away glaze in her eyes. *There's my answer.*

"She seems cool. I don't know her well enough yet to say whether I like her or not."

Okay, fine. Lauren *is* cool. And she might even be able to make Payton happy. Who the hell am I to stand in the way of that? "Give the girl a shot. What could it hurt? If nothing else, she has perfect bone structure." *Perfect mother effing bone structure!*

CHAPTER NINE

Payton

I've been in the study messing around with my MIDI program since the sun came up. I couldn't sleep at all last night. After dinner, I was sort of in a daze, and I still cannot believe it; I'm in California less than forty-eight hours and the universe presents me with an opportunity I would be stupid to pass up. Lauren. She's pretty, she seems cool, and she wants to "get to know me." It *must* be some kind of celestial intervention like Venus or Ishtar or whoever is screaming at me, "Here! Here's someone to concentrate your energy on who will actually return the favor!" I should go for it and be thankful, shouldn't I? I can't keep endlessly moping around like a lovelorn loser. She might be exactly what I need to get over Kendall. Nothing else I try seems to be working. *Yeah. I'll give Lauren a chance.*

I'm in the middle of mixing down a track when I feel a tap on my shoulder. I slip my headphones down around my neck.

I look up to see Kendall rubbing the sleep from her eyes. "Why are you up so early?"

Because I've been arguing with myself all night about the pros and cons of dating somebody in order to forget about someone else. "I was dreaming and had a stroke of musical genius," I fib. "I'm gonna try my hand at crossing classical with electronica."

She skulks over to the rolling office chair and slumps into it. "That'll be interesting," she croaks through a yawn.

"Yeah, hopefully, or it could be a disaster."

"Nothing you do could ever be a disaster."

Wanna bet? "Thanks. Why are *you* up so early?"

She hunches her shoulders. "I wasn't tired anymore."

"Would you like some coffee? I was gonna make a pot."

She nods.

We make our way to the kitchen. She sits at the breakfast bar and watches me as I work my caffeine magic. When it's finished brewing, I pour her a cup with hazelnut creamer, exactly how she likes it. She takes a sip then shoots me a wide grin. "I love your coffee. If you were a barista, you'd put everyone else to shame."

"That's the real reason I agreed to this move—not to be your music teacher, but your personal barista."

"That's fine by me," she retorts before taking another sip.

"So, I decided you were right. About Lauren, I mean. I'm going to give it a chance with her. If she's interested, that is."

"Oh, she's interested," she speaks into the side of her coffee mug. "I've been hanging out with her a lot lately. She's good people. Before you know it, the two of you will be celebrating your one year anniversary together in Paris."

A disbelieving laugh seeps from my mouth. "Counting your chickens before they've hatched much?"

"Whatever." She rolls her eyes, gets up, and saunters over to the fridge. She peers over her shoulder at me. "We've got no food."

"What did you expect? You're always eating out," I reply.

She looks at me straight-faced then starts chuckling uproariously.

I don't get it. "What?"

"You are the *worst* lesbian *ever.*"

"What?" I repeat. She strains her neck at me all like, 'Come on!' I take a moment to consider what could be so funny about the phrase, "you're always eating out." And then it hits me like a Mac truck. "Oh, *dude!*" I howl. "Your mind lives in the gutter, doesn't it?"

"Yes, right next door to the mind of a horny sixteen-year-old boy. They get along well."

"Good. I'm glad your mind has friends."

She wiggles her eyebrows at me then quickly goes quiet again. Something really serious must have popped into her head. "Let's go to Whole Foods. You've got time for grocery shopping before your hot date with Lauren, right?"

My hot date with Lauren. Yeah, there's plenty of time before that *happens.* "You're driving," I say.

"Okay. Go get dressed," she replies, and a puckish little smile flickers into being.

* * *

Whole Foods is ridiculous, and I'm not talking about the prices. It's like someone called a meeting of the Hollywood high council or something. Every famous person in the state of California must be here doing their food shopping. Normally "star-struck" cannot be used to describe me, because honestly, who cares? Celebrities are only people with deep pockets. But today, I feel downright out of place like a peasant in the presence of royalty. *This is no way to act like a rock star.*

"Will you relax, please?" Kendall grabs a bunch of bananas and places them in the cart. "They're just people. Isn't that what you always say?"

"Yeah, but that doesn't mean I'm okay with, like, regularly walking among them."

She laughs. "Walking among them? What are they, aliens? And if they are, what does that make me?"

"I don't know, the next queen of the colony?"

"Well, if you're keeping company with the person who's next in line for the throne then you must be a VIP, so start acting like one."

"Okay." I reach for the sunglasses she's pushed into her hair, slip them onto my face and adopt an "I am so amazing. You just don't know it yet" stance. "Better?" I ask in my most laid-back, surfer-dude voice.

"Yeah, much better."

I push the cart down the next aisle. "Cool."

We run into Rebecca Gordon, Kendall's co-star from *Idol Worship*, in the canned goods aisle. Kendall introduces us. Weirdly enough, my first thought is to ask her what it was like to kiss Kendall, because that's something I'd die to have the chance to do. Instead, I nod in her direction. "Hey," I say like I imagine a rock star who is thoroughly unfazed by anyone's fame would do. She and Kendall have a polite chat about stuff no one actually cares about. I pretend to be completely disinterested in the whole conversation and wander off to examine the nutritional facts on a can of creamed corn, which I already know has absolutely *no* nutritional value.

I pinch a jar of dill pickles from the shelf and place it in the cart. A little while later, I hear Rebecca call, "Glad to meet you, Payton." I lift the Aviators off my face. "Glad to meet you, too." I somehow manage to make it sound like I couldn't have cared less to make her acquaintance. *Kendall wants a VIP, then that's what she'll get—Payton 2.0.*

"That was very suave," Kendall says.

"What's that supposed to mean?"

"It means where did this Cooler than Thou thing come from?"

I put the sunglasses back on. "You told me to be cool, so I'm being cool."

"I meant be the awesome, charming person you are, Payton, not be an incredible asshole." She quickly turns on her heel and walks away from me.

Okay. Apparently Payton 2.0 needs some refinement. "I'm sorry," I mutter once I've caught up with her. "I need some time to get used to being out here in your world. I'm feeling completely out of my element right now."

She turns quickly to face me and throws a giant chocolate bar in the cart. "In my world, all you need to do to fit in is be yourself, okay? Do that and everyone you meet—celebrity or not—will like you. You were completely yourself at dinner last night with

Lauren, and she was so taken with you that she *asked you out!*" She sighs. "Don't you get it? You're so damn *likeable*. And if given the chance to really get to know you, you're actually loveable."

I am? Crap. I don't know how I'm supposed to respond to that. "I said I was sorry. I mean it, I'll try harder not to be weird."

"Please do. Now, let's finish shopping. I told Lauren I'd have you ready to go by one. I intend to do exactly that."

"Yes, ma'am," I reply and make a ridiculously goofy face.

She smiles. "That face."

❊ ❊ ❊

"I like how I introduced you to Lindsay Pratt on the checkout line and you were all like, 'Oh hey, you were really good in that movie where you played a prostitute. I think only you and Julia Roberts have ever pulled that off well.' And then everyone around us started laughing about it," Kendall says as she places the tangerines in the fruit bowl.

"She *was* good in that movie."

"Yes, she was. Hey, it's noon. You'd better go take a shower."

"Right."

"And wear something sexy," she shouts at my back as I'm retreating to my room.

"Feel free to go ahead and pick something out for me," I call to her.

When I get out of the shower, I'm not surprised to find a pair of destroyed hip hugger jeans and a cut-off black tank with the word "OBEY" printed across the front laid out and ready to wear. It's been a running joke between Jared, Sarah, and Kendall that my "boobs make everyone obey" ever since I bought the damn shirt. It's a little embarrassing, but sometimes I think it might actually be true, especially when I catch random guys staring at my chest.

I dry my hair, get dressed, and walk out into the living room. Kendall is sprawled out on the couch watching some terribly written, even more horribly acted soap opera. Once she notices me standing next to her, she does a double take. "Mmhmm, I should have been a stylist," she says, her mouth creeping into a satisfied grin.

"I'm stealing your Aviators. I think they'll complete the look."

"They will, definitely." She sits up and digs through her purse. "Come sit down."

Despite my qualms, I join her on the sofa.

"Look up."

"You're so weird," I reply as I raise my head.

"Pssh, not with your head! With yours eyes."

I look at her, momentarily confused. "What? Why?"

She clicks her tongue against the roof her mouth. "Will you do it, please?"

I shrug, lower my head and roll my eyes toward the ceiling. I feel all her weight shift on to me as she repositions herself to straddle my lap. My lungs deflate with a sting as though her body has literally knocked the wind out of me. I flinch so hard at the contact that I nearly knock her to the floor. She anchors herself by latching on to my shoulders.

"Don't jump," she says sharply. "I'm gonna do your makeup. How do you feel about the smoky-eye look?"

"Okay, I guess."

"Good, 'cause that's what you're getting."

Once she's settled and balanced, I become extremely aware of how petite she is. She can't be more than a hundred pounds soaking wet. She's *so* tiny and seemingly fragile, I'm almost afraid I'll break her. "Why are you sitting on me, anyway? I could've sat, and you could've stood."

"It's easier this way. We're at eye level."

Actually, we're more at lip level, but whatever. All I want is for her to finish doing my makeup and get off of me. Lying next to her is one thing, but I can't handle this much physical contact between us. If I die of a coronary, it wouldn't come as much of a surprise.

The intercom buzzes. Mike's voice calls up from the front desk. Unfortunately, Kendall ignores him to focus on my mascara. "Perfection," she murmurs, still straddling me.

"Excuse me, Ms. Taylor," Mike buzzes up again, "Ms. Atwell is here to collect you."

"She's here to collect me? I *knew* you famous people were aliens!" I guffaw.

Kendall leans into me and laughs, her forehead meeting my shoulder.

Oh, man. Move, Kendall! Please!

"All right." she scoots off me. Into the intercom she says, "Send her up, Mike."

As we wait for the elevator to reach our floor, she looks me over, admiring her handiwork. I spin around without her telling me to. "How do I look?"

She brings her thumb and forefinger up into a mock-pistol position and makes a popping sound with her lips. "Killer."

There's a knock at the door. She instructs me to take deep, steady breaths.

I haven't been on a date in forever. It's going to take more than breathing exercises to get me to unwind. I lean against the back of the couch, trying to seem cool for when Lauren walks in.

"Hey you," Lauren greets Kendall with a chipper note to her voice, her slight southern drawl ringing through.

"Hey," Kendall replies. They do that weird air-kissing-on-both-cheeks thing.

Lauren's eyes meet mine, and I can literally see her breath hitch in her throat. *Okay, it feels* pretty damn good *to get that kind of reaction from someone.* "Payton, you are a vision," she says.

"Thank you. You're looking quite fine yourself."

"Are you ready to go? I'm kind of double-parked," she snickers. "Oops!"

I nod.

"Oh, here," Kendall places her mirror-lensed sunglasses in my hair and smiles.

"Thanks."

Lauren offers me her hand. I take it. "See you later, Kendall," she says as she leads me toward the door.

I notice Kendall staring at our clasped hands. "You kids have fun," she hollers as she closes the door behind us.

❊ ❊ ❊

We arrive at the shop on Rodeo Drive and are greeted by the designer herself. Lauren embraces her like they're old friends.

She presents me as, "Payton, my lovely date to the Time Zone Ball."

"I'm a huge fan of your designs, Ms. Westfeld," I offer my hand for a proper introduction.

She shuns the norm and sucks me into the Hollywood pastime of the cheek-to-cheek greeting. "Please, my friends call me Victoria." *All right, then. Ms. Westfeld it is.* Victoria does an indiscreet lap around me then gets straight down to business. "How tall are you?"

"Five nine and a half, though I don't usually count the half."

"Models should *always* count the half," she replies seriously.

That's great, but I'm not a model. Why do people keep likening me to one? "Okay, thank you." I leave out the "that's good to know" I was planning to say in an attempt to quell my instinctual sarcasm.

"And you're what, a size four?"

I bury my hands in my jeans pockets. "On a good day. Most of my clothes are a five in juniors."

"Hmm. You found yourself a diamond in the rough with this one," she mutters to Lauren, then disappears behind a heavy black curtain.

"What is she talking about?" I whisper.

Lauren sniggers. "She likes your body-type. I can't say I blame her."

"Oh." I'm instantly uncomfortable. I feel like a piece of meat on display in a butcher's storefront, and I really don't appreciate it.

Victoria emerges from behind the curtain with a stack of dresses in hand. They're all dark colors and buckles and zippers—

extremely extravagant and expensive, no doubt. "Let's start with these." She hands over three dresses from the pile and leads me into a dressing room.

A few moments later, I step out wearing the first selection. It's a halter top—black and dirty-gold, long and tight. Its sides can't quite be called sides, since they're nearly non-existent; my hips and obliques are exposed for all eyes to feast on. *I might as well be naked.*

No joke, Lauren is practically dribbling on herself. It's kind of flattering, yet somewhat off-putting at the same time. Victoria is nodding her head up and down like one of those bobble head figurines on display in the rear window of ancient Volvos. "Don't bother with the rest of them," she murmurs. "This dress was made for you."

Lauren leers at me for a while longer. Eventually, she motions her thumb at Victoria. "What she said."

"Okay. That was easy," I mumble as I head back into the dressing room. I return with the dress draped over my outstretched arms. Victoria takes it from me and zips it into a garment bag before I've gotten a chance to take a gander at the price tag. "Um, I'm sorry, what does it come to?" I fish through my wallet for my credit card. *My mom will be thrilled when she sees the bill.*

Victoria shoots an amazed look at Lauren. "You haven't been in LA long, have you?"

"I'm sorry?" *Was that meant to be some kind of insult? It sure sounded condescending.*

Lauren catches the annoyance in my voice. She tries to explicate the situation to me. "Most of the time when a designer dresses someone for an event, it's more like they're lending the attire rather than selling it."

"In this case, it's my gift to you," Victoria adds. "Think of it as a welcome present."

It doesn't seem right to accept a gift from someone I met half an hour ago. It's like I'll be indebted to her in some way. Lauren must sense my hesitation; she reassuringly places her hand on the small of my back. A groundswell of pure exhilaration runs through me from head to toe. "It's okay, Payton." Her voice is as softhearted as the expression on her face.

Victoria pushes the garment bag toward me. "Please, I insist."

I take the hanger graciously. "Thank you. It's beautiful."

As we say our goodbyes, Victoria slips her business card into my hand. "Should you decide you might be interested in a modeling career, I'd love to have you in one of my shows."

No. I have absolutely no interest in peddling my body for a living. "I don't think so, but thank you anyway," I reply as lightly as possible.

❊ ❊ ❊

I open the car door for Lauren. A look of astonishment warps her features.

A small, self-conscious giggle slips through my lips. "What?"

"Nothing. It's just, I can't remember the last time anyone opened a door for me—anyone who wasn't being paid to, that is."

"I try to mind my manners," I reply. I hang the dress on the hook in the back seat then slide into the front.

"You know, that dress is almost as beautiful as you are," she says.

My cheeks instantly catch fire. I feel them redden with heat and have to bite my bottom lip to keep from calling her crazy.

She seems to notices the blush. "You really don't know how pretty you are, do you?"

Before I can stop myself, I roll my eyes. "I'm really not, though."

"Wow, polite and modest. I didn't know they still made people like you."

"*You're* polite."

"But I'm not modest?" she asks playfully.

"I'm not sure yet," I tease back. Somewhere inside of me, a current of courage surges. I'm not ready for this outing to come to an end. If I'm going to do this whole dating thing, then I'm going to invest myself fully. "If you don't have other plans, I'd like to take you to lunch." I hold my breath in anticipation of her answer.

"I would love that," she replies with a pleased smile.

She chooses a restaurant in Santa Monica called Killian's Kitchen. It has a homey atmosphere, small and quiet. To be honest, I'm surprised at the lack of attention she's garnered throughout the day. I was expecting her to have a ton of screaming fans following close behind like Kendall always does, but Lauren is only stopped by a few people. I'm glad that her presence doesn't send every person she meets into frenzy; it gives us the chance to talk in earnest.

Over lunch, I tell her all about growing up in New Jersey and how my grandfather gave me piano lessons twice a week until the week he died. She tells me all about how her entire family packed up and moved to California from Kentucky when she was ten so that she could go to auditions without having to commute constantly.

"My parents were so cool about it," she says. "Both my mom and dad were professors at the University of Louisville at the time. My mom got a job at UCLA, my dad got one at USC and snap! Just like that, we moved. My older brother hated the idea at first. He'd recently started high school, making new friends and all that."

"But he got over it when he saw all the girls strutting around town half-naked, right?" I jest.

"Yeah, basically."

"It sounds like you're very close to your family."

"I am. When I got my own place, my mother insisted that it be in the same neighborhood. So, of course, I live across the street from my parents now."

I laugh. "I get that. I thought my mom was going to have a conniption when I told her I was moving out here."

"And did she?"

"Not exactly. She was mostly concerned that I was doing it for the right reasons. You know, for educational purposes." *As opposed to what, following Kendall around like a puppy?* "So, what's your next project and when are you starting it?"

"Actually, my brother and I are working on a screen play together right now, so I'm taking a few months off from acting until filming for *The Relishing* starts."

"You're an actress *and* a screen writer? That's one hell of a resume."

"It's solely a passion project at the moment, but fingers crossed we'll eventually be able to make a movie out of it."

She tells me that her screen play is about the life of a fictional 1940's-era jazz songstress, which leads us into a forty-five minute conversation about our mutual love of the genre. "If there's anything I know, it's jazz—thanks to my grandfather, of course. I think *Lady Sings the Blues* is one of my all-time favorite albums."

She gasps. "Oh my god, I *love* Billie Holiday!"

"I've tried a few times to do my own rendition of 'God Bless the Child,' but that song is too amazing to ever be covered."

"Let's make a deal right now. If I'm ever able to get this script a green light, you'll do the score."

"You haven't even heard me play, let alone anything I've composed."

"Payton, you got into MALA without having to audition in person. Kendall practically swears by your talent. *And* you were taught by an underground jazz legend. That's proof enough for me."

"I guess I can't refute the facts, can I?"

She shakes her head. "We have a deal, then?"

It could be precisely the thing I need to get my foot in the door, and even if it isn't, I'd have a lot of fun doing it. I throw my hands up. "Why not? I'm in."

She smiles. "Brilliant!"

Our waitress mistakes my gesture as a signal for the check. She places it in the middle of the table and saunters quickly away. Lauren and I burst into synchronized laughter.

"She's eager to get us out of here, huh?" I speak through my giggle.

She glances at her watch. "We *have* been here for two hours."

"Yeah, it's time for us to leave."

Both of us reach for the bill and our hands accidentally touch. Her lips slide into a shy grin, but she doesn't pull away. Neither do I. It's nice for a change, not freaking out over making physical contact with a girl.

"I've got it."

"No, I do," she protests.

"I asked you to lunch, so I've got it."

She wiggles her eyebrows. "I can't refute the facts, can I?"

That's my line, only cuter. "No, you can't."

❄ ❄ ❄

The sun is beginning to dip below the horizon as we pull up to the apartment building. She throws the car in park and walks me to the front entrance. I want to invite her inside, but feel like that would be moving too fast. I don't want her to get the wrong idea or anything.

"Thank you. I had a great time"

"I did, too." I shift the garment bag from my left arm to my right and motion it at her. "Thanks for this."

"No problem. So I'll be here with the limo around nine on New Year's Eve."

"Okay, great."

She takes a pace toward me, closing the gap between us. My initial gut reaction is to move away from her, but I somehow manage to hold my ground. *Is she going to kiss me? Should I let her? What is the proper first date etiquette?* Before my inner turmoil can get the best of me, I pull her into a hug and kiss her cheek.

She's all smiles when I let her go. "I'll see you soon."

"Yes, you will."

She waves goodbye as she walks back to the car. I feel kind of awesome as I watch her drive away.

Upstairs, Kendall is lounging on the sofa reading *The Relishing* and enjoying a glass of red wine. *She's drinking just to drink? That's new.*

"Hey," I interject.

She looks up from her page. "You're home late," she mutters then returns her attention to the book. "I suppose that means you had a good time."

I shamble over to the couch, lay the garment bag across the back, and take a seat beside her. "I did, yeah. We went to lunch after visiting the dress shop."

"That's nice." There's a subtle note of indifference to her voice like she doesn't actually give a damn whether or not I had an enjoyable day.

I want to say something about it, but don't. "What did you do today?"

"Mostly this," she gestures to the book. "It's good. I can see why they want to make a movie out of it."

"Is it? Cool. I'll have to read it when you're done with it."

"Sure." She shrugs. "Looks like you got your dress. Can I see it?"

"Okay." I start to unzip the bag.

"Wait." She reaches out a hand to stop me. "I meant I'd like to see it on you."

"Isn't that bad luck?"

"What are you talking about?" She laughs. "Sounds like you're thinking of a wedding dress. Even then, it's only bad luck for the groom to see."

"Oh, I think you're right."

"So, will you try it on for me?"

I could say no, but why? Lauren thought it looked great on me. Maybe Kendall will think the same. "I'll be right back."

I'm so excited to see her reaction that it only takes a few seconds for me to wriggle into the dress. I nearly rush right past the mirror in my bedroom, but pause at the last second to give my hair a good brushing. When I'm finished, I inspect my reflection closely. At first, I couldn't fathom that I had the muscle definition to make the dress work, but on second glance, it's not too shabby. *Here goes nothing*, I think as I present myself. "Tada!"

She stands and her book falls to the floor, crashing on to the rug with a resonating thud. Her pupils dilate and fix on me. I swear, her gaze is boring into me so hard that I can feel it in the pit of my stomach. It's like taking a blow to the back with a two-by-four—heavy and alarming in the most extreme way. "What do you think?"

"I think pictures of you in that dress are going to be *everywhere* in two days' time."

"Shut up," I chuckle.

"You only want me to shut up because you know I'm right." She whistles a cat call at me. "Fashion magazines, look out."

I snort. "Victoria Westfeld wanted to hire me for a runway show. Can you believe that?"

"Yes, I can believe that."

"I don't get it. I'm not nearly emaciated looking enough for that. *Hello*, I actually like to *eat*."

"Yeah, but you also like to run. It equals out."

"So what are you wearing to this thing?"

"A sleeveless, powder blue sequined gown. I'm picking it up from De Leche the day of the party."

"Cool. Want some company when you go pick it up?"

She scuffles in place. "Gunner Roderick is coming with me. He wants his tie and cummerbund to match."

"Oh, sorry. I didn't know it was a date."

"It isn't," she says quickly. "The Time Zone Ball isn't a date either. Lawrence set it up with Gunner's people. I hardly know him."

"Maybe you'll like him once you've had a chance to get to know him." *And knowing you had a boyfriend would be a huge help to me. It might finally sink in that I have no shot with you.*

"Possibly." She pats her tummy. "I'm feeling a little flabby all of a sudden. Think I'm gonna head down to the gym."

"Okay, loony tunes. You have fun with that." *Get nice and toned for Gunner.*

"Thanks," she says acerbically and bounces out the door.

CHAPTER TEN

Kendall

Five miles in forty minutes and I'm still going strong. I'm not in the least bit concerned with the fact that my heart is pounding so hard it's likely to explode, or that there's a plume of smoke leaking from the treadmill's motor. I'm going to exercise Payton out of me or die trying.

It hurt more than I thought it would, her coming home happy from a date with someone who wasn't me. I shouldn't be hurt. I should be excited for her and delighted that she's getting involved with someone who isn't a complete asshole. I'm the one who pushed her to give it a stab with Lauren in the first place. But I'm not excited *or* delighted at all. The only thing I feel is rotten.

I jolt off the treadmill and over to the free weights. Normally, I top out at about thirty pounds, but tonight I'm pushing myself to the max with the fifty-fives. I'm all but completely spent after a few reps with my right arm, so I quickly switch to the left one. If I keep forcing it, I know I'm going to injure myself, but I don't really care. My forearm is just beginning to burn when my elbow snaps. Right away, a searing pain shoots down my arm and straight through to my wrist. Without a doubt I pulled a muscle somewhere, but whatever. I drop the weight on the rack, hurry down the hall to the ice machine and scoop a bunch of cubes into a towel. I stumble into the elevator with my elbow firmly packed in ice and make my way upstairs. *Damn! I cannot be bruised and swollen on the Time Zone red carpet.* Lawrence and James will take turns scolding me if I'm vilely black and blue in front of the press.

Payton is busy texting someone when I trickle pathetically through the door. She's at my side in a nanosecond after seeing the state I'm in. "What the hell happened to you?"

"I broke myself," I kid.

She cradles my arm gently and removes the makeshift ice pack. The inner elbow area is already a deep shade of violet. She gasps at the sight of it.

"Don't look at it! It's gross!" I try to pull my arm away, but she doesn't let go.

"Kendall, stop it. This looks bad. We should go to the hospital."

"So we can sit in the waiting room for hours only to have some know-nothing doctor tell me he can't do anything for it? Yeah, I'll pass. Thanks."

She sighs. "At least let me put an ice pack on it and wrap it in an ACE bandage."

"I don't have either of those things," I say, sounding like an out-and-out idiot. She's staring at me with a look of utter disbelief on her face. "What? I've never needed them before. I'm not usually this much of a klutz."

"Yes, you *are*." She shakes her head disapprovingly as she grabs her keys off of the coffee table. "I'm going to CVS. Keep that ice on while I'm gone," she commands and is gone before I can protest.

Twenty minutes later, she bounds through the door like a hunting hound tracking a scent. She unloads the contents of a plastic shopping bag onto the breakfast bar: two self-cooling ice packs, an adhesive compression bandage, a bottle of ibuprofen, and a chocolate bar.

"A chocolate bar?"

"Believe me, you're gonna need it." She motions for me to sit on a stool. I watch as she deftly cracks an ice pack, wraps it in a paper towel and presses it to my skin. She binds the pack to my arm with a bandage. "Is that too tight?"

"No."

"Good." She opens the fridge, pours a glass of water, and places it in front of me, along with two ibuprofen pills. "You'll feel better in a little while."

I swallow the pills and grin. "Thanks. How did you know what to do?"

"Don't you remember how beat up I used to get during soccer games?"

I laugh. "Oh my god, you were fierce on the field! They gave you that slogan junior year, 'Payton Brings the Pain!' I remember seeing it on those signs people in the bleachers were holding up."

"Yeah, I brought the pain all right. I wrapped my ankles, knees, and shoulders at least a thousand times each," she says as she guides me to the couch.

Once I'm seated, she kneels to undo my shoelaces and remove my sneakers. She sits down beside me, grabs the remote, and proceeds to flip through the channels. We settle on a documentary about genetic mutations and human chimerism.

"How's your arm feeling?" she asks half way through the show.

"Not too bad," I mumble and nuzzle my head against her bicep.

She lifts her arm around my shoulders. I lean into her and shut my eyes. I drift off to sleep, content with the knowledge that she loves me even if it isn't quite in the way I want her to.

※ ※ ※

It's the morning of the Time Zone Ball. The front desk buzzes up around ten to let me know Gunner has arrived. I don't bother inviting him upstairs, which I guess is sort of ill-mannered. My elbow is still pulsating with soreness, and I don't feel like going out. I know this whole day is something I can't bail on, so I force myself to get dressed.

Before I leave, Payton re-wraps my arm and stuffs the bottle of ibuprofen into my purse. "It's looking pretty good, but you don't want to aggravate it. Don't lift anything with that arm. Take some pain killers in a few hours if it starts aching again."

"I'll be back long before I need to take more pills. We're picking up my dress, stopping at his tailor, and then I'm coming home." He won't be getting an impromptu lunch invitation from me.

"Okay," she says as I depart.

Gunner greets me at the front desk with a polite hello, but is swiftly distracted by my swathed arm. His bright green eyes inquisitively comb over the bandage. Maybe I should have worn a long-sleeved shirt? *Jesus H. Christ, I am a hot mess.*

"That looks unpleasant," he remarks.

Genius he is not. The pretty boys never are. "It's not that bad."

We make our way to his car. We're silent for most of the ride downtown, until we hit a patch of traffic. *Great, now we're gonna have to make small-talk.*

He gestures to my elbow. "What happened, anyway?"

"I strained a muscle lifting weights a few days ago."

I expect him to burst into a round of obnoxious laughter, or say something sexist about how girls shouldn't bother with free weights. Instead, he flashes a sympathetic grin. "I've done that a few times, tried to bench press way more than I could handle."

"It was stupid of me. I knew I was pushing myself too hard."

He smiles. "Don't beat yourself up. It happens to the best of us. You'll heal and be at it again in no time."

So, he's handsome *and* friendly? I'm sure he could've found a date for this shindig without having to be set up by his handlers. It might be prying, but I feel the need to ask him about it anyway. "I hope you don't mind me asking, but why did you agree to this set up? It's not like there's a shortage of women who would enjoy an evening with you, and we don't exactly know each other all that well."

"That's sort of the reason. I was blown away by your performance in *In Heaven's Arms,* and I thought maybe if we got to know each other better, you might want to work with me someday."

"That's sweet, but you didn't have to go through all the trouble. I've seen one or two of your movies. You're a *very* good actor."

"Aww shucks. Thanks."

We arrive at De Leche with relatively little fanfare, which is surprising since that rarely happens when two movie stars are seen in public together—especially when said movie stars are of the opposite sex.

I speak with the manager while Gunner wanders around the studio. He's astounded by the plethora of eveningwear surrounding us. The wonderment in his eyes is entertaining. "Why is women's fashion so complicated? When guys want to dress up, we have two choices: suit or tux."

I chuckle. "I don't know. Women are more fickle than men."

He snaps his fingers. "That explains a lot."

"Don't quote me. I'm only hypothesizing," I reply as a member of the staff presents my gown. "Gunner," I call.

He turns around and focuses in on the dress. "Our stylists coordinated it perfectly. I think my white tux will go great with that dress."

"No, *my* stylist is abysmal. She wanted me in this hideously puffy magenta thing. I picked this one out."

"Magenta? Isn't that a day-glow color?" he asks, his tone somewhere between amused and horrified.

"Kind of."

"Thanks for *not* going with her pick. I'm plenty manly enough to pull it off, but I don't think any guy should ever wear a pink cummerbund."

He's gorgeous as hell and actually funny, yet I'm not the least bit enticed by him. I'll pretend there's nothing weird about that at all.

"Do you think we'll find a cummerbund to match?" I ask once we're back on the road.

He shrugs. "I was hoping you might be able to help with that. According to my stylist, I'm the kind of guy who wears plaid with paisley. That's why I need a stylist. I wanted him to take care of all the details, but I was told that you insist on handling the details yourself."

"I like to play dress up as much as the next girl, but I don't like letting others dictate what I wear."

"Independent. I dig that in a woman." He slips his hand onto my thigh.

There it is—the classic come-on. Won't he be surprised when I don't get all swoony about it? "Yeah, that's a rare quality these days." I grab his wrist and lift his hand off of me.

"It is," he retorts flatly.

From that moment on, he acts like a spoiled brat—and I mean he sulks right up until the instant I get out of the car in front of my building. "The limo will be here at nine," he says simply before speeding off.

God, I am so sick and tired of guys playing sweet to get into my pants! Does that crap *ever* work? Maybe it does on stupid girls, but not on me. I cannot wait for this party to be over. On the elevator ride up to the apartment, I decide that my New Year's resolution is to fire Lawrence before he can hatch his next lame publicity stunt.

I'm not even fully through the door when I pick up the fragrant, somewhat spicy scent of pasta sauce. "Are you hungry?" Payton hollers from beyond the stove. "I'm making lasagna. Or, I'm trying to make it anyway."

"I'm famished. And it smells delicious to me."

She grins. "How'd it go with Gunner?"

"I had to explain the difference between polyester and satin. Then he picked out a royal blue bowtie and cummerbund set and proceeded to give me attitude when I told him it didn't match my gown. And, oh yeah! He groped my thigh."

She mumbles a few choice words under her breath and flings a spatula into the sink. "He touched you? Without your permission?" I see her fists clench as an ember of anger ignites into a full-scale wildfire. Through gritted teeth, she mumbles, "I can kill him for you, if you'd like. He's a mediocre actor at best, so I doubt anyone would miss him. Then you could go to this thing tonight with anyone you want. Hey, bonus!"

Has she always been so protective of me? Come to think of it, yes she has. "It's okay. If I had people killed every time they touched me without my permission, I'd be living on a pile of bones."

"That would most likely be bad for your image, huh?"

"Yeah, I'd probably only ever get cast as a criminal or dominatrix. Though both of those would be fun to play."

"I'm sure your fans would *love* to see you in pleather or a prison uniform."

"They'll have to settle for me in chainmail. That's what's next for me at least."

"That'll do, I'm sure. Now, get your butt over here so I can check your battle wound." I simper over to her and hold out my arm. She undoes the bandage and presses lightly on the flesh around my black-and-blue. "Does that hurt?"

I grimace. "Only a little."

"The swelling's gone down, but the bruise is gonna stick around for a while."

"The makeup team will handle it. They'll be here early enough to figure something out."

"That's good." She turns her attention back to the stove, removes a pan from the oven, and examines its contents warily. She shrugs. "I suppose if it looks like lasagna and smells like lasagna, it must be lasagna."

She's so adorable, I have to laugh. "Aww, honey, you learned how to cook!"

"Wish my mom could be here to see it. She won't believe it when I tell her."

"Don't worry. I'll vouch for your newfound culinary prowess."

❊ ❊ ❊

Lawrence arrives at seven sharp with the makeup and hair team in tow. As soon as he walks in, he's droning on and on about "the giant bruise that will be very noticeable in a sleeveless gown." I tell him to relax, because I gave the crew a heads up. They've come prepared with an abundance of smudge-proof cover-up.

I'm already dressed and seated before a lighted mirror, enjoying a crisp, cold beer and waiting for Frank to finish prepping his curling iron, when I catch a glimpse of Payton's reflection. She is stunning in her gown. I'm talking every-last-bit-of-oxygen-sucked-out-of-the-room kind of stunning. Everyone pauses to stare at her. Her mouth slips into this frightened grin like she wasn't expecting five sets of eyes to settle on her so suddenly.

"Wow, Payton," Lawrence says as he jumps off the couch to his feet. He's met her a few times before—when he accompanied me on publicity trips to New York, and Payton reluctantly agreed to meet us in the city for lunch—but has never seen her fancied up. "You are going to steal the show tonight, my dear."

She blushes. "Thank you."

"Felicia," Lawrence calls, "why don't you do Payton's makeup while Frank and Brit do Kendall's hair?"

"Oh no, that's okay," Payton stammers.

"Let her do it," I direct. "And when she's finished, Frank will straighten your hair. You'll be flawless."

She sighs and sits down in the chair next to me. "Okay."

❀ ❀ ❀

"Flawless" doesn't cut it. If I knew of a better word to describe Payton in this moment, I'd use it. But flawless is the best I can do. Her hair is pin straight and shiny, like coffee-colored taffeta. She has shimmering gold eye shadow on her lids, which makes her amber irises stand out like I've never seen before. I'm afraid I might actually be salivating, so I force myself to look away.

"Okay, ladies, you are good to go," Felicia states as she closes up her cosmetic kit. I air-kiss her cheeks and thank the team as I escort them out.

"The limo should be here for us in a few minutes, Kendall," Lawrence notes. He hands me my purse and marshals me in the direction of the door.

"You look spiffy in your tux, Lawrence," I turn to him, straighten his euro tie. "I'm surprised a man with your outstanding fashion sense could possibly think that a complete oaf like Gunner Roderick would be a suitable date for me."

"Another guy you don't like?" he moans. "I'll add him to the list."

"Next time, try to find me an escort who won't get handsy with me, okay? I don't think that's asking too much."

"I'll do that." He nods. "Payton, hun, will you come down to the lobby with us? I'm sure Lauren will be here on time. She's very *punctual.*" He leers at me. *Yeah, yeah, I get the hint. It's yet another awesome quality Lauren has that I lack.*

"Yes, thank you," Payton says.

She and I are shoulder to shoulder during the elevator ride, even though there is no solid reason for us to be standing so close together. I can see she's sweating despite the fact that she's trying so hard to remain calm. "Don't be nervous," I tell her. "Pretend you're at one of those jock parties you always dragged me to in high school."

"I never wore a $5,000 dress to any of those jock parties. And no one tried to take my picture either."

"No one tried to take your picture because they knew you'd break their legs."

She snorts. "True."

The elevator opens to the lobby. We step off in stride, Lawrence following close behind. Almost immediately, a white limo pulls up the drive. Gunner and his publicist, Stacy, step out. Lawrence greets them with smiles and handshakes. I smile at Stacy and shake her hand. Gunner, however, can go straight to hell and roast for all eternity.

He offers me his arm. I loop mine through his and lean in very close to his ear. "I can pretend to like you tonight and continue to do so for however long we're forced to be seen out and about together, but do you see that gorgeous girl over there?" I signal toward Payton. "Her family is *very* Italian and *very* New Jersey. If you touch me inappropriately again, she might arrange your disappearance. And I won't stop her. Nod if you comprehend what I'm saying."

He shakes his head stiffly. I almost laugh. Instead, I call Payton over and introduce her. For a tick, I think Gunner might piss his pants. It's not always a good thing that people automatically equate the word "Italian" with "mob hit," but in this case, it's comical.

A moment later, a second limo pulls up. Lauren's posse hops out and she trails behind them. Right away, my attention is on her. She's in a white spaghetti strap gown adorned with black crystal accents down the back. *Well that's friggin' perfect. She looks to die for!*

She enters the lobby, ropes Payton into a hug, and kisses her cheek—not a faux-kiss, an actual lips-meet-skin kiss. A violent upsurge of nausea abruptly locks my stomach in a vice. I'm not sure whether I'm going to throw up or faint, but I'm positive something terrible is going to happen. To my surprise, Gunner steadies me by slipping his arm around my waist.

"I know you told me not to touch you, but you're looking kind of green," he whispers.

I hold onto him tightly until I'm able to regain my composure. "Thanks."

"You're welcome."

I suck it up, stutter out an overly pleasant 'hello' to Lauren.

"Your dress is amazing!" she returns.

"Yours too, sweetheart!" I turn to Gunner. "Please, get me out of here," I mumble.

He answers with a wide, genuine-looking smile that causes me to second guess my distaste for him. "Okay, people," he calls loudly. "We should get rolling. Don't want to miss the press!"

Everyone titters in agreement. We herd to our limos like cattle, and I can't help thinking that we're all a bunch of desperate fame whores. I get one last look at Payton before she vaporizes behind darkened glass windows. She's beaming. *Great.*

❄ ❄ ❄

We arrive at the Beverly Regency to a choir of screaming fans. They're penned up behind steel barricades, holding out pictures and posters. Some of my fans are clasping hardcover copies of *The Relishing*. It's noisier and crazier than usual, and word only *recently* got out that I've been cast in this film. There's a very good chance I could be trampled if I get too close. Still, I can't stand how these people are kept in cages—how the bloodsuckers in charge of these events separate the haves from the have-nots with impenetrable dividers and beefy security guards.

As we make our way closer to the fan zone, Lawrence hands me two silver sharpies. Even though I'm a righty by nature, I've recently mastered the art of hurriedly signing my name with both hands simultaneously. I like to fit in as many autographs as possible, because I really don't want anyone to be nearly crushed to death while vying for my attention.

Lawrence is ahead of me, making sure I don't pause for too long. People with cameras keep asking if I can take photos with them. Lawrence responds, "She's not stopping for pictures, only autographs" to every one of them. I keep moving along per his instruction, until I come across a man with a little blonde girl on his shoulders. They are wearing matching *The Relishing* t-shirts.

I'm about to sign his book when I notice that the girl has tiny braces on her thin, little legs. She's so quiet and well behaved, it damn near breaks my heart.

"Is that you daughter?" I ask the man. "What's her name?"

"Yes. Her name is Jessie." He reaches up, tickles her sides. She chuckles ever so sweetly.

"Should I make this out to her?"

"Yes, please. It's Jessie with an I-E. She loves this book so much. She wants to be just like Ciara when she grows up."

"Do you have a camera with you?"

He nods and pulls a cell phone from his pocket. I kick off my heels and literally start scaling the barrier. The exertion sends ripples of pain down my injured arm, but I ignore the sting and keep climbing. As I ascend, the crowd roars to a deafening decibel. It's as though these people think I'm a bona fide superhero. They friggin' *love* me. It's fabulous!

Lawrence grabs my shoulder. Through clenched teeth, he asks, "What *the hell* are you doing?"

"Being a superhero," I whisper and motion for the man to give his phone to Lawrence. "Take a picture of the three of us, Lawrence," I bark. He's so surprised by the demand that he snaps two pictures without complaint.

I jump down from the barricade, slip my shoes back on and take the phone from Lawrence. I check to make sure the photos aren't blurry before returning the phone. "Here you go."

The man is so stoked, he's tearing up. "Thank you so much."

"You're welcome." I wave to the girl. "It was so great to meet you, Jessie!"

Lawrence tries to hurry me away from the fans and over to the press section, but I stop him. "Get that man's name and address. I want four VIP passes to *The Relishing's* LA premier sent to him."

I expect him to object, but he simply says, "Okay, I'll handle it. Go over to the press box."

From out of nowhere, Gunner reappears at my side. "Are you feeling better now?"

Truthfully, all those people shouting my name and showing me so much adoration made me blank over that I haven't seen a shadow of Payton since arriving. "A little bit, yes. Thanks for asking."

"No big deal," he murmurs. "Now, let's look happy for the cameras."

We smile and pose for pictures—first together, then separately. I'm showing off the back of my gown when I hear the crowd behind me boom. I glance toward the penned-up area. Lauren is there signing autographs. Payton is standing beside her, looking completely overwhelmed and unnerved. She only gets worse as Lauren guides her down the red carpet. While Lauren jokes with the photographers and adopts perfect poses like a seasoned pro, Payton is stiff and tongue-tied.

Well, that was the briefest respite in history. So much for feeling better!

The cameras keep flashing. Reporters are hollering, wanting to know all about Lauren's mysterious companion. Lauren tells the world her name, says she's a musician, and then points to me. "She's also best friends with the lovely Miss Kendall Bettencourt," she says. Like a shot, everyone in the press box is yelling for Payton to strike a pose and comment on her gown. She's a statue; she doesn't move an inch.

Gunner hitches his head toward Payton. "I think she needs some help."

I consider being spiteful and letting Lauren deal with it, but my heart won't let me leave Payton in the hands of someone who doesn't know her well enough to understand how to disengage her from panic mode. I sneak over to her and take her hand into my own. "Twirl for me," I say at the top of my voice. She smiles and snaps into action, whirling in a series of slow turns. Cameras capture picture after picture as the photographers ooh and aww.

"And who are you wearing tonight?" I ask, lightly prodding her with my elbow as a hint to target the reporters with her answer.

She steps closer to the outthrusted microphones. "I'm wearing Victoria Westfeld. Isn't it beautiful? I feel like a princess."

Lauren leans in close and puts her hand on Payton's back. "And you *look* like a princess," she says in earshot of the reporters. *Sure, Lauren, throw out a lifejacket after your date has already been saved from drowning.*

I'm starting to feel sick again, and it couldn't come at a worse time. Lawrence and Stacy indicate that we should move into the ballroom, but I'm not ready to let Payton out of my sight. I don't trust that Lauren can handle her with appropriate kid gloves. They've both got a few minutes left with the press. If I lose them now, there's no way I'll be able to find them once they've gotten inside. I'm sure to be preoccupied with mandatory mingling and requisite dancing.

"Come on," Gunner says. "I think she'll be okay, now."

"Okay," I sigh and turn to Payton. "Try to have fun. I'll track you down later."

She nods. "All right. See you later."

As I move to follow Gunner into the banquet hall, I realize that Payton now seems much more relaxed. She's talking animatedly with a few reporters. Her hand is knotted with Lauren's. *It figures.* I *talk Payton out of her fit of anxiety, and* Lauren *reaps the benefits.* Don't think about it, I tell myself. Go inside, converse and dance.

"I hope you like to dance," I say to Gunner once we've made our way into the ballroom. "I'm going to keep you on your feet most of the night."

"I like to dance." He pauses. "I'm sorry about being an ass this morning. I'm bad at flirting and worse at being rejected. Can we start over? It would be cool if we could be friends."

He seems so sincere. Plus, he's been such a good sport about my mini-meltdowns this evening. He hasn't once asked me to explain myself, or looked at me like I'm a total headcase. Yes, I think we can be friends.

"Forget about this morning. Let's have a good time tonight."

"Cool. How about we make the rounds and then we can cut a rug."

"Cut a rug?" I chuckle. "Despite your use of archaic phrasing, you're on. Let's get some drinks first though."

CHAPTER ELEVEN

Payton

This whole evening is way too much for me. As if talking to reporters and having photographers take a boat-load of pictures of me wasn't enough, Lauren introduces me to practically every celebrity in the room. I meet actors, musicians, designers, everyone save for the freaking President of the United States. All anyone says to me is "your dress is gorgeous" and "you ought to get into the fashion industry." They don't seem to care about anything unless it's pleasing to the eye. I've overheard conversation upon conversation about clothing and sports cars and jewelry, but not a single mention of the sorry state of the planet, the struggling economy, global politics, the friggin' destruction of the rainforest—nothing that actually matters. It makes me wonder whether these people are truly shallow, or if they're simply ignorant to the world's problems thanks to the well-to-do bubble they live in.

For Lauren's sake, I maintain my composure while wading through the ever-flowing stream of mindless dialogue. She must gather that I'm having difficulty containing my contempt for these people, because she continually apologizes for their vapidity. "I'm so embarrassed," she says. "I swear, I think everyone is afraid to be themselves at these events. Most of my friends are really cool human beings when they're not all huddled together in a group."

"I'm sure it's difficult having to keep up appearances and all that," I agree, trying not to let my skepticism rear its ugly head. I want to ask her how she can possibly stand it. She's such a *normal* person. She's so *real*. At least, that's how she seems.

"I'm going to grab another glass of champagne. Would you like one?"

"Why not?" I know I should probably slow down. I've already had more than my fill of alcohol tonight. I hope I don't get so hammered as to discover tomorrow morning via the *LA Times* that I've done something stupid like streaking down Sunset Boulevard.

"Okay. When I get back we'll dance?"

"Sure," I nod and watch her retreat toward the bar.

In her absence, I am roped into a discussion about nothing of consequence with some annoying, self-obsessed pop singer. I notice that he is wearing a watch and interrupt his ridiculously implausible story to ask the time. It's 11:20. I haven't seen Kendall since the party began. She said she'd find me, but obviously hasn't made much of an effort to do that so far. Maybe she's off having an excellent time with Mr. Blonde-haired, Green-eyed, Perfectly Buff Hollywood Hottie, dancing the night away, or laughing with him in a quiet corner somewhere.

"Payton, your champagne." Lauren returns and hands me a glass. I drink it quickly and place the empty flute on a nearby table. "Wow," she says, sounding impressed. "Okay, ready to dance?" She smiles a sweet, heartfelt smile. I all but completely blank over the irritation I'm feeling.

I strain to hear the music over the dull rumble of chatting. It's up-tempo and thick with synths. "Yeah, I can bust some moves to this song."

"Great!" She grabs my hand, leads me through the sea of show biz aristocrats and onto the hardwood dance floor.

She sways gracefully in perfect time with the beat, changing her rhythm slightly to suit every passing track. Her smooth, hypnotic movements draw me in. She pulls me closer, slithers down my body and back up again. I can feel the warmness radiating from her skin, the wet-hot balminess of sweat bleeding through her pores. "You're good at this," she whispers. Her breath tickles my ear.

"So are you."

She wraps her arms around my neck. As if on cue, the music slows. The sudden variation throws me off, and I nearly trip over my own feet. "Want to take a break?" she asks, concern in her eyes.

"No. It's just been a long time since I've slow-danced with anyone. I'm not sure I'm fit to lead." I admit, feeling totally inept.

"Sure you are. Let the rhythm guide you."

I suck in a lungful of air, place my hands on her hips, then close my eyes and tune in to the song. The musician in me takes command. My brain sends signals to my feet, telling them to move in stride with the bass drum. Lauren follows step for step. I open my eyes to find her smiling widely. "There you go. It's kind of like riding a bike."

"Dancing with you is much better than riding a bike." I hadn't intended to make her blush, but her cheeks go rosy. She looks away and grins. Once she recovers from reddening, she rests her head against my shoulder.

It's an interesting feeling, being pressed against someone without having to worry if I'm reading the situation wrong. It's completely uncomplicated. She likes me. I like her. We're dancing and touching and having a nice time. There is nothing more to do than bask in the simplicity of the moment.

The song seems to go on for hours. When it ends, Lauren pecks me on my cheek. "Thank you. You've been a lovely date this evening."

Before I can reply, the DJ cuts the music. He lets the crowd know that midnight is upon us. The huge projection screen behind him flickers to life. A pre-recorded video of the Times Square ball drop rolls, and he begins the countdown to the New Year at thirty.

Lauren takes my hand, looks at me and shouts "twenty-nine" along with the rest of the crowd. By twenty-eight, I am giddily counting, too. "Twenty-seven! Twenty-six!"

She holds her dark, enigmatic eyes steady on mine. I'm fairly certain the secrets of the universe are hidden behind the eyes of pretty girls. I'm also fairly certain I'd like to unravel the secrets behind *her* eyes. "Twelve! Eleven!"

As the time dwindles, I remember what's supposed to happen at the stroke of midnight. Kissing. Kissing Lauren Atwell? Yeah, I can most definitely do that. "Three! Two!"

"One!" I turn to her and frame her face with my hands. "Happy New Year," I say, then press my lips to hers. She slips her hands into my hair, deepening the kiss intensely. All around us, people are yelling New Year's greetings. Wispy pieces of paper confetti fall from mid-air and brush against our skin. Somewhere, someone starts singing "Auld Lang Syne." Absolutely none of it fazes me. In this instant, we are unreachable. We're kissing each other as though our lives depend on it. I'd forgotten what it's like to kiss someone and mean it. It's wonderful.

I break contact with her only once the need to breathe becomes too great to ignore. She inhales deeply and exhales. "Damn."

I laugh. "I know."

"Well, now that we've made it past midnight, would you like to get out of here?"

I've wanted to do exactly that since we first stepped foot inside the place, but I don't know if she means get out of here as in *get out of here*, or plainly *to leave*. I should make it very clear I'm not *that kind* of girl. It'll take a few more dates to get me to give it up.

It's as though Lauren can hear my thoughts. She quickly says, "Wait! That sounded suggestive, didn't it? No, no, I didn't mean to imply that we like, you know. I'm just over the excitement. I thought we could maybe go someplace a tad less–"

"Jam-packed with famous folk?"

"With any kind of folk."

"Can you do that? Take off whenever you want?" Are her obligations fulfilled for the night? She can just go home like it was detention or something? "Where could we go on New Year's Eve that won't be packed?"

"There is this one spot I like. It's on the east side of Palos Verdes. You can see the entire city from up there. It gives the illusion that LA is actually kind of beautiful." She shrugs. "We could take the limo. I'll let the crew know we're leaving. They can take a cab home, they've done it before."

"Okay, but I should find Kendall before we take off."

She points to the far end of the dance floor. "I think she's over there. I see Gunner, so she can't be too far from him."

I turn and spot him right away. Kendall steps around him into my view. "I'll be right back. Will you wait for me here? I don't want to lose you in this giant horde of bodies."

She grins. "I'll be right here."

I'm gradually making my way through the throngs when Gunner spots me. He waves delicately and taps Kendall on the shoulder. She's caught up in conversation with a small group of fellow megastars. I envision her annoyance at being interrupted as she barks at Gunner. He hints for her to turn around.

As soon as she notices me, it's like nobody else exists. She doesn't turn back to excuse herself from the discussion before taking off in my direction. There's a remarkably dogged look on her face, an extreme determination to reach me. I basically had to fight my way through the crowd, but for her, it parts like the Red Sea. We meet dead-center of the dance floor.

"I'm sorry I didn't find you earlier," she mutters. "Every time I tried to get away, someone else stopped to talk to me."

"It's okay. I figured that would happen."

"Are you having fun?"

"Yes, surprisingly, but Lauren wants to leave. We're going to Questa Verdi or somewhere to see the view."

"Palos Verdes," she says with a chuckle. "Yeah, I've heard the view is nice there."

"I just wanted to let you know we were heading out."

She nods. "Okay. Enjoy the rest of your night."

"I will. See you at home," I say, then turn to walk away.

"Hold up!" She tugs me back to her side. There's a guise of restrained trepidation on her face like she has something earth-shattering to say but can't find the words. Maybe I'm imagining that something is wrong, or maybe I'm projecting. Either way, the moment is charged to be sure.

"You want to talk?" I ask, trying to gently nudge her into speaking.

She glances around the room, studies the mass of people surrounding us. "No. I just forgot to say Happy New Year." She pushes herself up onto her tiptoes, kisses my cheek, and quickly shoves me away before I even have time to get excited about it. "Now go on." She points at someone behind me. I follow her finger with my gaze and find that Lauren has quietly snuck up beside me. Kendall shoos me away and vanishes from sight.

Lauren smiles. "Hey there, ready to go?"

I sure the hell am. "Absolutely."

❀ ❀ ❀

Even through the faint light of streetlamps, Palos Verdes looks like something ripped from the blueprints of a fairy tale. The colossal houses stretch from the sides of gargantuan hills. Some homes face the ocean, some face the city skyline, and others are designed to have a split view of both.

The limo parks atop a bluff overlooking the Pacific. I exit the car, and Lauren meets me on my side. She takes my hand and leads me to a quiet perch on the cliff. We sit down, hanging our feet over the outcropping. I allow myself to become enveloped in the sights, scents, and sounds surrounding us. In the distance, the lights of Los Angeles twinkle like stars in the pitch black night sky. It's all very romantic. I can imagine this place at sundown, the sky resembling a watercolor made from paints with unusual names like *Strawberry Fields*, *Cyan Potion*, and *Marigold Sunshine*.

A while passes before I let myself interrupt the silence. "You were right. It's gorgeous here."

She lifts her head from its resting place on my shoulder and looks me square in the eye. "*You're* gorgeous."

My stomach flurries. Regardless of what I feel for Kendall, I really *do* like Lauren. Besides the fact that she is beautiful, she's honest in the most endearing way. She simply is who she is—no pretense, no apologies. Confidence. That's the most admirable thing about her.

Suddenly it's like the whole of me completely concaves; I realize how sick and tired I am of being a pathetic, love-sick idiot pining over my straight best friend. It's self-inflicted torture, and it's absolutely insane! I'm here in this beautiful place with a knock-out girl who is actually into me. Why shouldn't I revel in her? Life is too short! Who the hell am I saving myself for? *No one who wants you, that's for shit sure! You've got the champagne equivalent of beer muscles in your favor, so go ahead and let yourself be that kind of girl. 'Those kinds of girls' have more fun.*

I move in for the kill, not faltering in the slightest. Our lips meet once and separate slightly, then touch again. "Let's go back to my place," I whisper merely inches from her mouth. I should be nervous, considering my complete lack of experience when it comes to sex. But I'm not. There's something about her that puts me at ease; perhaps it's her sweet southern charm that convinces me of her graciousness. I know that even if I should fumble around like a clueless virgin—which I probably will—she'll be patient and kind about it. *No, I am not sacred. I'm cool as can be.*

"Or we could go to mine," she whispers back. "I don't have a roommate."

"Yeah, but my place is closer." *And I want to get this over with before I start to lose my nerve.* I kiss her again.

She laughs into my lips. "Fair enough."

CHAPTER TWELVE

Kendall

I wake up New Year's Day from an alcohol-induced coma, barely able to focus my bloodshot eyes on anything beyond the end of my mattress. I got so blitzed last night that I don't even remember crawling into bed. Drinking my face off seems to have become my new favorite pastime. And why wouldn't it? It helps me forget to care—not just about Payton, but everything else too. When I'm hosed I have no qualms whatsoever about my life. All God's creatures have their eyes on me? Well, that's cool! My mother wants to stunt every attempt I make at fully reaching adulthood by treating me like a perpetual child? I've got no problem with that whatsoever! Still, I know getting stewed on the regular isn't a good habit to have; I should stop before it becomes a problem.

Through the haze in my head, I hear that the TV is on in the living room. *Payton's up.* Even though I'd rather hide under the covers and pretend the entire universe doesn't exist, I force myself to my feet, throw on a pair of sweats, and shuffle out to say good morning.

I misplace my words when I find that Payton is not alone. Lauren is stretched out on the couch, her head in Payton's lap.

The two of them are watching the *Twilight Zone*, giggling like little girls. *That bitch is wearing Payton's Deadmau5 t-shirt!* Of all the tees Payton owns, that one is *my* favorite! I've worn it so many times before, but never because I needed clean clothes to put on after a long night of screwing Payton's brains out. *It should be me lounging there, wearing that shirt!*

All right, I've officially lost my damn mind. There it goes, right out the front door. I decide to follow it, and try to bolt out of the apartment before either of them notice that I'm standing here. Lauren must hear me grab my keys from the counter, because she sits up and looks over the back of the couch. "Hey, girl."

Rather than say what I want to say, which would be, "Oh hey, whore! Get the hell out of my house," I mumble the *second* thing that comes to mind—something about having a day jam-packed with appointments, and then rush out the door like I swallowed a mouthful of speed.

I haul my dumb, dazed ass down to the garage, hop into my car and proceed to drive around to stew in my jealousy. It's stupid really, that I'm brooding on like this when I could have anyone I want! I'm Kendall goddamn Bettencourt, the best thing to happen to this town since Grace Kelly! Or, so it's been said. I don't actually believe that, but whatever. Perhaps it's time to start acting like I believe it.

I'm half-way to the Hollywood sign when my phone chimes, adding to my already elevated stress level. As soon as I say hello, Gunner is hyperventilating in my ear. "Kendall? Is this a bad time?"

I sigh. "It's as good a time as any. What's up?"

"The dry cleaner shredded the damn black and red pinstripe suit jacket that goes with the pants I'm wearing to the New Year, New Hope thingy tomorrow, and I can't get a hold of my stylist! Man, he is going to bust my balls! He borrowed it from Van Ludwig! Anyway, I need to go shopping, and you know how much I suck at shopping."

"Whoa, okay. Take a breath. Where are you?"

"I'm at home scratching my ass."

"Do you have a plain black suit or tux? Either of those would be fine," I say through my laughter.

"No. I don't actually own any of the stuff my stylist makes me wear. I get it all on loan. I've got a closet full of holey jeans, Affliction t-shirts, and Diesel sneakers."

"All right. It's too late to get something custom fit, but I'm sure we can find you a suit off the rack. Meet me at Bourdain's on Rodeo in twenty?"

"I'll be there in fifteen," he says and disconnects.

It turns out Gunner is a pretty good guy, after all. We had a nice, long chat last night at the Time Zone Ball about all the wonderful expectations we, as celebrities, have to live up to. He has to be a ladies' man as much as I have to been seen in public with one, all so no one will suspect that he's actually a sensitive guy or that I'm into girls—or into *a* girl. Not that I told him about that.

I stroll up to the shop to find him standing on the sidewalk, looking kind of under the weather.

"Thanks. You're saving my ass."

"The same ass you'd still be at home scratching right now?"

"Yes," he says and pulls the door open for me.

"Are you okay? You seem like you're not feeling well."

He shrugs. "I'm getting a cold, but what can I do? I'd rather stay home and sleep than go to this banquet."

"If it weren't a charity thing, I'd say you could skip it."

"Yeah, skipping a charity event is an asshole thing to do," he concurs. He turns to the clerk. "I need a black double-breasted jacket, size thirty-eight R and pants to match, size thirty-two."

"Look at you, all knowing your size and stuff. See, you didn't need me at all," I joke, expecting him to laugh. He doesn't.

"Do you ever think about bailing on life? The Hollywood life, that is. I do. Sometimes I think about going to college, or moving back to Wyoming to raise horses. It's like that saying, 'nothing gold can stay.' I'm not sure I'd mind much to find out if that were true."

"I'm still kind of getting used to it, but yeah, I've thought about it. Then I remember that life sucks no matter where you are or what you're doing."

The clerk returns, suit in hand. Gunner takes it from him and slips into the fitting room. I wait quietly for him to finish. A few moments later, he emerges with the suit on its hanger and a goofy grin on his face.

"I guess that's the one," I say.

"Deep down inside you always know when it's the one, even if it's hard to tell at first. Or hard to accept."

"We aren't talking about suits anymore are we, Master Yoda?"

"We both know what—or *who*— we're talking about," he replies as he pays at the register. He heads for the door without saying another word.

"Do we both?" I holler at his back. After a few stunned seconds of silence, I catch up to him outside.

"When Lauren showed up at your place last night? Yeah. It was kind of obvious you wanted to punch her in the face. I figured out why pretty quick. *Ehem.* Payton."

I click open the car doors, reach for the handle. "Gunner, you don't know the first thing about it."

"I've got four sisters. I'm in-tune, all right? I know when a girl has it bad for someone, and you've got it bad for Payton. Personally, I think you should go for it." He leans over the roof of the car and lowers his voice. "It's the twenty-first century. I doubt anyone would care that you're gay."

Dude, a little discretion would be appreciated. "I am not talking about this with you on the sidewalk. Get in the car."

"All right," he says and scoots into the passenger seat and closes the door. I do the same on the driver's side.

"Firstly, don't give me the 'it's the twenty-first century and everyone in America has reached enlightenment,' bullshit. Watch the damn news; hate crimes still happen. Secondly, I didn't say I was gay."

"Semantics," he grumbles.

"I wasn't finished!" I whirl around to him. "Thirdly, it's not really any of your concern is it? This thing between us is a business arrangement. It's not like we're actually dating."

"Because you don't want to date *me*, you want to date Payton."

You can have anyone you want, eh, Kendall? Prove it; want him. *Everything will be infinitely easier that way.* "Would you please shut up?" I grab him by the collar of his shirt, tug him toward me, and plant the hardest, most desperate kiss on him. He's stunned at the outset, but then I feel him pucker into it. He leans across the center console. I think that he's going to put his arm around me. Instead, he puts his hands on my shoulders and softly pushes me away.

Seriously? "Are you off your meds? I just made a pass at you!"

"Look, you're totally hot and you can be cool, but I know you aren't into me."

I wave him off. "Like that matters! You're a guy."

"Yeah, but I'm not a Neanderthal. If I'm going to hook up with a girl, I want to know that she at least *likes* me. And you don't." He pops open the door and steps out into the harsh light of day. "Go home and figure yourself out, Kendall. Trust me, you'll be happier for it."

❋ ❋ ❋

There's nothing quite like being rejected to make you feel like shit. Worse than that, he was right to do it. I've been walking on eggshells for so long, protecting myself from what? Acknowledging that my biological imperative may not include the drive to procreate, that I just might be attracted to XX chromosomes instead of XY? That's so stupid—minor in comparison to the fact that I might actually be in love for the first time in my life. It's with a girl… so *what*? Lesbian, bisexual, whatever! This isn't about categorization *or* chromosomes. This is about how I feel about another person.

I am fully worn out by the time I stagger into the apartment. The first thing I notice when I walk through the door is that every light in the house is on. I hear music streaming softly from the studio monitors upstairs. A sense of dread takes hold of me. Payton is home and entirely awake. I'm certain I would be more at ease if I had walked in on the damn place being burglarized.

Why isn't she out with Lauren painting the town red? I decide I had better alert her to my presence before she realizes that she's not alone and calls the cops or something. "Hey, I'm home," I yell up to her.

She turns the music down and sticks her head over the railing. "Hi."

"I'm surprised you're here. I thought you'd be out with Lauren."

"Not tonight. I've been trying to call you all day. I wanted to talk."

"About what?" I place my clutch on the coffee table and take a solid, steadying breath. I jump nearly a foot in the air when I unexpectedly find her standing right in front of me.

"About how you ran out of the house this morning. What was up with that?"

"How I ran out…" I scoff. "Since you're so concerned, I'll tell you exactly what was up with that!" I realize how unfair it is to be yelling at her, yet I'm powerless to stop myself from doing it. I'm so wound up that every last sensible part of me has shut down. There's not an ounce of stability left in me. "I'm pissed, Payton! Pissed at myself because I'm a stupid, gutless coward! I couldn't just tell you how I was feeling. I couldn't tell you that I think I want to be more than just your friend, and that it scares the shit out of me! It doesn't matter now. It's too late! You're sleeping with Lauren, and–"

"Are you fucking kidding me?" she yells over me. "I tried to sleep with Lauren! Oh my god, did I try! I was *this* close, and then I started crying! Do you have any idea how embarrassing it was for me, curled up in a half-naked ball at the edge of my bed telling a girl I really *liked* all about how I couldn't be with *her* because my heart belongs to you? It does, you know! My heart has belonged to you for as long as I can remember! Jesus Christ, Kendall! I've been killing myself since I was twelve, trying not to notice it was there, trying to make it go away!"

She's been feeling this for years? Years! I am such an idiot! "I'm glad it never went away," I mumble. Here she is, chilling in the middle of the living room, staring at me with her big honey-colored eyes. *She is so lovely. I can't...*

I rush at her, slamming her back against the kitchen wall. I run my fingers through her velvety tresses and kiss her *hard.* She kisses me back—tentatively at first, but soon I feel her tongue dance across my lips, begging for entrance to my mouth. Immediately, I realize how different it is, kissing a woman as opposed to kissing a man. It's inquisitive rather than demanding, pleasurable rather than acceptable, more delicate, yet so much more tantalizing.

My lips are wild, ravenous from waiting longer than they should have to be introduced to hers. Now that our mouths have become acquainted with one another, I never want them to be apart. I want to kiss her a hundred times a day, every day, for the rest of my life.

I kick off my shoes and suddenly, I'm climbing her—wrapping my arms around her neck, my legs around her waist. She puts her hands on my butt and props me up higher. Kissing her is simply not enough. I need more. I need *everything.* "Please, Payton," I whisper into her mouth. "I want to be with you."

She jerks her head back and gazes at me curiously. There is so much reverence sparkling in her eyes, but they are flecked with traces of apprehension, too. "I... We should probably..."

We *should* probably slow down, but I'm afraid if we do I might chicken out completely. "Don't second guess me. I want this."

As soon as I say it, her lips stretch into a smile. She pushes off the wall with her foot and carries me to the couch. In one fluid motion she gently lays me down and rests herself on top of me.

Her kisses move from my lips down to my neck, and I shudder unrestrainedly. A ripple of ecstasy runs though me as she pulls my shirt down my shoulders and licks my collarbone. I am so turned on. I claw like a rabid beast at the buttons of her shirt. My greedy hands hunger to caress *every single inch* of her skin. Furiously, I peel away the layers of her clothing: shirt, bra, jeans, boy shorts. She wrestles the last bit of my pants down my legs along with my panties. Before I can blink, we are both fully naked. She's hovering above me, holding herself up with her strong, lean arms. And then she stops.

Shit! What if she *doesn't want this? Did I do the wrong thing, attacking her face like some kind of feral animal in heat? Maybe we should've discussed it more; made sure we were on the same page.* "What's wrong?" I'm panting so hard, I can barely form words.

"You're just so..." She looks me over, head to toe. It feels like the first time anyone has ever really seen me. "You are *so* beautiful."

I'm beautiful? I've been told as much by a million different people, but when Payton says it, I truly believe it. I want so much to thank her for making me *feel* beautiful and for constantly reassuring me that I'm smart enough to do anything I set my mind to. But I know I could never in a thousand years express my gratitude in words, so I close my eyes and resume kissing her.

She cups my breasts in her palms. Her tongue slides down my stomach. Then lower and lower still. She halts again, looks up at me from between my spread legs. "Are you sure?"

Sure? Are you serious? I've never been surer of anything, ever. "I'm positive."

That's all the affirmation she needs.

I can tell that she's nervous at first, kind of twitchy and uncertain of where and how to touch me, but soon she finds her rhythm. My frontal lobe sends a signal to my lips, like 'let her know she's right on target.' "There. There, there," I mumble.

It's only a matter of minutes before the shock waves begin to surge through every nerve ending in my body. My synapses fire on automatic. *Repeatedly.* I've never felt anything like it. It's the most startling, marvelous sensation.

Are those her fingers? Holy…

I hear myself whimpering and place my hand below her chin to force her to stop doing the magical things she's doing. Her head snaps up at me questioningly, but I've got nothing to answer with. I lie motionless, struggling to take in air. She pulls herself up, rests her head on my shoulder.

When I can finally breathe normally, I flip on top of her. All my weight is on her and I'm kissing her hard, like before. All of a sudden I get *stupid* anxious. I have the most extreme longing to make her feel as magnificent as I do, but what if I can't do it right? What if I'm seriously bad at it? What if there are rules like in playing sports? I don't understand sports! I fucking *suck at sports*!

The moment before the panic alarm in my brain goes off, Payton stirs. "Hey, it's okay," she says, almost as if she has absorbed my thoughts via osmosis. "You don't have to do anything you don't want to do." She sounds so incredibly earnest, it completely renews my determination. *I'm gonna do this like a boss!*

"I *want* to," I reply breathlessly, then tease a trail down her body with my lips. My tongue finds its way to the space between her thighs. Her muscles go instantly rigid. I'm surprised at how I can actually *feel* her pulsating, like there's a tiny drum beating somewhere deep inside her.

"Kendall!" she purrs as her hips jerk upward. My name has never before sounded so sexy. As she reaches climax, she grabs fistfuls of my hair and lightly tugs my head back.

All my strength is drained. I collapse on top of her in wonderment, thinking of how I'd slept with guys before but it never came close to being this amazing. It was never once so powerful.

She folds me in her arms and kisses my forehead. We lie together for the longest time, wordlessly basking in the afterglow. I don't know exactly how much time passes before she breaks the silence. "Are you all right?"

I just had the most mind-blowing sex imaginable with someone who just happens to be a girl. *Well,* that *formula only works for one very specific equation.* Suddenly, I'm laughing harder than I've ever laughed before, because solving said equation is cathartic in the scariest, yet most exquisite way. All the pieces of the puzzle have finally come together: why I never really connected with the guys I dated, how I always felt like some inexplicable thing was missing. Now I know it wasn't them; it was me. *Shit.* "I think I'm gay."

"Yeah? That's awesome. Maybe we can do this again sometime," she jokes.

I want so badly to tell her that she might just be the only person I *ever* want to do this with. I want to tell her that I love her, but I'm petrified that one little word will change everything. I mean, *she* didn't drop the L word. She said her heart belongs to me. That's not the same thing as "I love you." The nomenclature matters. *Right, Kendall, because having sex with her on the couch is so much less life-changing than words.* "Maybe we can." I kiss her and then push to my feet. I take a few steps toward my bedroom. When I notice she isn't following, I turn back to find her staring at me. She looks so frightened.

"Um, did I say something wrong?"

I shake my head.

She sits upright and her muscles go taut as though my lack of explanation has literally scared her stiff. "Where are you going?"

"To bed," I say nonchalantly. "Are you coming?" *An invitation to share my bed… What a pathetic consolation prize to "I love you."*

She continues to eye me up and down for a moment before her face alights with a smile. "Yes."

CHAPTER THIRTEEN

Payton

I am coaxed into wakefulness not by the golden rays of sunlight flooding through the bedroom windows, but by the tingle of puckered lips and sultry breath against my neck. "Good morning," Kendall whispers, her voice scarcely registering through the fog of slumber I'm trapped in.

"Good morning," I reply, still groggy. I clear the gritty remainders of sleep from the inner corners of my eyes and focus on the sensation of bare flesh touching mine. It's all the silky smoothness of skin on skin, unadulterated by the weighty coarseness of clothing. I ruffle the sheets and take a peek beneath them. We are both totally nude. *She's... I'm... Holy shit! Last night wasn't a dream. I didn't imagine it. It happened. What if it was a one-time thing? What if she regrets it? What if this totally fucks up our friendship forever? Payton, you twat, say something!* "So I haven't died and gone to heaven, have I? Please tell me this is real."

"Died and gone to heaven, huh? That is *so* cheesy," she says with a snigger. "Yes, it's real."

"Will you pinch me so I can be sure?"

"I'll do better than that," she says, then kisses my lips.

I laugh when she pulls away. "I knew this was a dream! You don't even have morning breath!"

She huffs and hits me with a pillow. "Shut up and hold me, would you?"

"Gladly." I stretch out my arms.

She snuggles into me, nuzzling my cheek with her nose. "Can we stay in bed all day? I don't want to move from this spot."

"Will your calendar allow for that, you being a highly in-demand superstar and all?"

"Screw my calendar," she mutters and squeezes me tight around my waist. "I'm not going anywhere."

"I think we should try being productive today."

"Boo," she sighs. "I don't want to do anything that requires me to put on clothes."

"What I had in mind doesn't necessarily require either of us to be dressed."

"Oh, really?" Her eyebrows arch in the most overtly sexy way possible. She pounces to her knees and mounts me with all the stealth and expertise of a panther. I'm caught between her legs, which are spread on either side of my torso. She's leaning over me, staring straight into my soul. The bedcovers have fallen away, allowing for a full view of her stark-naked frame. *Kendall, you are perfect.*

She slides her hand down my stomach, stopping just inside my left thigh. I nearly die from lack of oxygen to the brain. "Is this what you had in mind?" She grins devilishly.

"Not exactly. I was thinking more along the lines of a music lesson."

She presses her lips against my sternum. "This could turn into a music lesson," she mumbles between kisses. "I can teach you to sing."

"I already know how to sing."

She moves her hand farther inward. "Then maybe *you* can teach *me* how to sing."

"Wait." I grab her wrist. "Do you think we're moving a little fast? Don't get me wrong, the physical stuff is *incredible*. But I don't want sex to be all there is for us."

Her lips narrow into a stone-cold frown. "Sex isn't all there is for us. I *care* about you. It's just that last night was the first time I've ever had, you know, *The Big O*."

She *cares* about me… *Cares*. I try not to focus on the non-committal nature of that word and instead choose to address the fact that sleeping with me resulted in her first orgasm *ever*. "Seriously? You've never?"

"No," she says quickly, her face coloring a bit. "I always thought I was one of those girls who couldn't *get there*."

"Why haven't you told me this before?"

"We never made a habit out of talking about sex, Payton. It's the *one* thing we've hardly ever discussed."

"That's because I didn't want to know *who* you were doing *what* with," I admit.

"Yeah, I didn't really want to know who *you* were doing anything with, either. That makes so much more sense to me now." She smiles, then jumps off me. "Now, how about you teach me some piano?"

"You might have to get dressed for that, after all. I'll probably be too distracted to teach you anything if you're hanging out in all your stimulating, bare-assed glory."

"Fine!" She stalks across the room, grabs a bathrobe from her closet, and slips it on. "You'd better put something on, too. I can't keep my hands on the keys when all they want to do is roam all over you."

"That's fair," I say. "I'll meet you upstairs in five."

❄ ❄ ❄

Kendall is so precious when she's confused. I've been trying to introduce her to reading treble clef sheet music for the last hour, and it just isn't working out. "Every line on the staff and every space in between those lines has a name, a note. The lines from bottom to top are EGBDF. The spaces from bottom to top are FACE."

"That is so retarded. Why isn't it BDEFG? Alphabetical order! I could *remember* that. And why the hell are A and C in the *spaces*? Who made this shit up?"

"Some Roman guy." I laugh. "All right, let's try it this way," I point to each line and recite its respective note, "EGBDF, Every Good Boy Deserves Fudge."

"Every good boy... damn it!" Her cellphone rings, breaking her concentration. "Uh, hi," she answers tepidly. "You're *where*? And you didn't give any consideration to the fact that *that* might be kind of creepy? Yeah, okay, we can talk." She hangs up, turns to me, and says, "Gunner is here. Is it cool with you if he comes up for a minute?"

Odd. "Should I get dressed?"

"No. This is your house. He's the visitor. He can deal with seeing us in our robes."

"Okay," I nod.

She saunters down to the intercom and reluctantly gives Gunner permission to enter her breathing space. Five minutes later he's standing in the doorway, looking totally uncomfortable. I stick my head over the railing to watch their interaction from the safety of the loft.

"I'm sorry about yesterday," he starts. "I had no right to tell you to sort yourself out. I've never been into another guy, so I can't even imagine what you're going through."

"No, *I'm* sorry. You were right. I did need to sort myself out; consider me sorted." She pitches her thumb over her shoulder, up toward me.

Gunner looks up and smiles. "Hey, Payton." He then thrusts his hands deep into the pockets of his jeans. "So, what do we do now? It seems wrong parading you around as my arm candy when you're... involved with someone else."

Involved with. Sure, I'll take that.

"I don't know..." Kendall turns to me with questioning eyes.

All I can do is shrug. It took me years to become comfortable enough with who I am to tell anyone else about it. I can't expect her to be prepared to make that kind of leap after only just realizing that she's gay, or rather, thinking that she might be. It wouldn't be fair. "There are all these rules one needs to abide by in order to survive in Hollywood, right? I don't know exactly how it all works, but I know it's complex. I think Gunner should remain your escort for the time being, until you're, you know, good and settled with yourself." The disbelief on Gunner's face is bested only by the shock on Kendall's.

"I'm sorry," she mumbles. "I'll get there eventually, I promise."

"I know."

"Okay," Gunner affirms. "You're cool with it. I'm cool with it. What about Lawrence? Do we clue him in?"

"No," Kendall shakes her head. "He's my publicist, not my shrink. When it's essential for him to know, I'll tell him."

"Right then, we're good." Gunner rubs his neck and shuffles anxiously in place. "I'll let you ladies get back to whatever it is you were doing."

Kendall suppresses a chortle. "Yeah, I'll call you."

❊ ❊ ❊

Two months into the exploration of formerly uncharted territory and we're still muddling through it like two little girls lost in the woods. We're intimate with each other—exclusively—but we still don't have a proper title. I want to give our relationship a new name, one that outlines exactly what we are; "friends" doesn't seem to cut it anymore. It's such a frightening subject, and I'm such a wimp that I won't dare broach it. Seriously, where would I even begin? "Hey, Kendall. What the fuck are we doing? Because I love you, you know, and it would be great if you felt the same about me." That's so lame. Besides, what if she *doesn't* feel the same about me? What if this is just a fling for her? I know I couldn't handle that. She is everything I've ever wanted, but what if she isn't really mine?

The thing that complicates this situation even further is that we have so little time to talk. Life has basically become an enormous ball of chaos for Kendall. Between script workshops, costume fittings, strength training, martial arts and fencing classes for *The Relishing*, and all the preparation for her upcoming *Idol Worship* press tour, I really only get to see her when we cuddle up in bed at night—which we do every night—or when she manages to squeeze me into her schedule for breakfast.

In the interest of fairness, it isn't only her agenda that's overloaded these days. My spring semester is in full swing and I feel like I'm so far behind the curve that I could eat, sleep, and breathe music composition and never be able to catch up. Every MALA student I've met so far is light-years ahead of me when it comes to large-format composing. And the competition is cutthroat! Some days I leave campus wondering whether I enrolled in college or joined the cast of *Survivor: Songsmith Island*.

Kendall pops her head into the bedroom, effectively tearing me away from my thoughts and the task of orchestrating a piece for a string quartet. "Whoa, that's a lot of blank staff paper," she says distractedly.

"Tell me something I don't know," I joke. "Wait, what are you doing here?"

She beams. "My fencing classes were cancelled today, which means my Friday afternoon is now free! I thought we could hang out for a while, just the two of us—you know, since you basically blew off our dinner plans last night."

"Kendall, I was working on a group project. *Group*, meaning I had to take into account the schedules of three other people. They decided last minute that the only time we could all meet was last night in Pro Tools Studio B, so that's where I needed to be instead of at a dinner where we'd sit across the table from each other in a sparsely lit restaurant pretending to be 'just dear friends.' And I didn't blow you off, I left you two voicemails about it and texted you half a dozen times. I'm sorry you were in training and didn't check your messages until seven. Besides, I'm not sure you really have the right to be upset with me for missing *one* dinner when you're hardly *ever* home."

"Oh, don't even…" she starts indignantly, but catches herself mid-sentence. "Okay, I see what you did there. You're not wrong, things have been crazy hectic for me lately. But I'm home *now*, and I'd like us to *not* fight so we can spend some time together before everyone arrives because I miss you."

At first I only digest the part where she says 'I miss you.' I look at her, befuddled until I process the 'everyone arrives' part of her speech. "Hold on, before everyone arrives?"

"We're going to the Gay and Lesbian Cinema Committee Awards tonight. Did you forget?"

Yes, of course I forgot. I'm up to my ears in college kid problems. Son of a bitch. "Well, technically, *we* aren't going. We'll only be in the same place at the same time."

I'm going to the awards with Lauren, which is totally unfair. It's one thing for Kendall to keep up the charade with Gunner, but it's utterly uncool that we're using Lauren as a pawn to keep our *whatever this is* under wraps. After a long, awkward conversation between the three of us, Lauren agreed to help us out: I will appear publicly with her at events that Kendall and Gunner are scheduled to attend, that way I can be in the mix without anyone suspecting I might be there with Kendall.

The hitch is Lauren still kind of likes me, and I'm not the only one who knows it. The tension between her and Kendall is unbearable sometimes. I can't help thinking that it's my fault. They were friends before I came between them. It's weird, feeling like I'm the cause of a dynamic shift in the way these two people—both of whom I care about—view one another. It's almost as if they're enemies now, or in some kind of heated competition with each other.

But the fact that I know the whole evening is going to be uncomfortable for everyone involved is not the reason I don't want to go to.

"I think I should stay home. I really need to concentrate on this. I've got two weeks left to finish it and still so much to write. I haven't even started on the cello part yet."

She stands there, arms folded, lashes batting away as though nothing I just said is of any consequence. "Please," she mopes. "The Visibility Award means so much to me. I want you there when I receive it."

"All right, I'll go." How could I refuse her?

She skips happily into my arms, tenderly kisses my lips. "Lawrence will be here with the makeup and hair team at six. Gunner and Lauren are coming later."

❋ ❋ ❋

Gunner and Lauren show up just as I'm throwing on the pair of dangling ruby earrings Kendall bought me especially for this evening. They're not quite my style, but they complement my gown seamlessly. With bated breath, I watch as Kendall greets them. She kisses Gunner on both cheeks without reluctance, but flashes an ill-at-ease smile at Lauren.

"Hi guys," I call from my chair as Felicia finishes painting my face. She gives me a thorough once-over then releases me. I saunter over to the group, hug Gunner and then Lauren in direct defiance of the freshly suggested hostilities between her and Kendall.

"You look beautiful," Lauren says after I pull back from our embrace.

My eyes instinctively flutter to Kendall. Her jaw muscles flair as I reply, "Thank you. So do you."

"Yeah, you and Kendall are both stunners," Gunner adds with such swiftness. It's as if he's aiming to defuse a live explosive. I'm so appreciative of his quick input, I could kiss him.

"Okay kids," Lawrence chimes in, "now that we've made it abundantly clear every woman in the room looks great, we need to leave." He aims a stiff finger at Kendall, "You can't be late to an awards show if you're an honored guest."

"Right," Kendall says. She shuffles to the kitchen table, picks up her clutch, and trundles back to us. She holds the door open for everyone, and then locks it behind her.

✳ ✳ ✳

We arrive at the Navarro Theater to fewer screaming fans than I expected. The photographers and reporters, however, are out in full force. Lauren and I trail slightly behind Gunner and Kendall as they make their way down the red carpet. We all pose for pictures, forcing smiles the size of Texas.

Once we enter the building, Kendall steps off to the side of the hallway, away from Gunner and their combined party of handlers. I realize she's waiting for me and quickly join her. "I can't wait until this thing is over." She takes a step closer to me and whispers in my ear, "I'm *dying* to get you out of that dress."

I shudder, awkward from the remnants of her breath against my skin. "You'll take care of that later, I'm sure."

"Oh yeah, you can bet on it with confidence." She arches her eyebrows with a slight insinuation of naughtiness. "I guess I'd better go find my seat before I lose control of myself, huh?"

"Yeah, you'd better." I watch her slink away into the amphitheater.

❋ ❋ ❋

"You two should be more careful," Lauren whispers once I've returned to her side. "It looked like y'all were gonna make out right there in the corner."

"Damn, really?" I am all but completely troubled at her insight.

"Yeah, you're lucky the press isn't allowed inside."

I nod. "Thanks for the heads up."

"No problem. Ready to do this?" She slips her hand into mine. I quell the itch to pull my hand away and nod.

Our assigned seats are to the right of Rebecca Gordon and Spencer St. Germaine. Gunner and Kendall are seated to their left.

As we scoot into the aisle, Kendall's glare locks onto mine and Lauren's clasped hands. I watch her lips twist into an irritated grimace. Gunner also notices the change in her demeanor. I'm relieved I'm not the only one. He mumbles a troubled "chill out" in Kendall's direction. She lets out a vexed sigh followed by a muted, yet forceful, "Okay."

The lot of us watch the show for a good hour as presenter after presenter calls the winners of various categories to the stage: Best Male Performance, Best Female Performance, Best Screenplay, Best Film, Best Director. Finally, the chairman of the Gay and Lesbian Cinema Committee gets to the Visibility Award, but not before going off on a tangent about how "it's out of the usual practice of the committee to present accolades to the stars of a film that has not yet been released." He goes on to laud Rebecca and Kendall for their poignant performance of two female characters who are struggling with the difficulties of living in the spotlight. Once he finishes his grand discourse, he calls Kendall and Rebecca up to receive their trophies. As they scramble their way onto the stage, the room rumbles with applause—mine included. Mr. Chairman hands them each a gilded bronze statuette, and the whole place goes silent in anticipation of their individual speeches.

Rebecca gives an unoriginal speech, thanking everyone involved with *Idol Worship* and her agent for bringing the role to her attention. She finishes, and Kendall steps up to the microphone.

"I'd just like to say, I've come to realize the importance of LGBT characters being represented in films and on TV, because visibility really *does* matter. When audiences get to see LGBT characters dealing with the same tough issues as everyone else, when audiences get to know and love those characters, I believe it's the most humanizing thing in the world. I'm proud to have had the opportunity to play a wounded yet very real character in *Idol Worship*, and I am truly grateful to the Gay and Lesbian Cinema Committee for recognizing the deeper message of the film. Thank you."

If the theater was loud before Kendall's speech, now it is downright thunderous. Every single person in the room is on his feet, clapping and cheering. The raucousness continues right up to the second Rebecca and Kendall get back to their seats. Kendall graciously bows her head and lifts her hands, miming the classic signal to "settle down." I'm staring at her in awe, surprised at the passion she's displayed, when Lauren—still clapping, herself—leans in close to me. "Beautiful speech," she says cynically. "It's so nice to see how proud she is to have played a LGBT *character*. She's gay, for fucks sake."

"Okay. First, that's for *her* to say, not for you, me or anyone else. Second, considering you and I both know how difficult it can be for openly LGBT people, I'm surprised at your attitude."

"I'm just saying. How long can this go on, really? The very definition of fame is that everyone in the world either knows your business or *tries* to know it."

"Give her a break, all right?"

"Okay. We'll see how much of a break you'll want to give her in a few minutes."

"What's that supposed to mean?" I ask defensively. The crowd's cheering has long since ceased; my voice reverberates, unobstructed, throughout the auditorium. I blush in recognition of my volume.

"Nothing," she whispers. "Forget I said anything."

"All right, everybody," the voice of the host blares through the sound system. "We've reached the part of the evening where we stop talking and start doing. It's time to auction off some celebrity kisses!"

Lauren turns her attention to the stage, abruptly putting an end to our conversation. I'm all too thankful for the interruption. "As you all know, the proceeds of this auction go to various charities, including the California Equality Project and the True Colors Higher Education Fund. Without any further ado, I invite tonight's participating celebrities to take the stage."

From my peripheral view, I see Kendall stand up. She makes her way down the row, pauses to talk to me as she reaches my seat. "It's just for charity. Don't be upset."

Upset? Does she really think I'll be upset about her kissing some rich fool for *charity*? What am I, a jealous child? Or some kind of asshole who isn't interested in helping my community? "It's fine," I wave her off. "Go be altruistic."

Kendall takes the stage again, along with two other people—a singer named Lenore and some football player I've never heard of whose team is the Los Angeles Crusaders. The host opens the auction with Lenore. A flurry of bids descends on the host, who seems so overwhelmed that he can hardly keep track. The winning bid of $2,900 goes to a woman seated a few rows behind me. She screams in delight after the host tells her to come down to the stage and stand next to Lenore. The football player is auctioned next. A woman sitting way up in the nosebleed section wins with a bid of $3,700. She also squeals in excitement as she heads for the stage.

"Last, but never least, we have the lovely Kendall Betten-court," the host says. "She's the star of the blockbuster film *In Heaven's Arms*, and, as everyone here knows, winner of this year's GLCC Visibility Award. Let's begin the bidding at $1,000. Do I have a measly grand from anyone?"

A tide of chatter ripples around the room. From somewhere in the back of the theater, a man shouts, "Right here!"

"There we go! Can I get two? $2,000, people! Come on, Ken-dall's dress is worth more than that!"

"Two thousand," shouts a woman in the front-left of the au-ditorium. The original bidder ups his offer to $2,400 and a small bidding war ensues between the two. The highest bid comes from the woman; she's gone up to $4,000. The man is about to make a counter offer, when a third voice chimes in.

"Eight thousand!" The voice belongs to a man. It sounds fa-miliar and relatively close to me. I look over to my left, and lo and behold, Gunner is on his feet.

What the shit is this!

"Sold!" The host hollers. "Give it up for Mr. Gunner Roder-ick! Who knew he was such a romantic?"

The crowd goes wild as he heads for the stage. It seems like every last person in the theater is cheering him on—every last person save for me and Lauren. Lauren reaches for my hand. She slides her fingers between mine and holds firm. "It's a publicity stunt," she says. "Lawrence put them up to it. Are you all right?"

No, I'm not all right! We're on shaky ground to begin with, and Kendall thinks she can just go around kissing people who aren't me?

I've tried to be understanding and supportive, if not downright accepting of this whole confusing thing, but I'm only human. We all have our breaking points, and I have unquestionably reached mine. "I need some air."

"Okay," Lauren jumps out of her chair, pulling me up with her. The last thing I see before we turn to leave the theater is Kendall's face as pale as a cadaver's.

We make a beeline for the doors leading to the street, but don't stop until we've reached the sidewalk. "Breathe." Lauren gently pats my back. "I know you're shaken up, but I also know Kendall will be out here looking for you in about two minutes."

"Oh, yeah? How do you know that?"

"Because she would be stupid not to."

"Payton?" Kendall calls from the doorway. Lauren and I both turn to face her.

"That's my cue to exit," Lauren says, then starts toward the theater. She stops when she's about six inches away from Kendall and shakes her head almost imperceptibly. I don't think I'm supposed to hear her say it, but I do: "If you break her heart, I'll be right here to pick up the pieces."

"Don't worry," Kendall fires back. "I'll never give you the chance."

CHAPTER FOURTEEN

Kendall

Lauren's snide remark angers me in the most dangerous sense of the word. Prior to this moment, I was unaware that anger had a flavor, but I guess there's only so much the human body can take before it has to either explode into a fit of full-blown rage or find another way to expel the fury. To my surprise, rage has a metallic tang to it—something very similar to the taste of blood. Actually, it isn't rage I'm tasting, after all. In fact, I'm pretty sure I've bitten my tongue.

Luckily, Lauren is smart enough to head inside before I let myself fly off the handle. She's not the most important person I'm standing in front of, anyway. I take a quick step toward Payton and reach for her hand. She jolts away from me in a hurry. *Oh Lord, please help me get out of the deep shit I'm in.* "Payton, I am *so* sorry. Lawrence set it up and I–"

"Stop talking." she interrupts, her voice so unforgivingly stern that it physically stings me. "'It's for charity. Don't be upset!' Well, I am upset! Maybe I'm overreacting, but I can't help it!" Without warning she goes deathly quiet. The next thing I know, I'm watching tears assault her face. The shiny droplets fuse with her mascara and stain her cheeks with long, black smudges. *Oh shit, I made her cry.*

A putrefied glob of remorse congeals in my throat. *Whatever you say, Kendall, it had better be damn good.* "Acting like I'm with Gunner is easy… No, that's not right. What I mean to say is, I just… I don't know how to do this." I sigh. "I don't know how to balance being the huge superstar everyone thinks they know and who I truly am. It's like I'm walking on a tight rope, and there's no safety net beneath me. On one hand, I have all the people and things I'm *told* to care about, and on the other, I have all the people and things I *actually* care about. I feel like everybody in the world wants everything, every last part of me. But I'm not ready to give them all of me. I'm not even ready to *be* me. Do you understand what I'm saying?"

She wipes at her eyes with a shaky palm and fixes her gaze on me. "I get it. I've been where you are. It's a process, coming to terms with yourself. But I'm not asking you to come bursting out of the closet on some nationally televised five o'clock news program. I'm asking you to tone down the façade a little bit. I don't need to be by your side at premiers and parties, but I'm *not okay* with you going around kissing anyone who isn't me."

All right, that is a reasonable request. The *idea* of Payton kissing someone else is enough to break me. I don't know what I'd do if it ever actually happened. "I swear I will never kiss anyone but you again. Lawrence can choose whoever he likes to be my escort, but I won't let him talk me into doing anything that might upset you. And I'm going to make him clear my schedule for the rest of the week. I'm not leaving on Friday for a three-week promo tour without spending every second I can with you before I go."

"What about the Ellie Nominations party tomorrow night? You can't miss that. Even if you don't get a nomination, you absolutely have to go. You have to go *especially* if you aren't nominated. If you don't at least make an appearance that would be like flipping the bird to the most important people in Hollywood. Then you definitely won't get nominated for anything you do in the future."

"I'll go if you come with me," I say, arms folded across my chest so she knows I'm serious.

She rolls her eyes. Her pupils reel so far back into her skull, I'm afraid they'll get stuck there. "Oh, man, Lawrence will have a fit. He's crafted this thing between you and Gunner so perfectly."

"You're right, he *has* crafted it perfectly. But I don't give a shit. I want to go to the party with you."

"Really?"

The question was posed in the faintest pitch, but hits me harder than a fist to the chin. "*Of course.*"

She sniffles. "Okay."

I reach my hand out to her again. This time, she takes it. "Come here." I pull her close to me and buff away the traces of her runny eye makeup with the pads of my thumbs. I realize we're standing on the sidewalk of one of the most well-traveled neighborhoods of downtown LA, but right now I can't afford to be concerned that some random passerby might recognize us as lovers. "Do you want to head back inside? The show is almost over. Or we could blow it off and go home."

"Let's go inside. It would look bad if you bolted from the theater and didn't come back. You'd probably offend the entire gay community."

"Hmm, yeah. That is not a good position to put myself in."

"No, it's not."

"Okay, here's the plan. We sit out the rest of the show then get out of there real quick before anyone else has the chance to. We hop in a cab and make our way home without any further badgering from the media, or anybody else."

"Great plan. But what are you going to say to Lawrence when he calls you up later, bellowing about how you disappeared?"

"I'll send him to voicemail."

"Good. I don't want his screaming at you impeding on my quiet cuddle time—which I am in dire need of, because my head is pounding harder than a sailor on shore leave."

"Okay, it's settled. If he calls me tonight, I'll send him to voicemail. Now, let's get the rest of this horrible evening out of the way."

❅ ❅ ❅

We walk through the door of the penthouse literally twenty minutes after the show ends. The host said "good night," and Payton latched onto my arm so quickly, it made my head spin. Before anyone else had the chance to exit the theater, I had already hailed a cab. It must have been destiny or an uncanny coincidence, because finding a cab in downtown LA is generally as easy as solving a *Where's Waldo* puzzle. *I never was any good at spotting that elusive little bastard.*

Payton drops her clutch on the coffee table and swiftly kicks off her shoes before flopping backward onto the couch. "I hope Lauren is all right," she mumbles once I'm seated next to her.

Seriously? She's worried about Lauren right now? I want to ask her what the hell *that's* about, but opt not to; my drama quota for the night has been surpassed. "Lauren is fine. Gunner promised to get her home safely—not that I'm particularly fond enough of her to care at the moment."

"Okay, *you* might not be fond of Lauren, but she's *my* friend," she reprimands me. "Do me a favor and try to be civil to her. Do *yourself* the favor. You still have to work with her on *The Relishing,* and it'll probably be easier for both of you if you're not at war with each other."

Damn it. She has a point. "Okay, you're right. I'll pass the peace pipe or whatever tomorrow. Gunner is going to call you tomorrow, too. He wanted to apologize to you in person, but I told him he'd have to wait because we're making a quick getaway."

She doesn't have the chance to respond before my phone starts to ring. I pluck it out of my purse and breathe an agitated sigh. "It's Lawrence."

"Give me that stupid thing!" She yanks the phone from my hand and prods at the end-call button until the screen goes black. She hands it back to me once she's sure it's turned off. "You can turn it on again before we go to sleep. I know tomorrow is a big day, and your 'people' will all have seizures if they can't get in touch with you."

"Thanks," I chuckle. Then, for some weird reason, a memory from our childhood pops into my head and gets me laughing harder. Payton ruffles her eyebrows at me, wordlessly asking for an explanation. "Do you remember that time we were playing in my back yard? I think we were in, like, fourth grade—I jumped off the swing in mid-air, landed the wrong way, and fractured my ankle?"

"I remember you having a fractured ankle."

"Yeah, but don't you remember the rest of it? I screamed, and you jumped off your swing so fast to help me up. When you realized I was really injured, you sort of threw me on your shoulders and gave me a piggyback ride into the house. I was crying and scared, but you were *so* brave about it."

"Oh, right! I carried you into the house, dropped you on the couch, and you called me your knight in shining armor. And then–"

"I kissed you. My mom ran upstairs to get her car keys so she could take me to the hospital, and I kissed you right on the lips."

She snuggles farther into my embrace and laughs. "How could I have forgotten that?"

"I don't know. That was our first kiss."

"Does that count, though? I mean, we were nine."

"It counted for me. From that moment on, I knew I was safe with you. Other than my dad, you're the only person who has ever made me feel like nothing bad could happen to me."

"I'm not actually a knight, and I definitely don't have any shining armor, but I'm glad you feel safe with me."

"I do. But right now, I'm also feeling very tired. Wanna go to bed?"

She stares at me for a while before hopping to her feet. She bends over, scoops me into her arms, and plants a quick kiss on my lips. "Fair lady," she says in a horrible British accent. "I shall carry you to the ends of the earth! Or to our bed, whichever we should first encounter!"

❋ ❋ ❋

The persistent buzz of my Blackberry startles me awake from the sweetest dream. The fantasy of riding off into the sunset on horseback with Payton is still fresh in my mind when I notice the digital clock on the bedside table. It's half past five in the morning. *Whoever the hell is calling me better have something really important to say.* I fumble around in the darkness, determined to find my phone without having to turn on a single light. When I do ultimately find it, I rip it from the nightstand with an irrational viciousness. *Damn it, I was enjoying that dream!* I yawn as I check the caller ID. *Home.*

"Hello?" I ask groggily, my voice hoarse and thick with hints of sleep. Out of the corner of my eye, I notice Payton stirring beneath the sheets. *She has to be up for class in, like, an hour.*

"Kendall, honey!" My mother's voice bursts through the receiver. "Did I wake you?"

"Yeah, Mom, you did," I cough. "What's up?" I'm wracked with dread. There's only one reason she would be calling me this early. Something must've happened to my dad. "Oh my god, is Daddy okay?"

As soon as the question leaves my lips, Payton is wide awake. Even in the shadowy murkiness of early morning, I can see the spark of alarm in her eyes. She springs up and turns on the bed-side lamp. In the full light of day, I realize that she is more than alarmed, she is downright distraught. She shoots a questioning look in my direction. I hold up my hand, letting her know that I need to concentrate on the call.

"Yes, honey. Daddy is fine. I can't believe you were sleeping," Mom laughs.

I can't believe you're bothering me at this hour for no good reason. Snootily, I ask, "You do know that California is three hours behind Eastern Standard Time, right?"

"I'm sorry. We thought you would be up. Your father and I are just so excited! We wanted to call to congratulate you before he left for work!"

"Uh, what are you talking about?"

She harrumphs. "You honestly don't know?"

"No, Mom, I don't! What the hell is going on?"

"Kendall Ann Bettencourt! The language," she warns, but in her second breath she twitters with enthusiasm. "Honey, you were nominated for an Elite Award!"

At first, the phrase doesn't register like there's earsplitting static or a raging beehive inside my head. My vision is hazy. I must have been sucked into some kind of time warp, or black hole or something, because nothing around me seems real. Every single object in the room has a foamy, cartoonish halo around its edges. *Maybe I'm dead?* Then I remember that I've got the phone to my ear. *No, how could I be on the phone with my mother if I were dead?* "Wait, Mom. *What?*"

"You were nominated for an Ellie! We just saw it on TV!"

This time the words reach my brain, but I can't say anything in return. I'm not sure how long I sit in absolute silence before my mother's shrieking wrestles me back to the land of the living. "Kendall, did you hear me?"

I nod my head, forgetting that she can't see me through the phone. "Uh huh. Yes, I heard you. Thank you for letting me know. I've gotta go. I'll call you back later, okay?"

"Okay. We love you! Congratulations again!"

I mumble a quick, "Love you too," and let the phone slip out of my hands. It hits the bed and bounces back into my lap with a thump. I follow it the whole way with my eyes, and that's when I realize Payton is soundlessly staring at me, anxious for me to speak.

"Is everything okay?" she asks. When her voice finally penetrates my skull, I crumble into a mess of tears. It's the most idiotic thing to do, but I can't help myself. "Kendall, you're scaring me. Please, tell me what's going on." She wraps her arms around my waist and pulls me in close to hold me tight as I cry. I'm sobbing so hard, I can barely breathe much less speak.

"Best Actress," I simper.

"What?" She relaxes her grip and looks at me. *There,* I think. *That twinkle in her eyes. She gets it.* "Oh my god! You got the nomination?"

I press my temple to her shoulder and nod.

"Kendall! You were nominated for an *Ellie!*" She laughs a great big laugh. "Why are you crying? That is awesome!"

"I can't." I hiccup. "I can't."

She swooshes my bangs away from my eyes. "Shhh, sweetie. Calm down first."

I draw in a mighty mouthful of air and settle myself before I speak. "I can't believe it. I really cannot. It's some kind of mistake."

"It isn't a mistake. The list of nominees must be so carefully chosen, there's no way your name could have slipped in by accident. And it shouldn't be so hard to believe. Haven't people been telling you this would happen for months now?"

"Payton, I mostly don't listen when people talk—especially media people, you know that."

"Kendall Bettencourt, Elite Awards Nominee." She wipes a tear from my cheek as she considers the phrase. "Doesn't it sound fantastic?"

"I don't know." I sniffle. "I guess I'll have to get used to it though, won't I?"

She smiles. "Yes, you will. Don't worry, you can handle it."

"I love how you always manage to talk me down from a panic."

"Of course I do." She places her hands on the sides of my face. "And I'm so proud of you. You deserve this."

"No, I don't."

"Obviously you do. This wouldn't be happening if you didn't deserve it." She smirks and goes to kiss me. Our lips are just inches apart when my goddamn Blackberry rings again. I shoot a scornful look at the thing, release a peeved huff that lets Payton know I'd rather throw it off the balcony than answer it.

"Pick it up," she says. "I'm gonna go take a shower."

"Okay." I let it ring a few more times, choosing to ignore it in favor of watching Payton retreat to the bathroom.

"Hi, Lawrence," I finally answer.

"Hi? Is that all you have to say to me? First, let me tell you that I don't appreciate the way you took off last night without saying a word about it to me. I don't need to know where you're going or who with, but I *do* need to know that you're leaving. Second, congratulations. You're an Elite Awards Nominee."

"Thank you, I know. I spent the last ten minutes crying about it."

"Did James call you? Son of a bitch! I told him that *I* wanted to tell you." He sounds like a spoiled brat throwing a tantrum. It cracks me up.

"No, my mom called me. My parents saw the announcements on TV."

"Oh. That's okay, then. Anyway, I need you to lay low today. My phone has been ringing off the hook with media people begging for interviews, and I don't want you answering any questions until you hit the Nomination Party Red Carpet. "

My stomach does a slow, sickening somersault at the mention of the party. "Yeah, about the party. I'm not going with Gunner."

"What?" His pitch drops a solid two octaves.

Crap. "I know it isn't what we agreed on, but I asked Payton to come with me. I already talked to Gunner about it. He's cool with it."

"Kendall, is this your way of telling me you're done with him? Sweetheart, I can't keep switching out your escorts. Jumping from guy to guy isn't going to help your image any."

"No, I'm not saying 'I'm done' with him," I reply, swallowing my budding frustration. "And I have no intention of jumping from guy to guy either. Please, can I just *not* have to seem cooler than I am tonight? I want to be myself for once, and that means I get to take whoever the hell I want to this stupid party."

"All right. Bring Payton," he forfeits. "By the way, I'm going to have to meet you at the Hilton instead of picking you up. I'll be too busy setting up your interviews to get away."

No skin off my ass. "Fine. I'll meet you at the party," I end the call with a grump.

"I can always tell when you've been on the phone with Lawrence. After you hang up, you look beyond stressed out," Payton says as she saunters out of the bathroom in a towel. "What happened?"

"Nothing much. He was being exhausting, as usual, trying to tell me what to do. He instructed me to avoid the media, which means I'm basically under house arrest for the day."

"I'm sorry he's a perpetual jerk." She slinks over to me and puts her hands on my hips. "But the house arrest thing could be fun if I play hooky."

I wrap my arms around her neck and stand on my tiptoes to kiss her cheek. "You're getting me wet."

"Oh, yeah?"

"I mean your hair. It's dripping on me." I press my finger to the tip of her nose. "Dirty mind... No, you're not playing hooky. Hurry up and get dressed. I refuse to let you take over the job of being the 'late one.'"

She throws on a faded Pink Floyd t-shirt and a pair of jeans and grabs her messenger bag from floor. "See you later," she says before making a mad dash out the door.

✸ ✸ ✸

My phone continues to blow up throughout the day. Every person I've ever given my number to, including those I haven't spoken to in years, calls to congratulate me. It's just beginning to get on my nerves by the time Payton gets home at five. "Hey, I'm home," she calls from behind the couch.

"Have a good day?" I ask over my shoulder, before getting up to kiss her hello. The first thing I see when I turn around is a giant bouquet of flowers—a spray of electric blue orchids mixed in with hot pink stargazer lilies. The sight of the loveliest soul I've ever met holding a cascade of blossoms is too much beauty for my senses to handle. Tears blur my vision as I jump into her arms with so much force she's barely able to keep from toppling over.

"I didn't know buying you flowers would be hazardous to my health," she mumbles through the series of quick kisses I plant on her lips.

"I'm sorry! Here you are, congratulating me all proper like, and I nearly kill you. They're beautiful. Thank you."

"It's okay. I forgive you. And you're welcome."

I take the flowers from her and search the kitchen cabinets for a vase.

"Have you been out at all today?" she asks at my back.

"I went for a swim earlier, but other than that, no. I've been a good girl, following orders."

"Then it's safe to assume you haven't noticed any of the sweaty guys with cameras lurking around outside?"

"Damn. No, I haven't. Did they bother you?"

"Not really. A few of them recognized me as your friend and asked about your reaction to being nominated. But I didn't say anything, don't worry."

"I'm not worried." *I am totally worried. Those disgusting leeches might try to use her to get to me.* I don't want to tell her that, though. So far, we've been pretty successful at avoiding any unpleasant run-ins with those unfeeling interlopers. Of course, that's only because we've rarely been seen alone together in public. *I really want to change the subject right now.* "Did Gunner ever call you?"

"He sent me a series of *extremely long* texts. Let me tell you, that boy knows how to turn a phrase. I had no clue that there were fifty-two different ways to say 'I'm sorry for being a turd.'"

"Is everything okay between you two now?"

"Yeah, we're good. I told him that if he ever does anything like that again, I'll take a cleaver to his balls and make *apizza gain* out of them."

"That sounds mortifying."

"I know," she retorts. "Should we get dressed? It's getting late."

"Probably. The crew will be here soon to make us up."

※ ※ ※

My nerves decide to heave themselves into chaotic unrest just as we're about to leave for the party. I don't know why I'm so convinced that this whole evening is going to be a catastrophe, but the feeling takes over me as soon as the limo arrives to transport us to the Beverly Hilton. In the ten seconds it takes us to get from the lobby to the car, we have to shirk the annoying inquiries of roughly twenty paparazzi. I'm honestly too preoccupied with reminding myself not to clasp onto Payton's hand to be bothered by the garish flashing of their cameras.

"You're jumpy tonight. It's weird," she says as the limo departs. "Want to tell me what's on your mind?"

"The massive number of rapid-fire interviews I'm slated for. Plus, I know once we arrive I'll have to focus on everyone else in the room but you. I don't want to leave you alone, but odds are I'll have to."

"Don't worry about me. I can fend for myself. Don't worry about the interviews either. Try to have fun and celebrate, all right? You're one of the select few who have ever been nominated for the most prestigious award known to Hollywood."

"It doesn't help at all when you put it like that."

"Nervousness looks cute on you," she says as the car pulls to a stop in front of the hotel.

"Okay. Let's do this."

We step out of the limo and are immediately drawn into a whirlwind of insanity. More members of the press than I have ever encountered at once are crowded around the red carpet. I haven't felt this intimidated in the presence of the media since I first broke into the business. I can't decipher which direction my name is being shouted from; there's one colossal wall of sound surrounding me.

"I need to find Lawrence," I bellow so Payton can hear me over the never-ending whir of voices.

"I think he found us," she points to a man jockeying his way through the crowd. I'm not tall enough to see him clearly, so I'm forced to trust that her height has not betrayed her. Fortunately, she's right, and I soon see Lawrence hustling up to us.

"This is wild, Lawrence!" I yell.

"I know. First thing's first. Pictures on the red carpet." He gestures to Payton. "You know how it goes by now, right? Big smiles and all that. After pictures, we head inside to the scheduled interviews. Payton, I'm sorry, but that means I'm going to have to steal Kendall from you for a while. I've arranged a booth for our party in the VIP section, so you're more than welcome to hang out there or at the bar. Are we ready to do this, ladies?"

"I'm good to go," Payton says.

I nod. Then, we're off.

* * *

The red carpet photo session is over quickly, and I'm whisked away to the conference area. I must go through thirty different journalists before realizing that I've been giving identical answers to approximately the same questions directed at me by entirely different people. "How does it feel to be an Elite Awards Nominee?"

Terrifying like my blockades have been overrun and I can no longer hope to avoid being conquered. "It's an incredibly humbling honor."

I sit through a few hundred more interviews until Lawrence lets me know that I'm done.

* * *

Lawrence escorts me into the ballroom, and I instantly catch sight of *her*. She's standing at the bar—drink in hand—conversing with a group of guys who are blatantly staring at her chest. She notices me coming toward her, and her eyes zero in on me. I smile, determined to keep my gaze trained on her until she looks away. *Damn it.* The longer I stare at her, the harder I have to fight to stave off the impulse to yell, "Payton Taylor, I am absolutely crazy about you!"

I turn to Lawrence. "Excuse me. I'm going over there," I say and jostle my way through the ballroom. Without any regard for the fact that it may be a faux pas, I ignore the multitude of people who try to get me to stop and talk. The only person I give a damn about right now is Payton with her perfectly straight hair pulled back into a high ponytail and her barely made up, yet entirely spectacular face. She is decked out in that white satin floor-length dress and all of its low-cut, V-necked majesty. Payton. *Thank God for her.*

I reach out to her in what feels like slow-motion, take her by the hand, and pull her away from her conversation. She holds tightly to her wineglass as I lead her through the crowd, out a well-hidden back door and into a secluded alleyway.

She looks at me confused. "Are you okay?"

"I needed to do *this*," I say and kiss her as though all the love I feel for her has flown through my veins and culminated in my lips. The wineglass slips from her hand. I hear it shatter against the pavement. Shards tinkle down around our feet. Still, I keep on kissing her.

"We are *so* gonna get caught," she whispers into my lips.

"No, we aren't," I pull away. "Look around. There's nobody here but us."

"Except for the ton of people inside. But hey, I don't care if *you* don't."

"Right now, I don't," I reply and move in to kiss her again.

She presses her palms to my shoulders, halting me. "You don't care right now because there's no one else around. But the second someone pops through that door or wanders down the alley, you'll care. We'd better quit while we're ahead."

"I don't want to quit while we're ahead. I don't want to quit *ever*." *I want to kiss you until the sun collides with the earth and chars us both into dunes of ash.*

She scrutinizes me, her face a mask of uncertainty. "Okay," she repositions her hands from my shoulders to the nape of my neck. "What are you waiting for?" She grins. "Kiss me."

And I do—for a very, very long time.

❀ ❀ ❀

I wake up a little after noon totally disoriented, head pulsing. I roll over to find a note on Payton's side of the bed. It reads, "Sorry for leaving without saying goodbye. I didn't want to wake you. I caught a cab back to the house so I can get ready for school. See you at home after class. –P." *A cab? What?*

Then I remember exactly what happened last night. Our epic alleyway make-out session got a little carried away. We ended up sneaking back into the Hilton, but didn't return to the ballroom. Instead, we checked into a suite and had a little party of our own, apparently involving two (now empty) bottles of champagne and lovemaking worthy of an Olympic event. I smile to myself. *That explains the headache and why this whole room smells like sweat.*

I reach for my cell phone and am horrified to realize that it's turned off. I power the thing up. The voicemail notification pings: six new messages. The first five of them are from Lawrence, each one sounding more heated than the last. He left the fifth message about an hour ago: "Kendall, how many times have I told you to keep your goddamn phone on? We need to have a serious conversation. Come down to the office as soon as possible." *Oh, he is* pissed. I continue on to the last message. It's from my dad. "Hey Pumpkin, not sure if you've seen this morning's *Daily Post*, but, you know what? Give me a ring later, and we'll talk."

Okay? I weigh my options. Call my dad back or call Lawrence back. Lawrence sounded much angrier than my dad did. I should let him know that it's going to be a while before I can make it to his office anyway. I've got to go home, take a shower, and put on some normal clothes. I can't very well show up in the gown I was wearing last night, can I? *It's decided.* I distractedly dial Lawrence's iPhone while foraging around on the floor for my dress.

"Where the hell have you been?" he says into the receiver without bothering to say hello.

"Sleeping," I say gruffly. "Sorry, my phone died."

"We've got ourselves a serious situation here, sweetheart. I need you to get your ass into this office immediately, got it?" There's worriedness to his tone. He so seldom sounds alarmed that when he does, it piques my interest.

"Did someone croak?"

"No, but something came up that we need to address before it flatlines your career."

I laugh. "Calm down. If it's a naked picture of me, it's fake."

He doesn't do the same. "I'd rather not discuss this on the phone. Get here when you can," he replies and hangs up.

I'm so not in the mood, I think as I slip into my dress and embark on a very long walk of shame.

❊ ❊ ❊

"What's the problem?" I ask as I stroll into Lawrence's office.

He slams a copy of today's *Daily Post* onto his desk. "Open it to page thirteen."

I flip through the paper until I reach the thirteenth page, where I find a huge photo of Payton and me in the alley behind the Hilton. I've got my arms wrapped around her neck, and she's kissing me while dipping me backward as though we'd been dancing in the moonlight. It's actually a really beautiful picture of us—or it would be a beautiful picture, if it weren't printed in the gossip section of some second-rate national newspaper with the caption "Kendall Bettencourt Celebrates Awards Nod with Lesbian Lip Lock" slapped across the top of it.

Who took this picture? I didn't see anyone around us! *Get real, Kendall. Like you were paying attention to what was going on around you! It doesn't matter anyway. You're busted.* Oh my god, Dad saw it! Which means Mom also saw it! I have a shit load of either lying or explaining to do. *Okay, stay composed. One thing at a time.* "I see the problem here. The page eight column is on page thirteen. That's confusing. We should definitely notify someone about that."

"That isn't funny, Kendall! How am I supposed to spin this to the press? 'She was so drunk that she stumbled into a poorly lit back alley, tripped over her own feet and collided lips-first with her friend?' Tell me what you want me to say! Illuminate me in ten words or less, because that's all you can get when it comes to the short attention span of the media!" he yells then takes a seat on the corner of his desk and folds his arms.

Oh no, he did not *yell at me.* "Okay, you incredible asshole! Here it is, in ten words or less!" I shout and count the words on my fingers. "I think I'm in love with her. Is that clear and direct enough for you, or do you need a complete oral history of where, when, and how it happened?"

"No, that will do," he says, his tone suddenly and surprisingly sympathetic. He taps his fingers on the glass desktop. I can practically see the cogs of his brain turning in time with his drumming. "I wish you would've told me about this sooner. Now we have to do damage control. 'Kendall Bettencourt, the Lesbian' is such a salacious gossip column headline. We are in for a shit storm of media hassle."

"Christ!" I manically flail my hands in his face. "You're so focused on the 'lesbian' thing. You're totally missing the 'I think I'm in love' thing! *Why* does the label matter? *Why* can't I just be a girl in love?"

"Because you're not *just a girl* at all!" He sighs. "Listen. I know you're young. You're falling in love, and you feel like you're on top of the world because of it. If you were any other kid in America, you'd be able to be a girl who happens to be in love with another girl and remain gleefully invulnerable to anyone's opinion. But you are not the average kid, Kendall. You live in the limelight! You are universally *adored* and looked up to! Every decision you make will be analyzed whether you like it or not, and it's possible that the opinions of others *can* hurt you. You have to think about Payton in all of this, as well. She's going to be subjected to the same kind of unpleasant attention that you will be: the paparazzi, the incessant hassle of reporters, the celebrity stalkers."

"You're a little late to the party, Lawrence! I've already thought about all of that—what it could mean for my career to live my life out in the open, what it could do to Payton to have her every move publicly examined." *All I've ever wanted to do is give our relationship a chance—on my own terms, without anyone's intrusion. But now, intrusion is inevitable, isn't it?*

And then, like an idiot, I start to cry. "I don't hold Payton's hand when we're walking down the street. She isn't the person by my side on the red carpet. We hardly ever leave the house because I know we'd be hounded by the media, and I don't want to lie about who she is and what she means to me, but I'm scared to tell the truth! I'm caught between a rock and a hard place. I feel guilty because I'm *not* being honest and ashamed because I don't think I *can* be honest! The whole planet wants me to be someone I'm not. Some days I feel like I'd rather rip my own heart out with a pair of pliers than live up to these stupid standards."

"Calm down and listen to me." He hands me a box of tissues. "If you want to be out, be out. I can't say for sure what the reaction would be should you decide that's what you want to do.

Maybe you'd become some kind of champion for the gay community, or maybe it would become very difficult for you to get the straight romantic lead. Either way, we'll make it work. But you must be prepared to deal with anything."

"There's the problem. I'm *not* prepared to deal with anything. I haven't even told my parents yet." My tears rage on, assailing my cheeks with a searing vengeance. "God! If I were a drug addict or an alcoholic that would be fine! People could get over that. But because I'm a lesbian, I'm gonna have to deal with relentless backlash? This world is so screwed up!"

"I agree, it is," he says then places his hands firmly on both of my shoulders. "I think you need to have a talk with your parents. That's the first step in the right direction. Go home, call them up, and tell them the truth; if anyone deserves that, it's them. We'll formulate a plan from there, depending on how it goes over." He gets up to walk me out and unexpectedly folds me into a hug. I've never let him hug me before, but it's kind of nice to know I've got someone on my side. "Let me know how it goes and keep in mind I'm behind you 100 percent, no matter what happens."

"Yeah, okay," I say and hurry through the door.

CHAPTER FIFTEEN

Payton

I get home from the longest day of classes ever, and the first thing I see is Kendall slumped over the kitchen island with her head in her hands. Initially I think she has a hangover. Every single muscle in my body is stinging from dehydration, and she's always been such a lightweight that I can't imagine how much worse *she* must be feeling after polishing off a bottle of bubbly on her own. After gently dropping my messenger bag on the floor and sneaking up behind her with the intention of giving her a back rub, I realize that it's not a hangover we're dealing with at all. I barely get my hand on her shoulder before she straightens up in her chair. She doesn't quite push me away, but I notice her balk a little at the contact.

"Okay, tell me what's up."

She spins the chair around to face me. My breath catches at the sight of her face—not in the good kind of way. The whites of her eyes are bloodshot, as though every last capillary in them has burst. The skin beneath her nostrils is red and raw like it gets when she's sick and has to blow her nose constantly. Without fail,

Kendall has gotten sick every winter for as long as I've known her—usually with the flu and generally around this time in early March. Every winter she'd miss school for a week. Every day of that week, I'd bring her chicken soup my mom helped me make and the classwork she'd missed that day. I'd try to teach her the day's math lesson so she wouldn't fall behind. She was never particularly good at math. Of course, I never told her that.

This is different though. She hasn't been coughing or sneezing—not once. It scares me. I know how to deal with the flu, but I don't know how to deal with whatever *this* is. "Really, what's going on?"

"The *Daily Post* outed me," she says matter-of-factly. "I thought for sure you'd have heard by now."

"No, I hadn't heard," I reply, genuinely taken-aback. "You know, because none of our friends actually *care* about what's going on in the world, and my mom prefers papers that print news as opposed to useless gossip."

"*My* mom has definitely heard." She grabs her phone and plays the voicemail on speakerphone mode.

Mrs. Bettencourt's voice seethes through the handset; it is so irate—so *forceful*—it literally echoes throughout the kitchen, encasing us in high definition surround-sound. "That is *it*, Kendall! I've questioned a number of the decisions Lawrence has made for you in the past, but this takes the cake! This is the worst possible publicity stunt that man could have concocted! First you play gay in a film, and now he's manipulated you into playing gay in your everyday life to ensure that film makes money? How could you let yourself go along with that? We raised you to have such integrity! I cannot believe…" The message cuts off.

"I've been avoiding her all day," Kendall says. "I'm not exactly eager to have this conversation with her."

"I can imagine," I say kind of sourly. That isn't a message I would've liked to receive. "Call your mom back and put it on speaker. I'm here now. I'll help you through it."

She takes a measured breath as she punches the speed dial for 'home.'

"Hello?" Mr. Bettencourt answers.

Kendall's lips creep into a small, somewhat serene smirk. She replies with a delicate, "Hi, Dad."

"Hi, Pumpkin. Had a rough day, huh?" he queries, his tone amazingly unruffled.

"It's about to get worse. I need to talk to Mom. Is she there?"

"She is. But let me ask you something before I hand the phone over to her."

"Sure."

For a second, we hear rustling on the line—the sound of a palm covering the mouthpiece, followed by a few muffled, indecipherable words. Then Mr. Bettencourt's voice returns clear as day. "Your mother couldn't see it, Kendall, looking at that picture, but I could; you girls love each other very much, don't you?"

"Yeah, Dad. We do."

If this moment were less horrible for Kendall, I'd just about jump for joy. That was the first time I've heard her reference me and love in the same sentence.

"I think that's wonderful." The sincerity in his voice is un-questionable. After a beat, he continues, "hold on. Here's Mom."

A lone, bitter snicker leaks out of Kendall. "At least my dad is cool," she says to me. I sit down in the bar stool next to her and instinctively grab hold of her hand.

"I was beginning to think you weren't going to call me back," Mrs. Bettencourt declares. She doesn't sound angry anymore. Her voice is as neutral as a robot's, completely devoid of emotion.

"I didn't want to call you back. I know you aren't going to like what I have to tell you, but I need you to really listen to me and not gloss it over like you do with *everything else* you don't wanna hear."

"All right, I'm listening. Say what you have to say."

"Lawrence didn't concoct this. No one did. It's not a PR stunt. I'm not playing gay for publicity. I *am* gay. In real life."

Mrs. Bettencourt remains wordless for longer than I've ever experienced. Anyone who has ever met this woman knows how easily she can talk your ear off. That's what makes her silence so daunting, so much more painful than a thousand obscenities.

"I don't know how to respond to that," Mrs. Bettencourt mutters finally.

Kendall blinks hard and fast in a brave last stand against the tears brimming in her eyes. I squeeze her hand a little tighter. Ultimately, she loses her battle. "You need me to tell you how to respond? Okay, *Mom.* Respond by telling me that this doesn't change anything and that you still love me."

"Of course I still love you, Kendall, but it does change things. I don't understand where this is coming from. You've never had any of those tendencies before. You've had boyfriends in the past. You probably haven't met the right man yet."

Kendall groans. "Yes, I've had boyfriends in the past—a ton of them! But it never felt right with any of them. I had to force myself to connect with all of them. It never happened on its own. And really? I haven't had any *tendencies*? I spent every waking hour of my life with Payton. That should have been your first clue. That should've been *my* first clue!"

"I knew this was about Payton! Honey, she is your best friend. There is a fine line between platonic and romantic love, and it's easy to mistake one for the other. Maybe the fact that she is gay has confused you. I don't think you should reject the possibility that you could fall in love with a man someday."

Kendall's cheeks color with exasperation. "I know the difference between loving someone as a friend and being *in love* with someone, thank you. And this isn't about Payton. This is about me. Even if Payton weren't in my life, even if I had *never* met her, I would still be gay. I finally *get* that."

"No, I don't think you do 'get' the gravity of this decision. You don't seem to comprehend what a risk you're taking by living this way. It's hard enough for the average person to lead a gay lifestyle, but you're a public figure!"

Sheer repugnance flares across Kendall's face. She's clearly trying so hard to keep her temper under control, but I fear she's been pushed beyond her boiling point. Her rage is slated for a volcanic eruption of monumental proportions. I feel like a citizen of Pompeii, helpless against a fuming Mount Vesuvius.

"Decision! Lifestyle!" she shouts. "Like I had a choice! Do you really think I woke up one day and said to myself 'I'd like my life to be more difficult than necessary, how can I make that happen? I know! I'll become a lesbian! That's sure to complicate the hell out of everything!' That's not what happened, Mom! I didn't *decide* to be gay. It's the luck of the draw, okay? I was dealt these cards, so I'm gonna have to play my hand."

"I don't accept that, Kendall!" Mrs. Bettencourt fires back. "There is *always* a choice. Unfortunately, I can't make your choices for you, because *legally* you are an adult. I can tell you if it were up to me, this thing between you and Payton would *not* be happening. You claim it has nothing to do with her, but it clearly has everything to do with her! She's a bad influence on you! You were normal before you found out she was *that way*."

"Mom, you're being crazy!"

"I am *not* crazy, I am right! You know what? Do whatever you want, but I suggest you keep your affairs private. People in this country have an aversion to homosexuality, and those same people are the ones lining up to see your films."

"Those people are called homophobes," Kendall snipes. "Sounds to me like you fit right into that camp, so let *me* suggest something to *you*—keep lining up to see my films, because that's the only way you'll be seeing me at all from now on. And by the way, I'm still *normal.* So is every other gay person on this god-forsaken rock of a planet!" She ends the call and slams the Blackberry against the counter so hard that the screen cracks. "Damn it! Now I need a new phone *and* a new mom—too bad I can't go out and buy both!" she yells. It's an act though. I can see right through it. She's not half as heated as she is hurt.

"I'm so sorry." It's the weakest thing in the world, but it's pretty much the best I can do. I'm too caught up in being thankful for my own amazingly accepting mother to even know how to begin to console Kendall. I'm totally stunned at the level of Mrs. Bettencourt's hardheartedness. I knew she wouldn't be ecstatic about it, but I never imagined she would react with such concentrated ugliness.

"What if she's right?" Kendall asks. "Lawrence said it, too. What if I come out and people start hating me? That means I become a liability rather than an asset as far as the studios are concerned. And that means there's a chance I might not be considered for a lot of the roles I'd like to play. I've worked so hard to get where I am, and I could lose it all because of this one small part of who I am. But my career isn't even the main thing I'm worried about; I'm worried about *you*. You'll never be able to escape the attention. Every time you leave the house someone will be in your face with a camera and a microphone. I don't want that for you."

I already know what the press is like. Between showing up to big events with Lauren and just being around Kendall, I understand what it means to be famous. The media can haunt me until my dying breath, for all I care. It would be worth it if it meant Kendall and I could be together without having to creep off into alleyways or duck into dark corners. Nevertheless, there's no denying that her reservations are justified. But it's a bit late to be thinking this over now, isn't it? There's a two-page spread of us making out in the *Daily Post*, for crying out loud. How can that be explained away?

"Don't worry about me. I can handle the hype. You are the key player in this; none of this is fair to *you* at all. You should be allowed to take as much time as you need to come to terms with who you are. But the story seems to have broken wide open. I mean, there's photographic proof floating around that you're not quite straight. So the question is, how do you avoid being out?"

"I have no idea," she laments.

Neither do I. "All right." I hand her my phone. "It's time for Lawrence to earn that phenomenal salary you pay him."

❅ ❅ ❅

"Can't we just—I don't know—say the picture is a fake or something? There are a million different editing programs capable of forging a photo!" Kendall yells then gets up to pour herself a *second* glass of wine.

Lawrence lets his breath out lightly into his mouthpiece. Speakerphone amplifies the sound into the wailing of gale force winds. "Regrettably, no; there is a legion of software experts who could prove the photo's authenticity."

Damn you, Lawrence. Why couldn't you have said yes? "So, what are her options? How do we make this go away?"

"The only foreseeable way to make that happen is if we present this incident as a one-time deal. We can hold a press conference where we will chalk the whole thing up to a mix of alcohol and Kendall being so overcome with joy about her Ellie Nom that she shared a kiss with her oldest, closest friend. From there, she will have to redouble her public appearances with Gunner.

Essentially, she'll have to be semi-permanently attached at the hip with him in order to 'prove her heterosexuality.'"

"No," Kendall takes hold of my hand. "I told you there'd be no more of that and I meant it."

"That was before anyone had proof. But it's out there now. I don't like this one bit, but I'm going to have to roll with it."

"Payton, that isn't all," Lawrence continues. "If we're really going to sell this cover-up, you'll need to steer clear of Kendall for a while—in every capacity. The two of you cannot be seen together at all."

"Steer clear of me!" Kendall yells again, but much louder this time. "We live together! How the hell is she supposed to steer clear of me?"

He doesn't have to clarify it for me, I comprehend precisely what he's getting at. I detest the idea *and* him for even hinting at it, yet I have no choice but to concede that he's right. I'm no good for her career. Or it could be that her mom is spot-on, and I'm just plain no good for her in general. *The road to hell is paved with good intentions*—isn't that how the old adage goes?

"It's simple, right, Lawrence? I have to leave. And stay away."

The quiet on his end of the line is my answer. I hear him loud and clear.

"How long is 'a while'? Ballpark estimate?" I query.

"Indefinitely."

Kendall's bottom lip quivers as she forfeits to her tears.

I force myself to ignore the agony saturating her face and charge past her into the bedroom. I grab one of my duffle bags from the closet and start shoveling handfuls of clothing into it before I lose my resolve. I'm not even conscious of what I'm doing; I'm just operating on autopilot. It's like I'm caught in some kind of trance made up of equal parts righteousness and remorse.

I hear Kendall say, "Fuck you, Lawrence," before thundering into the bedroom after me. "I am not going to let you do this!" She charges at the bag on the bed, grabs it by the shoulder strap, and violently chucks it onto the floor. Everything I've packed away goes spilling all over the carpet.

"Damn it, Kendall. Please don't make this any harder on me!" I kneel down to gather up my belongings. Miraculously, I'm able to keep myself from crying. "You can't come out to the world. You're barely out to yourself... And that's *okay*. But the press will never leave you in peace as long as I'm around; that will only raise more suspicion. You need me to do this, so please just let me *do it*."

She stands there, staring down at me. There is so much grief, so much *guilt* in her eyes. It pains me to see it.

I hoist myself to my feet so that we can be face to face. "This is not your fault."

"Yes it is!" she sobs. "You deserve to be with someone who loves you and can say it out loud, regardless of who may be around to hear it."

"Hey, remember when you promised you'd get there eventually? You haven't broken that promise. You're taking it slow, that's all."

"This isn't the end of us, is it?" she whimpers.

Maybe it is. I hope not. I flash a frail smile. "We're taking a break. You of all people should know that breaks are temporary—fleeting at best."

"Right," she nods. "Where are you going to go? Please don't say back to New Jersey." Her voice is getting hoarse from sobbing.

"No, silly, I still have school. As much as I bitch about it, I'll never quit. You know I relish a challenge." I shoulder my bag and turn to look at her. "I'll come back tomorrow for the rest of my stuff once you've left for the press tour. There won't be any paparazzi squatting behind the bushes if they know you aren't home."

"Okay," she murmurs as she sponges away her tears.

I move to exit the room, but before I can leave she latches onto my bicep and tries to pull me closer. I grind my sneakers into the ground. This is the first time I've ever *not wanted* to kiss her. "I won't have the strength to leave if I kiss you."

"I won't have the strength to *let* you leave if you *don't* kiss me." It's the closest to begging she can possibly get without falling to her knees; I don't doubt it would come to that if I were to refuse.

I slip my arm around her waist, press our bodies so tightly together that I can scarcely tell where mine ends and hers begins. She kisses me as though it were our first kiss and our last rolled into one.

I slide out of the embrace and scuttle toward the front door without looking back.

❋ ❋ ❋

I drive around for a while before ending up at La Cienega Park. I'm sitting on the hood of my car, seeking comfort in the warm twilight air, when I realize that I'm not simply drowning in anguish. I am profoundly lost.

There *is* someone who can help me find my way. I claw through the pockets of my cargo pants for my cell and dial the only number I know by heart. The familiar voice answers from 3,000 miles away. "Hi, Kiddo."

"Hi, Mom.

I relay every last detail of the affair to her, including how I'm fairly certain it has ended and how devastated I am about that. She isn't at all surprised to hear that Kendall and I had been dating for months. She tells me that she figured it out long before the *Daily Post* broke the story, long before Grace Bettencourt called her to complain about how I ruined her daughter's life—which was the call she received a few minutes after Kendall hung up on Mrs. B. Somehow, my mom just knew, like she's always *just known* about everything. She says she didn't want to bug me about it. She figured I would talk about it eventually, because I talk to her about everything sooner or later. She lets me know that she was happy for me because I was happy, and she's heartbroken for me now because I'm heartbroken.

"Kendall may just need time to put everything into perspective," she says. "It was so difficult for you to realize that you were as entitled to happiness as everyone else. I can't fathom how much more difficult it must be for someone as renowned as her."

Or maybe Kendall and I were doomed from the very beginning. We live by different sets of laws in two separate realities. She is Hollywood, west-coast glam. I am New Jersey, east-coast drab. Those two universes are so vastly different from each other that they cannot possibly intersect for any significant amount of time. That's why she moved out to LA—to allow her star to shine at its brightest, to cut through the dullness of normalcy. I'm just a remnant of her old life, a leftover who should've given up the ghost a long time ago. "I know how difficult it is for her, Mom. That's why I left. I was only complicating her life. It wasn't fair to either of us, wasn't right that our relationship was going to become more burdensome than it was blissful."

"Oh, Kiddo," she utters. "No matter what happens from here, remember the main reason you moved out there in the first place. You're getting an invaluable education, and you have to finish what you started."

"I want to finish what I started more than I've ever wanted anything, but I can't afford the Music Academy. I doubt I can find a job that pays enough to cover the tuition unless I become a drug-dealer or a prostitute."

"That certainly isn't going to fly," she says with a laugh. "The rest of this year is paid for, isn't it? We'll figure something out before the fall semester. In the meantime, do you have any friends you can stay with? At least until you find a job that will get you on your feet."

Gunner? No, I'll take a hard *pass on him. But there might be some-one…* "Um, I think so. I don't know. I'd have to make a few calls."

"All right, then. Make those calls and let me know how it goes. If worse comes to worse, get a hotel room for a few days and put it on your Visa."

"Okay. Thanks, Mom. I love you."

"Love you, too."

I don't bother putting my phone back in my pocket. Instead, I shoot off a text to Lauren. "Hey. Sorry to bother you. I kind of need some help. Are you busy?"

It only takes a moment for her to text me back. "No bother, hun. What's up?"

"Things are so screwed up." She stops me from cluing her in to the details of my foray into homelessness and says she's at an industry-sponsored event where the "atmosphere is hardly conducive to conversation." She insists that I meet her at her place. The next text she sends includes her address, which makes me think about how weird it is that I've never gotten around to seeing where she lives. Every time we hang out, we do it in public. It's kind of funny. Lauren is always eager to hang out with me in open spaces, coffee shops, or the boutiques on Rodeo Drive—while Kendall is so afraid to run the risk of being seen with me. The thought is a switchblade to my heart. I floor the gas pedal, fly down Wilshire Boulevard toward Westwood going well over the speed limit.

My GPS leads me to a chateau-style house on Birchwood Drive. Its façade is made of large gray stones and timber. There's a circular tower off to the right of the glass front door. I notice Lauren's electric blue BMW coupe parked in the driveway. I trek up the concrete staircase, ring the bell. *No answer.*

I take a seat on the top step and listen to my phone ring over and over as I wait. Jared calls three times; Sarah calls four. *They must have seen the article, after all.* I'm too downcast to talk to either of them, so I hit the end-call button seven times. *I wonder if they've called Kendall at all. She needs friends so much more than I do right now. She's all alone in this now.* I shoot them each a brief text asking them to check up on her, and then turn the phone off and bury my face in my hands. It's all I can do to keep from completely falling to pieces.

I'm not sure how long it is before the silhouette appears at my feet, blocking out the light from the streetlamp.

"Hi," Lauren says, looking down at me.

"Hi. You look nice," I say, because in her black leather vest, skinny jeans, and biker boots, she's really does. I may be brokenhearted and miserable, but that's no excuse for impoliteness.

"Thank you." She sits down next to me. "I heard about the picture. I wanted to call you, but figured it wouldn't be a good time. Did y'all sort it out?"

I didn't say anything about it via text, but I'm probably radiating so much sadness that the International Space Station could hone in on it like a beacon. "If you can call me voluntarily moving out and agreeing not to see her for the next however-long sorting it out, then yeah. We're all good."

"Oh my god, that sucks." She frowns as she gently cups my knee. "I'm sorry you're hurting. But look on the bright side; you're not homeless! You can stay here as long as you'd like, no strings attached. It'll be good to have someone here while I'm away for the *Idol Worship* tour anyway."

"Kendall's leaving tomorrow. Are you?"

She shakes her head. "I've got tomorrow off. Spencer and I are doing some interviews here on Saturday. We're catching up with Kendall and Rebecca in New York on Monday."

"Wanna help me move the rest of my stuff then? I didn't have time to pack everything."

"Sure."

"You know, at present I'm thinking it was wrong to ever hope to get out of Kendall's friend zone," I exhale in frustration. "It's all fucked now."

"Oh, come on, that must be one of the stages of grief talking! It's nauseating how crazy you are for her. You didn't have a choice, your *heart* wanted her. You never stood a fighting chance against that. You know, believe it or not, I wanted you and Kendall to work, because I knew how much you wanted it to work and because I wanted you to be happy even if I wasn't the person making you happy. Who knows? Maybe someday it will work out for the two of you. Don't give up hope, okay?"

Perhaps it is her uncomplicated reasoning or her urging me to stay optimistic in spite of the tremendous feeling of defeat taking root in my chest—or maybe it's some twisted amalgamation of both that finally brings me to tears. All I know is it happens, and I let it.

"I hate to see girls cry," she says after a while. "Why don't we grab your stuff from the car, go inside, down some liquor, and watch zombie movies until we realize how great our lives are because at least no one is trying to eat our faces off?"

I wipe at my sodden eyes and smirk. "Okay."

❄ ❄ ❄

Two weeks into living by myself in Lauren's house, and I'm still not used to being alone with my thoughts. Kendall and I exchanged phone calls every other day for the first week, but they were painfully brief and both of us always ended up bawling. It hurts too much, talking to her, wanting so badly to be with her and knowing that I can't. The last time she phoned I didn't have it in me to pick up. I let her go to voicemail. We've progressively fallen into communication blackout since then.

I basically don't know what to do with myself, so I've configured an unfussy routine to help me function: wake up, go to school—where everyone treats me like I am at the epicenter of the biggest scandal since Watergate, thanks to a press conference brilliantly orchestrated by Lawrence—come home, plunk into bed.

I'm afraid I have literally stopped caring about everything. I don't care about writing music, don't care about the clef or the key signature or the time measure. There is no difference between the flags of eighth notes versus sixteenth notes, because guess who doesn't care? This girl right here.

I don't even care about talking to anyone—with the exception of Lauren because she is the only person who has proven herself capable of providing any relief from the wretched existence I'm living. She's chronicling her press tour adventures on digital video and e-mailing clips to me every day.

I wake up Sunday morning to find her latest video already in my inbox. I click the play button. The camera pans around a pub with lots of Red Sox gear on the walls then cuts to Spencer St. Germaine, Rebecca Gordon, and Lauren sitting at the bar. Lauren turns the camera on herself and declares, "Okay. We're at Fenway Faithful's in Boston, which I thought you would find especially excellent, and Spencer is totally *bombed*." She points the lens at Spencer and Rebecca and instructs them to "Say hi to

Payton." Rebecca smiles and says hello. Spencer waves tawdrily and yells, "Hi, Payton, you sexy thing!"

The video cuts again to the girls carrying Spencer into a hotel room. He crawls on to the bed and promptly passes out. Lauren and Rebecca proceed to draw on his face with magic markers while giggling like madwomen. It makes me laugh. I'm so grateful for it that I dial Lauren's number straightaway.

"Did you enjoy that?" Lauren chuckles.

"Yes, I did. Thanks for sending it."

"You're welcome. I figured you'd find it funny. What are you up to?"

"I'm applying for a Recording Engineer work-study position because I'm so broke I can't even afford to go window shopping. What about you?"

"That is way more exciting than what I'm doing. I'm waiting for room service to bring me a salad. I'm hungry, but too lazy to go down to the bistro." Then a distant knocking sound begins in the background. "Speak of the devil," Lauren continues. She brings the phone with her to answer the door. "Um, hey, can I help you with something?" she asks. I can tell by the uneasiness in her tone that she isn't talking to a room service attendant.

"Oh, you're in the middle of something. My bad," Kendall's voice smacks me from clear across the country.

"No, it's fine. What's up?"

"Rebecca wanted me to ask if you'd like to come shopping with us," she says.

Silence passes between them until Lauren breaks it. "Kindly tell Rebecca that I politely decline, but appreciate the invitation."

"Yeah, okay. I'll do that."

"Thanks."

I hear the door creak as Lauren closes it. "She looks like death warmed up. Clearly, she loves you something awful. I wish she was strong enough to own it, for both your sakes."

"I don't have any idea what to say to that."

"I'm sorry. You were starting to get over feeling crappy, and I've dragged you right back into it."

"Don't worry about it. I'll be okay. But I think I'm gonna go. I haven't showered in days," I joke.

She plays along with me. "That's attractive. I'm sure you smell de-lightful." She sniggers. "I need to ask you something before you go."

"Whatever it is, the answer is yes. I owe you big time."

"Please, let me ask first before you say yes. Believe me, you're gonna want to think about it."

I'm instantly worried. With a caveat like that, maybe I *shouldn't* say yes. "Okay. Ask away."

"Will you come to the Elite Awards with me? It's my first time being invited, and I'd like to share the experience with someone cool. I also thought you might like to be there, you know, in case Kendall wins."

"Shit. I forgot I have other plans that night."

"You don't even know what a terrible liar you are, do you?"

"Sadly, yes, I do," I whine. "It doesn't seem like a good idea. I'm not supposed to be in close proximity to her."

"Payton, she doesn't have a restraining order against you. You'll be there with *me*, legitimately for a change."

True. I might not be allowed to talk to her, but perhaps I could be there in support of her if I keep my distance. "All right, I'll go on one condition."

"What's that?"

"I want a new Victoria Westfield gown."

She snickers. "It's a deal. And this time, we'll have three weeks to prepare. She can probably make you a custom dress."

"We are *so* going to her shop when you get home! Better let her know we'll be in to see her next week."

"Will do."

❆ ❆ ❆

Monday and Tuesday go well. Today is a different story. I'm in a strange mood, caught somewhere between calmness and restlessness. This morning I found out I got the work-study job. The hours kind of suck—mostly nights and Saturdays, because that's when the school rents out the studios to off-campus artists—but the pay is great: fifteen bucks an hour. Of course, that's only because it's a school-sanctioned job. No recording engineer makes that much once they've graduated unless they're lucky enough to get a contract with a record label. But whatever, I don't want to be a professional engineer. I'm not thinking about what the future holds for me. I'm too busy focusing on my daily survival.

Anyway, the joy of finding out that I am gainfully employed is short lived. I'm in the student lounge working on some drum charts, when I notice that the TV in the background is tuned into MusicTube, NY. The VJ announces the start of a live Q and A session with the cast of *Idol Worship*. I try to immerse myself completely in my sheet music, but every last bit of concentration I possess drains out of me when the guy working the sandwich station ups the volume.

Kendall's slight, solemn voice bombards my ears. My eyes take it upon themselves to wander up to the screen. There she is, golden hair all jagged and sharp-edged down to her elbows, baby blues alight with shimmer, lips plump with pastel pink balm—and none of it does a damn thing to conceal her listlessness. There's no life left in her, whatsoever. She's nothing more than a marionette performing at the command of an invisible puppeteer.

"Is that Kendall Bettencourt?" A girl at the table next to mine points the back end of her pencil at the TV.

"Yeah."

"Is she *high* or something? I thought she was supposed to be the poster child for beauty."

"Ask her," the other girl gestures to me. "Yo, Payton, your girl is looking beat. Must be missing all that lesbian sex she wants us all to think she's never had."

"Go to hell." I grab my notebook and bag from the table and haul ass out through the exit into the courtyard. By the time I take a seat on the low retainer wall, I'm crying—wondering if the pain will ever go away or if it'll always feel like I swallowed a stick of lit dynamite every time I see Kendall's face on TV or in a magazine.

Man, these last three weeks have been the longest of my life. *I miss the days when I didn't have to fight to get out of bed in the morning.* I decide right then and there to skip the rest of my classes for the week and spend Thursday in bed with the curtains drawn across the windows to help me forget that the sun exists. I know it's melodramatic, but again, I don't care. Being conscious only means that I play that night on repeat in my head: the sparsely lit alley, Kendall kissing me as if it were the end of the world. I wish that it actually had been the end of the world. I haven't just lost the person I love, I've lost my best friend.

CHAPTER SIXTEEN

Kendall

My plane is twenty minutes away from LAX. After forcing myself to smile for three weeks while giving bogus answers to intimate questions about my fake relationship with Gunner, the prospect of being home is uplifting. Until I remember that Payton won't be there when I get in, then I throw my sunglasses over my eyes and cry as quietly as possible. I've gotten so good at concealing my blubbering that no one seems to notice anymore.

Lawrence is in the seat next to mine. He knows I'm crying, but doesn't say anything to comfort me. Instead, he hands me a cocktail napkin. "I arranged for Gunner to pick you up at the baggage claim. Dry your eyes before you get off this plane and for God's sake, act like you're happy to see him."

I snivel out a meek "okay" and do as I'm told. I doubt I'll have to act happy to see Gunner. I'll probably be genuinely happy to see him. It'll be nice to be in the presence of someone who isn't either an interviewer prodding me for information, or cast mates who pity me for being such a remarkable tool.

The plane touches ground. I'm on my feet the second it rolls to a full stop. Lawrence catches me by the arm before I can take a step forward. "Is there something else I should do?" I ask in all seriousness. *I'll do whatever you want. I just have to get off this giant steel bird.*

He shakes his head. "It didn't have to be this way. I told you that from the get-go. I hate seeing you so unhappy."

Oh, it didn't have to be this way? No shit! I made it this way. My mom sure thought it was a great idea though! That was the second hint that I had made the wrong decision, bested only by the first hint, which, naturally, was Payton walking out on me. "Lawrence, you said it yourself—I am universally adored and looked up to. Don't I need to be exactly that in order to be a successful actor? People admire me so much that they want to *be* me. I'm America's Sweetheart… not because I have to be, but because I choose to be. Obviously, I've made my decision, now I have to live with the consequences." I move away from him and scamper down the aisle toward the exit.

As promised, Gunner is waiting for me at the baggage claim. He smiles at me as I approach from the gangway. I'm so sincerely happy to see him that I run at full speed into his arms. He lifts me into the air, twirls us both around, and then sets me back on my feet. "Welcome home," he says. He nods over his shoulder at a small crowd of people with cameras in hand. He leans in close to my ear. "Media alert. I'm sorry. They followed me here from my damn house!"

Right. I know what they're after, a photo that will sell for big money. If that's what they want, I'll give it to them. Screw it. Who cares anymore? "Kiss me," I mouth to him. "And not like you'd kiss your mother."

The directive shocks him. He doesn't have to verbalize it — it's written all over his face. Despite a moment of hesitancy, he does it—takes me in his arms, bends me backward into a dip, and plants his lips on mine. It is so reminiscent of the kiss with Payton that got me into this whole mess that I have to battle against having a breakdown. My single saving grace is how different his lips are from hers. His lips are a little rougher, a little dryer, and my heart doesn't come close to skipping a beat when they meet mine. I close my eyes and kiss him back. *Fake it for the cameras.* I see the bright, achromatic flashes through my closed eyelids. I hear the shutters click in quick succession. Then it's over. He stands me upright and releases me. I smile and ask, "Honey, can you grab my bags?"

He nods. "Let's get you out of here."

❈ ❈ ❈

Since arriving home from the press tour a week ago, I have very deliberately been making sure my schedule is packed with public appearances so that I won't have to spend any significant amount of my waking hours at home. This apartment is haunted by her essence. Yesterday, I realized the sheets still held her scent; her aroma vigilantly invaded my dreams, disturbing my attempts at peaceable sleep. I ripped them off the bed, sent them out for cleaning.

With every passing day it becomes more and more apparent this place will never be the same without her around. It's too quiet, too empty, and too dead. It's amazing how after only three months of living with her, she managed to make this house a home.

Christ! There are seven billion people in this world; how many are lucky enough to find love with their best friend? And to think that maybe I could have been one of them! I think I could have built a very happy life with Payton—had children with her, grown old with her. But I've messed that all up. I am so spineless I may as well be a jellyfish.

"Hello? Ms. Bettencourt? Mr. Roderick is here for you," a voice from the front desk disturbs my pity party.

No! I forgot about lunch with Gunner! I buzz down to the lobby to let them know I'm on my way, then race out the door.

The elevator's mirrored interior obliges me to come face to face with my reflection after sidestepping it for days. The girl staring back at me from the other side of the looking glass comes across as naturally high-end—with her posh clothes, expensive makeup and chic hair style. It's almost effortless to overlook the fact that she sold her soul to save her status.

The doors spring open when the lift reaches the lobby. Gunner receives me with a standoffish smile. "We need to talk."

❋ ❋ ❋

Our waitress sets a plate of salad down in front of me. I thank her and proceed to push the greens around with my fork.

"She's pretty," Gunner nods at the waitress as she walks away.

"I guess."

"You didn't even look at her."

"So?" I shrug.

"So, you're a lesbian. You should act like one."

The fork drops from my hand, trills shrilly against my plate. "Excuse me?"

"You heard me. It's killing you, pushing away the person you love so you can pretend to be something you're not. It isn't thrilling me either."

I take a quick glance around. The closest occupied table isn't very far from ours. I don't doubt the couple seated there could eavesdrop if they cared to. "Must we discuss this *here*?"

"Does it matter where we discuss this? In a restaurant, in your penthouse or in the car, the conversation will be the same. This has to end. I should've put a stop to it after everything that went down at the Visibility Awards."

I lean across the table and lower my voice to a near whisper. "Don't act like you're doing this for me. We both know you went along with it to begin with because it was good for your reputation to be seen with me."

"Sure. I knew it would benefit both of us if the world thought we were dating. But it's not benefitting either of us anymore. I hate how it's nagging at my conscience that I've taken any part in this smoke screen, and you've been marginally this side of suicidal since Payton moved out. For the record, Payton's been miserable, too. She looks like she only just survived an exorcism."

My ears perk up like a curious dog. "You've seen her?"

"Last night," he confirms. "She was with Lauren at the West Hollywood Arts Gala. I'm actually glad you stood me up to stay in and sleep. It was nice to have the chance to hang out with her. She would've taken off in the opposite direction if she'd seen you."

"Wait. She didn't look good?"

"She looked great. On the outside, anyway—all dolled up. Her eyes gave her away though. The kind of pain she's feeling leaves scars. In all honesty, I think if she could choose between breathing and seeing you, she'd choose seeing you."

I throw my napkin on the table. "Was it absolutely necessary for you to tell me that? Do you think hearing that kind of shit makes this any less insufferable for me?"

"Well, it's all on you, darlin'. You're doing this of your own free will. I don't see anyone holding a gun up to your head, making you choose between being loved superficially by the masses or deeply by Payton. Who even knows if you'd have to make a choice? Hell, I'm a small town boy from the High Plains, and I was raised not to care whether a person is straight or gay."

"You're 100 percent right about one thing; loving her *should have* trumped my fear of being rejected by people I don't know from a hole in the wall, but it didn't—clearly. So now instead of taking a break, I'm pretty sure we're just plain over."

"Seeing as how you've been totally down in the mouth since, I think it's safe to say you know you screwed up. Luckily, there's a real easy fix to this predicament. Come out, be with Payton—to hell with *theoretical* adversity."

"There's an easy fix," I mock him. "What alternate reality do you live in? I'm so deep in the closet I can't see the light of day.

Everything that has happened over the last month… It's all just nails in the coffin. This is my life from now on."

"No use trying to talk sense into you, is there?" he asks loudly. "That woman loves you so much she's willing to sacrifice her own happiness to protect you, to help you hoodwink heaven and earth. Good Lord, people spend their whole lives wishing to find that kind of love. You have it at your fingertips, and you're pissing it away because you're too scared of what others *might* think to reach out and grab it. If you ask me, it's not worth it."

"I know you mean well, but I really didn't ask you."

"All right, *Honey.*" He fishes a wad of cash from his pocket and tosses it onto the table without counting it. "I'd say we're about done here."

"Yeah." I stand up. He follows.

As we're leaving, he takes me by the hand the way a parent would take a tantrum-throwing child. "Gotta save face," he mutters under his breath.

* * *

The instant Gunner drops me off, I start calling up everyone I know who resides in the greater Los Angeles Area—well, *almost* everyone—and invite them over for a rager party. My second call is to Jason's Wine & Spirits for what I'm sure is the single largest order they have ever received. I'd put money on it that I've damn near cleared their shelves. That is easily my favorite thing about living in LA: liquor stores that make deliveries and delivery guys who are more than happy to double as personal bartenders once their shifts are over.

By the time the sun goes down there are roughly three hundred people staggering around my apartment, half of whom are naked and crammed into the pool within two hours of arriving. Mark Carter is upstairs spinning sick tunes on Payton's multi-thousand dollar equipment. He plays his signature remix of Giuseppe Ottaviani's "Lost for Words," and everyone starts hollering like they're in a club. I watch people break out party favors in the form of tiny plastic zip-baggies full of white crystalline powder. Nose candy definitely isn't my thing, but far be it from me to deny anyone else their fun.

So very many beautiful people, countless Hollywood movers and shakers, some totally average yet exceptionally cool human beings I don't remember ever having met before—all in my penthouse because I invited them to come over and get inebriated for absolutely no reason other than I was feeling incredibly lonesome.

I stand in the center of the living room, taking it all in. These people don't actually give a shit about me. They're just here for the free booze. Whatever. I could use some alcohol myself.

"I need Tequila! Right now!" I scream over the music. Almost as soon as I shout it I am holding plastic shot glasses in each of my hands—I don't even have to take a single stride toward the improvised bar near the ranch slider doors.

I down both shots and close my eyes. When I open them again, everything around me has gone from moving in real-time to slow motion. I have surpassed maximum awesome, so I pull my hair up into a ponytail, squeeze my way into the crowd of sweaty, swaying carousers, throw my hands into the air, and dance my ass off.

❋ ❋ ❋

I wake up, head splitting, to the sound of empty glass bottles clanking against each other. The last thing I remember is the cops showing up to break up a fight between Spencer St. Germaine and a paparazzo who snuck his way into the gathering. *Why the hell is my bed shaking? Holy shit, it's an earthquake!*

I'm not fully coherent, but I know enough to get my ass to a doorway or risk being crushed by stuff falling off the walls. I sit up quickly to find Lawrence rocking my footboard.

"And the princess awakens!" He helps himself to a seat on my bed. "I was starting to think you were dead."

"Not dead, only asleep. And by asleep to say we end the heartache and the thousand natural shocks that flesh is heir to, 'tis a consummation devoutly to be wished!"

"Thank you, Mel Gibson—that was very nice."

"You're quite welcome. Be sure to tell everyone you know that I can spout Shakespeare through a fucking monster hangover, and with my eyes half open, no less. Now, why are you here?"

"You haven't answered your phone in two days," he says calmly.

"Two days? And it took you this long to check on me? My, how you've changed since my spirit died. It's nice, isn't it? Knowing that I'll capitulate to whatever demands you make of me without mouthing off."

"I came over to make sure you'd be on your A-game for the Elite Awards tomorrow evening. If I had known you disappeared because you were in a drug-induced coma, I would have been here sooner. This is out of character for you, sweetheart. You've always been too motivated, too 'together' to fit the hard-partying, self-medicating Hollywood starlet prototype."

He's right, of course. That isn't me. And it's not who I want to become either. I just needed to be a lighter shade of blue for *one fucking minute.* "I swear to you I didn't do any drugs. But I did drink a lot. I must have been roofied."

"One spiked drink—that is how it starts. Before you know it, getting drunk isn't enough. You start messing around with the hard stuff and then you're caught in a tailspin. I've seen it happen more times than I can count on two hands." He sighs. "Kendall, I've been in this business for thirty years and I have never worried about any of my clients as much as I'm worrying about you right now."

He should be worried. If my existence is going to be this shitty from now on, I think I'd rather opt-out. Everything sucks, and it is always going to suck, no matter how many awards I win, or how many millions of dollars I make, or how many people scream my name and tell me they 'love' me at my movie premiers. "I have all the money I'd ever need, but it can't buy me anything that makes life worth living, can it? All this recognition from my peers, the adoration of millions of strangers—it means a lot to me, but not as much as Payton does. I can't believe I'm doing this to her. I can't believe I'm doing this to myself. I mean, honestly! I love her more than I ever thought I was capable of loving anyone. Maybe I can *survive* without her, but I can't *live* without her."

"Then you know what you need to do?" He slaps his knees. "Put her above everything else, above your fear, above whatever judgments anyone may pass. You're the first person to tell someone to go to hell when you need to, so go on—be the Kendall Bettencourt I know and flip a great big middle finger at any haters who slither out of the woodwork. Be you, be in love, be *happy*. I was wrong to insinuate that you ever should've done otherwise."

"Even if I try the 'being myself' slant, it's too late for me to be in love and happy. Payton won't talk to me. She doesn't even take my calls anymore. I'm persona non grata, not that I blame her for that. I wouldn't want to talk to me either, if I were her."

"She's doing all of this because she thinks it will benefit you, not because she wants to. I bet she's as forlorn as you are and not talking to you is her attempt at easing her own pain."

"Wonderful. So, what the hell do I do about it?"

"I have an idea. It involves me intercepting information that is more sensitive than classified CIA communications, so if I manage to pull it off it has to stay between us, okay? Otherwise, I'll be drawn and quartered."

"Dude, if your super-secret information can help me make things right, I'll sew my mouth closed until you hand me the pair of embroidery scissors I'll use to open it."

A shadow of amusement washes over him. "You're a funny girl, have I ever told you that before?"

"No."

"Well, you are." He stands up and kicks a few bottles out of his way. "A funny girl who's living in a goddamn pigsty. Praise the lord you're going to come out—another month's worth of you trying to party away your pain and this place would be a towering garbage heap. I'm getting a team of housekeepers over here pronto."

"Thanks," I smile. *For everything.*

❄ ❄ ❄

A bitter chill charges down my spine as our limo pulls up to the Providence Theatre, the highly revered venue for this year's Elite Awards. Tonight is the most crucial night of my life, and I have never felt closer to coming unglued. There's a knot roughly the size of Rhode Island in my abdomen, and I can't remember a time when I've wished for the gift of clairvoyance as much as I'm wishing for it now. I've rubbed my rabbit's foot, stuffed my lucky penny into my handbag, and prayed to every deity known to humankind. *But what if that isn't enough?*

"Are you going to be sick?" Lawrence asks, his voice quivering with atypical agitation. "You look like you're going to be sick."

"She's fine!" Gunner asserts through gritted teeth. "Jesus, man! Leave her alone. She's nervous, that's all. You would be, too, if you were in the running for an Ellie."

I wish I could tell him 'being in the running' for an Ellie is *not* what I'm anxious about. But if I told him that, I'd have to explain what I *am* anxious about—and then Lawrence would execute me slowly with a dull butter knife.

"I'm nervous *for* her," Lawrence murmurs under his breath.

"What was that?" Gunner questions sternly.

Clearly, *everyone* is on edge, which means tempers are running hot. It's only serving to intensify my uneasiness. "*Both* of you shut up! Just keep quiet and let me do my thing! Okay?"

"Okay," they say in tandem, each of them pouting like little boys who've been scolded by their mother.

The chauffeur opens the rear passenger-side door. "Ready to do your thing?" Gunner offers his arm. I nod, giving him the go-ahead to lead me on to the red carpet.

We step into the cool night air. The photographers begin their pictorial blitzkrieg. They remove their fingers from their triggers just long enough to bark directions at me. All I hear is Kendall, Kendall, Kendall! I'm beginning to hate my own name, if that's even possible.

"Kendall?"

"What?" I whirl ferociously on Gunner.

"Payton is *here*," he says, gesturing behind me with a subtle flick of his head.

"She's *where*?" Here, as in, on the red carpet? *Oh my god, this was not part of the plan!* She's supposed to be home watching the show on TV! Better yet, she's supposed to be home, not watching at all! If someone were to relay the details to her later, that would be perfectly fine… but to be able to watch her reaction to tonight's proceedings in real time? These are not things my heart can take.

Sure enough, Payton is a few feet behind me, looking superb in a black and dark maroon asymmetrical cut Westfield and posing for photos with Lauren. She's become a natural, talking and giggling coyly with reporters as if that's what she was born to do. She knows how to handle these barracudas better than I do—by being herself. I feel like I should be taking notes so I can learn by example.

Gunner protectively takes hold of my hand. "If you need to, we can bunk off the Press Q and A and head inside."

He is such a good friend, in spite of how coldly I treated him the other day. I should really apologize. "No, I'm fine. But listen, I wasn't very nice to you at lunch. It was uncalled for. I wanted to say I'm sorry."

"It's water under the bridge."

"There's something else I need to apologize for in advance. I'm going to do something tonight that's sure to change my life—and maybe even yours."

He shrugs his shoulders. "That's why we have publicists, isn't it? We make messes, they clean 'em up. Don't worry about it. Just do what you gotta do."

I throw my arms around his neck, pull him into the tightest embrace. "You're so awesome."

"I know," he smirks as I release him. "Now put your brave face on and let's go do this."

CHAPTER SEVENTEEN

Payton

Lauren and I just finish up our first lap around the Press Q and A box when I catch my first glimpse of Kendall. She's in a wispy, iridescent taupe gown, and she looks *sensational*. The make-up and hair people did an amazing job at faking her hallmark glow.

"You're a real sickly shade of gray," Lauren says.

Of course I am. It hurts me to *think* about her, let alone be physically near her. To make matters worse, she's still the most beautiful creature I have ever laid eyes on. "When can we go inside?" I wonder. "It's getting a bit too hectic out here for my taste." I definitely don't want to be standing here when Gunner and Kendall arrive to make their rounds.

She consults the PR guy who's standing next to her. "We can go inside now, if you'd like. I'm done here."

"Yes, please."

Arm in arm, we make our way into the theater.

We're hot on the Maître D's trail. The deeper into the gigantic, glittering banquet hall he leads us, the wider Lauren's eyes get—until we finally arrive at a table only yards away from the stage.

"Oh my god," she gasps. "I didn't know I merited a table so close to the stage. I thought I'd be lumped in with the peanut gallery." She snatches two flutes of champagne from a passing waiter and giggles. "We are *so* VIP, and I am *so* not complaining."

I relieve her of one of the glasses. "You'd better not be complaining. This is a dream come true for most people, I imagine."

"It is. I can only hope to be nominated someday. But this is a helluva good start, for sure."

"Well, cheers to a helluva good start," I raise my glass to hers. They make a louder *clink* than either of us anticipates.

"Thought they might've broken there, for a second," she beams. "You can't take me anywhere."

My amusement is interrupted as Kendall enters my sight-line again. She follows Gunner down the aisle to their designated table, which is rather inconveniently located diagonally across from ours. She notices that I've seen her and brandishes an ill-at-ease smile. I return the gesture, pretending to be unaffected by her presence. *Great. She's gonna be three feet away from me all night, smack in my view.*

"Christ, I'm sorry," Lauren says, motioning her head at Kendall's table. "That has to suck for you more than words can express."

"Kinda," I affirm. "It's okay, keep that champagne coming and soon I won't care."

"I got this." She signals to a roving server holding an uncorked bottle. He scurries over to us faster than a rat on speed. "Please make sure my friend's glass is full at all times," she says and slips him a hundred dollar bill. He nods graciously as he pours more bubbly into my flute, then returns to his place at the end of the aisle. I take a sip, but nearly spit it out after realizing he is eyeing me like a hawk.

Lauren also notices that he is focusing penetratingly on my flute. She erupts into a booming fit of laughter. "Tonight is gonna be *awesome*," she says, then taps her imaginary wristwatch and mouths to the waiter, "every twenty minutes."

An hour and three alcoholic beverages into underage drinking night at the Elite Awards, and I'm feeling quite fine. I do, however, decide to cut myself off after the third glass. Both Lauren and my vigilant waiter frown at me, but I shoo them off good naturedly. The plan was to drink enough to loosen up, not enough to get tanked—and at this point, Kendall's occasional peeps in my direction aren't bothering me half as much as they did in the beginning of the ceremonies. In fact, we locked eyes a moment ago, and my stomach didn't lurch one bit.

She isn't looking so well anymore. She's tense and panicky and utterly unable to hide it. She tried to play it cool by saying that winning an Ellie wasn't important to her, but I know in actuality it's one of the most significant things that could happen to an actor. I never thought she would be freaking out as badly as she is though. I want to go over there, drape my arms around her, and whisper the most relaxing things I can think of into her ear. However, I know that would be a detriment to the mental health I've been working so hard to repair this last month.

"Best Actress is coming up in ten," Lauren murmurs.

I clamp my gaze on Kendall again. "Cool."

Lawrence notices me eyeing her up, but doesn't alert her to it. Instead, he excuses himself from the table and starts very gingerly making his way toward me. Kendall doesn't track him with her eyes, just continues to gawk uneasily at the stage.

"Hi, sweetheart." He squats down in front of me, resting his elbows on his knees.

Oh, a good scolding! That is exactly what I need right now. "If you've come over here to remind me of how I should be staying as far away from Kendall as possible, I'm sorry. This is where Lauren and I were told to sit," I reply to his greeting with a hint of brazenness.

"On the contrary, I'm here to encourage you to go wish her luck. She could use some support."

I thought I was supporting her by keeping my distance. "Isn't that what she has you for?"

"Yes, but I know she would much rather have you than me sitting next to her."

"What about…"

"You're not a box of rocks, so stop being dumb." Lauren chimes in. "The man told you to go talk to her. Best get to steppin'," she shoos me off.

"All right, jeez."

Lawrence escorts me to the table. I make myself at home in the seat he previously occupied, and he moves over to a vacant chair. Kendall doesn't seem to notice that I've arrived; she's stuck in some kind of eerie stupor. I clear my throat. She turns her head. I watch her scrap through the tears clouding her irises so that she can focus on me. *Oh, to hell with doing the right thing for her. I'm going to do what's right for me for a change.* I take hold of her hand and squeeze it tight. "It's okay. No matter what happens, you're going to be fine. Win or lose, you will always be the best actress in the business as far as I'm concerned. But you're going to win so don't worry."

"Thanks," she whispers as the presenter takes the stage.

He clears his throat and begins reading from the teleprompter. "The Elite Awards Nominees for Best Actress in a Leading Role are…" After each name he calls, he gives a short speech about the actress' career. Four names are announced and four speeches are made before he gets to Kendall. "Kendall Bettencourt," he starts, "this is your first Elite Awards nomination, though it surely will not be your last. You bring the enthusiastic passion of youth to every role you play and particularly to your breakout role as Heaven in *In Heaven's Arms*. All of Hollywood looks forward to watching you grow throughout what is sure to be a long and impressive career."

Kendall smiles bashfully and mimes an earnest "thank you" to the announcer as a round of applause rings throughout the room. Then she looks at me stolidly. "Please don't cry. If you do, I won't be able to get through it without crying myself," she murmurs.

I don't get the chance to ask her what she's talking about before the presenter opens the velvet envelope. "And the Ellie goes to Kendall Bettencourt!"

The crowd roars to life with a standing ovation and wild cheering. We stand up simultaneously, and I'm in her arms, hugging her gleefully without the slenderest hint of foot-dragging. "You won!" I shout, both of us still cleaving tightly to the other's shoulders. I repeat myself in immeasurable elation as she releases me from our embrace. "You *won!*"

"I know," she counters my excitement with a staggering soberness and a tepid grin. Lawrence leans over, gives her a light cuddle, a kiss on the cheek, and an anemic "Congratulations."

I watch her take off toward the stage. As she ascends the stairs, I turn to Lawrence. "Why isn't she ecstatic? Why aren't *you* ecstatic?"

He answers with a shrewd smile and a wink. That's when it hits me: They already knew she was going to win. Both of them knew it as certainly as they know that the sun rises in the east.

"Here comes the interesting part," he utters once he realizes I've figured it out. "You'll want to pay close attention."

Of course I want to pay close attention! It's her acceptance speech! I watch intently as she takes the golden statuette into her hands and steps up to the podium. The audience takes a seat and quiets down in anticipation of her address.

"Okay, I'm going to try and get through this as quickly as possible. Firstly, I'd like to thank the Elite Awards Council for this amazing and kind of terrifying moment," she begins and the crowd chortles collectively.

"Lawrence Mackin, James Sovkov, and everyone at the Sovkov Agency, thank you so much for helping me achieve this. To the *In Heaven's Arms* cast, crew, and director Michael Jarvis—thank you for putting your faith in me; I appreciate it so very much.

To my dad, David Bettencourt, thank you for being a voice of reason in my life. Mom, I want you to know that I love you. A huge thank you to all my friends and all my fans for being awesome, and lastly," she pauses and scans the crowd. She finds me and gestures to me with an outstretched arm and open palm. A thousand pairs of eyes target me and a vast silence blankets the room. I feel the heat of blood furiously whooshing to my cheeks. "To Payton Taylor, the woman who taught me how to use that thing in my chest commonly referred to as my heart—thank you for always, *always* being there for me." She stops again to wipe away a tear that has rolled down her left cheek. "I love you more than words can say. Letting you walk out that door was the biggest mistake I have ever made. I hope that someday we can start again."

Music pumps through the sound system signaling the end of her oration. The usher motions for her to exit stage left, but the audience explodes into Fenway Park style applause—complete with loud whooping and wolf whistling—before she can leave the stage. She folds her hands around her trophy and takes a cordial bow then withdraws backstage.

I witness it all, but none of it penetrates. I'm in an advanced state of dumbfoundment or something. *Did she just out herself on prime time television, and tell the entire universe that she loves me? Yes, she did. And* you *cannot breathe. Breathe, Payton!*

"Payton," Lawrence grabs my shoulder, gives me a gentle shake that brings me back to earth.

"Yeah," I exhale. "Why is my face wet?"

His brows furrow. "Because you're crying."

"I am?" I touch my fingers to the skin below my right eyelid. "I am."

He chuckles, then removes his VIP lanyard-badge and places it around my neck. "Follow me." He takes my hand and leads me through a side door out of the auditorium and into a long, bright hallway.

"Where are we going?"

He shakes his head and pushes open another door. *This* room is bustling with reporters, photographers and recording devices. I'm under fire as soon as my arrival is noticed. People are tossing questions at me and cameras are snapping pictures in automatic mode. "All right, everyone back off!" Lawrence yells. "She's not going to answer any questions." We cut through the sea of press and stop at a roped-off area. There's a hairy, muscular security guard standing next to a sign that reads 'Awards Staff /Award Winners and Handlers Only.' Kendall is standing in the distance with her back to me.

Lawrence takes me by the shoulders. "The ball is in your court, sweetheart. But if I were you, I'd go over there and tell the girl you love her, because honestly, outing herself to the entire world on television took more courage than I can imagine. And she did it because she can't live without you."

With that, my mind makes *itself* up. I make a beeline for Kendall. I reach out for her shoulder and spin her around. We stand vis-à-vis, but remain silent until I can no longer stand the sound of my own respiration. "I cannot believe you did that."

"I *had* to. I never should have let you leave in the first place. All that fear and confusion I was feeling… it was like a dark cloud blocking out the sun, it just needed to pass so I could see things clearly. Payton, I love absolutely everything about you. You are the kindest, most thoughtful person I have ever met. You're smart, and brave, and beautiful in every way. And I love that I can be myself with you; I love that you let me be a dork who makes lame puns."

I can't help but smile. "Yeah, but you're a cool, sexy dork." That's the last thing I say before I wrap my arms around her waist and pull her into the most fervid kiss—the kind of kiss that makes your lips go numb, lingers on your tongue and on your mind long after it's over. She rests her hands on the back of my neck. "I'm sorry I didn't get there sooner," she whimpers softly into my lips.

"Shhh," I mutter. "I love you."

"I love you, too," she beams. "There's nothing keeping us apart anymore. Will you please come home?"

Home. I miss everything that word involves. "Yes, absolutely." I say. "I've been waiting for you to ask."

EPILOGUE

Kendall

"Holy Christ on a cracker! Why didn't you warn me Atlanta was going to be hotter than hell?" Payton gripes as she drops her duffle bag on the hotel room floor. I laugh, hand her a bottle of ice water, and smack a proper kiss on her lips.

"Yeah, like LA is any better right now? It's *July*."

"Why do you think I was hanging out at Gunner's place so much before he left for Paris? And why the hell is it *so* much cooler in the Valley anyway?"

I flash an amused grin. "Because it's a *valley*, Payton."

She gives me the evil eye and tackles me onto the bed. I swat at her hands as she tickles me. "Listen, smarty-pants," she says. "I spent four and half hours on a plane to come visit you on set and maybe catch a glimpse of you in chainmail. You'd better be nice to me, or I'm gonna go home."

"You can't go home." I feign a scowl. "It's my birthday tomorrow! Besides, isn't this the first time you've had two consecutive days off since you started your new job?"

"Oh, man." She yawns. "I had no idea an assistant composer's job would be *so* intense. And to boot, the lead composer is a neurotic mess. But at least I've been keeping myself occupied. It's totally a bonus that *The Relishing* is going to have a killer score. It might even make this film worth watching."

I whack her arm lightly. "What? Lauren and I aren't enough to make it worth watching?"

"Of course you two are enough—especially you, you gorgeous thing."

"That was a very good answer." I kiss her nose.

She climbs off the bed, stretches her arms. "I'm gonna hop in the shower. Then what do you say we take a nice, long nap?"

"I am *so* down for a nap before dinner," I holler after her as she disappears into the bathroom.

"Oh, I forgot to tell you," she pokes her head into the room again. "I made a reservation for 8:30 at that Sundial place you wanted to check out."

"Aww, baby! You're so good to me."

❄ ❄ ❄

Eight o'clock rolls around, and I'm still stranded in front of the bathroom mirror trying to finish up my makeup. Payton's reflection appears in the glass. She folds her arms across her chest, leans against the doorframe, and proceeds to scrutinize my every move. "You know, for a movie star you are ridiculously typical," she says with a grin on her face. "Primping yourself to perfection, throwing our whole schedule into total upheaval. Such a *girl*."

"Oh my god, it's not my fault I'm not as inherently beautiful as you."

She slinks up behind me, snakes her arms around my waist and rests her chin on my shoulder. "Oh *please*. You're stunning, and you *know* it."

"Sure, I do."

"For real though. We're running late. Lauren's already in the lobby. She just texted me that our car is here along with the *paparazzi*," she sing songs. "By the way, I had no idea there were paparazzi in Georgia."

I gurgle. "Like, eight months into dating me, and you've yet to learn there are paparazzi everywhere?"

"I guess not. But I wore my sexy vest just in case." She pops her collar and does a little jig. "It won't matter how desperately they want to capture a photo of 'MusicTube's *hottest celebrity couple*' if we never get out of this room though. So, brilliant strategy—I adore the way you think."

"Okay, okay. Let me put on lip gloss, and we can go."

❅ ❅ ❅

"It took you guys long enough," Lauren says as we enter the lobby.

"I'm starting to miss the days when we didn't talk to each other, Lauren." I impishly stick my tongue out at her.

"And I'm starting to miss the days when the two of you avoided going out in public together. Let's go get this meet and greet over with."

Payton smirks and slips her hand into mine. "Ready?"

"As I'll ever be."

We push through the revolving door and head out into the muggy night air. Once we're a few steps into the courtyard, camera flashes begin to light up the darkness.

"Hi guys," Lauren waves at the front line of photographers. "How are y'all doing tonight?"

The paparazzi respond with pleasant retorts and flattering comments on her outfit. If there's anything I've learned from Lauren's unflappable southern temperament, it's that you definitely catch more flies with honey than you do with vinegar. The more cooperative you are, the less they get in the way. It helps that I don't have any secrets left to uncover. They don't get on my nerves as much anymore.

"Kendall!" A guy with a video camera beckons for my attention. "I've heard you and your mom haven't been getting along since you came out. Is that true?"

Okay, I might be more comfortable with these guys than I have been in the past, but that doesn't mean I want to discuss my family problems with them. "All families hit a rough patch now and then, but we're working through it. I'm sure you've butted heads once or twice with your parents, right?"

"You bet I have," he replies with a snigger. "I've got one more question for the two of you and then my buddies and I will get out of your hair."

"All right," I concede.

"Payton, seriously, when are you gonna put a ring on it?"

"Dude," Payton says. I see her cheeks flush pink. "You seem like you're good at your job, you'll probably know when it happens. But I think you've got a while to wait." The whole group of photographers chuckle at her answer. And then, as promised, they back off into the dimness with a few friendly 'have a good night's.'

"You've gotten so good at dealing with unwanted attention," Payton says as we slide into the limo.

"Yeah, I'm impressed," Lauren concurs. "I know paparazzi can be annoying, but they can also be kind of amusing if you're cool to them."

"I'm figuring out it makes my job easier if I talk to them with a little bit of respect."

"Baby, I'm so proud of you," Payton says. She kisses my cheek and nuzzles into my neck

"Okay, if you two are going to be this adorable the entire ride to the restaurant, I'm going to get out and walk."

Payton and I look at each other and crack up.

❄ ❄ ❄

We make it to the restaurant by 8:35. Payton is delighted that we're only five minutes late instead of the usual fifteen. The Maître D receives us with a smile, and we follow him into the dining room.

I stop short when I notice the table we're being directed to already has people seated around it, and then a second time when I realize who those people are: Sarah, Jared, and my parents. "Surprise!" They yell in chorus. I hurry over to the table to greet everyone. Jared hugs me so hard that my back literally cracks. Sarah kisses my cheek and ruffles my hair. I throw my arms around my dad; he lifts me off the ground like he used to when I was a kid. My mom smiles at me blearily until I make the first move to hug her.

"I'm sorry, Kendall," she says as she embraces me. "As long as you're happy, that's all that matters—and I can see how happy you are with Payton."

"Thanks, Mom. It means a lot to hear you say that."

She releases me and gently pats my cheek.

I'm still in utter disbelief by the time Payton finishes introducing Lauren to everyone and takes her seat beside me. I hardly catch the bit of conversation between my dad and Lauren where he talks about Payton flying them all out here for my birthday.

"Wait," I grab Payton's hand, "You flew them out?"

"You're not the only one with a big Hollywood job anymore," she wiggles her eyebrows. "Lawrence will be here later. He said something about having a conference call or whatever with some director. My mom really wanted to make it down, too. Unfortunately, she couldn't get off work. She sent you a birthday gift though. I'm not allowed to give it to you until your actual birthday, so you'll have to wait until at least midnight. You'll have to wait until we get back to the hotel for the rest of your presents as well."

Tears spring to my eyes, "All of the most important people in my life are either here in this room, or keeping me in their thoughts. That's the best birthday present ever."

With a smile, she recalls the words I said to her on her birthday last year. "No crying on your birthday. Not even happy tears."

Letter from Kristen

Thank you so much for reading
The Gravity Between Us—I hope that Kendall and Payton's story
touched your heart as much as it did mine. If you did enjoy
The Gravity Between Us, I'd be eternally grateful if you would write
a review on Amazon or Goodreads. Getting feedback from readers
is amazing and also helps to persuade other readers to pick up one
of my books for the first time!

If you'd like to be notified by e-mail when my next book is
released, just sign up for email notifications at
www.authorkristenzimmer.com. For regular updates on my
writing process, or if you fancy saying hello, feel free to follow me
on Facebook or Twitter.

Thanks again!
-Kristen

facebook.com/authorkristenzimmer
@kristen_zimmer

Made in the USA
Middletown, DE
03 July 2021